BLOOD RED WINE

Lawrie Hammond

A BLACK TWIST BOOK

Design and photography by Patrick Nugent

Typeset in 11.25/16 point Bembo

ISBN 9781 549941689

First Printing

I had lots of help along the way, primarily from Patrick Nugent of the Waveney Valley Writers Guild, Black Twist Books and from Zibba George of Barsham City. Thanks.

Chapter 1

They had been travelling for over three hours now. Graham preferred to drive and Julie preferred not to. Both knew that on long journeys it was safer to stop and change over every couple of hours or so, but they were nearing the Channel and there wasn't that much time to spare. Graham liked to get to the dock in plenty of time and hated being late, he liked to plan things such as journeys to the last detail. Julie had always been a bit more cavalier about time, a bit more laid back. Most of her journeys to the Channel ports had been either tight for time or very tight for time but only occasionally had she missed a ferry. This had never seemed terrible. The only really bad miss was when she arrived a bit late for the Friday night Eurostar to Paris from London. It was her first time on the train – heading for a romantic/dirty weekend – which was completely screwed by arriving in loads of time, at least ten minutes before the train was due to leave, and was then, astonished at being barred from getting on. The most galling thing had been the knowledge that the gate was still open – but only for first class passengers, several being hurried through after her arrival. She had stood helplessly at the barrier, trying in vain to flirt with the guard-come-ticket checker who was seemingly gay with aspirations of being a future SS commandant.

She mulled over these old memories with a half-smile as the car cruised on. Graham seemed a little anxious – there was only about an hour to spare before the ferry gate closed and, as he had said several times, they hadn't yet picked up any cheap wine.

'We may still have enough time to dash into that big Carrefour near the ferry, but we'd have to just get the wine and maybe a bottle of gin, but we won't have time to wander round the cheese counter.'

'Yes dear,' said Julie, with that slightly musical note that was taking the piss. Graham didn't seem to hear. He was well aware that his pedantic timekeeping, or, as he put it, 'the attention to detail', got on her nerves a bit. But that was how it was, and they still got on pretty well. As Julie sat in a half dream, a car had slowly pulled level on the Autoroute. It was French and the driver was determined to pass them even though Graham was cruising at the speed limit and in a newer, more powerful car. The other car was fully loaded with luggage shoved against the back window, completely blocking it. There were several children in the back, all playing on hand-held game machines. They came to a slight incline and the older car struggled to keep level but still the driver held his foot down. There were now three other cars behind him, all tailgating and all flashing their lights. Julie smiled to herself and wondered, not for the first time, what it was that made French drivers so aggressive. She looked at the children in the back of the car, all oblivious to the tussle of egos going on around them. It would be nice to have children, she thought, somehow it made sense of being here, on Earth. The small girl nearest her looked up from her gaming and stared back at Julie, who smiled. The girl poked out her tongue and resumed her electronic battle. Julie was a little shocked and the idea of having children disappeared from her mind.

Julie and Graham's relationship had not really got going as yet. They had met at a 'do' arranged by Julie's father at his golf club, a posh one with a ridiculously high annual fee and a waiting list. Her father, who was President of the club, had encouraged her to go along as she had 'just-come-out-of-a-relationship' and so she had gone more to humour him than actually seeing it as any kind of matchmaking set up. Most of the attendees were around her father's age but with a sprinkling of younger noveau riche. The sprinkling included quite a lot of music and media people who presumably saw the golfing fraternity as a networking opportunity, which of course it was.

There was an excellent buffet and a series of entertaining short lectures around the themes of cooking and wine. One speaker explained how the vintage wine system had developed and another showed the audience how high-quality kitchen knives were made by the same process that had been developed for Samurai swords. The knife man was Graham. They got chatting, which ended in a dinner date a few days later, which ended with a stay over at her house. Since then they had met up quite often when he was in town and it was all very 'pleasant'. Julie looked over at Graham and thought back over their short relationship. He was actually rather good looking and certainly very accomplished in the bedroom department, but she had never thought of him as a permanent partner and certainly not as the father of any children, if that ever raised its head. The word 'pleasant' had formed itself again, which had always been a hugely insulting euphemism in her family. She and her sister had often used it to great effect. Yes, pleasant, but not very... what? Sparky? Emotional? Just not very... but pleasant.

Julie was woken from her brain rolling by Graham saying, 'Oh look, they're selling wine in the lay-by ahead. If it's OK then that will save us some time', and within a few seconds they had pulled off the main road onto the loop road that constituted the Aire, had stopped beside the make-shift stall and Graham was out of the car. Julie opened one eye, surveyed the scene, and noticed that there was some sort of conversation going on, but she couldn't hear so she snuggled back down in the seat and tried to get back to the warmth of her day dreaming.

'Are you go back to Folkestone, England now *M'seiur*?' said the shorter of the two as Graham sampled the wine.

'Bah, *oui*, Folkestone' said Graham.

'The wine is good, yes?'

'Yes, good.'

'But you lay down for three months before drink, yes?'

'*D'accord*,' said Graham.

After just a few minutes a case of the wine, having been sampled, approved and paid for, was put into the boot and they were back on the road on the final short leg to the ferry and England.

★★★★★★★

As soon as the car was out of sight a dapper man in his fifties stepped out from behind a fence and gave simple instructions. The two younger men quickly took down the roadside sign, put it into the back of the white un-marked van, closed the doors and drove off. The older man surveyed the Aire for any signs of them being there, disappeared around the fencing again and along a track for about half a kilometre to where a narrow road bridge crossed the main road. He looked around one more time, got in his car and drove off. No one saw him leave.

For the previous half hour Jean-Paul had stood by the parapet on the road bridge watching the approaching traffic through binoculars. There had been no traffic across the bridge – which was hardly surprising as it really only took cows to and from milking and the occasional tractor, but not even that at this time of year. Jean-Paul had been given very specific criteria. He was looking for a British-plated car, with two people, older rather than younger. No children as they could cause problems. When Graham's car was spotted Jean-Paul had phoned through to the Aire, and the sign was put up.

Just to be sure Jean-Paul had given simple instructions to the two brothers to ask in their broken English if the car was heading straight to the Folkestone ferry and also to tell them the wine would improve in time.

From his office ten minutes later, Jean-Paul used his pay-as-you-go mobile to call a Paris number. He just said that the package had been delivered, gave the description of the car and number plate and confirmed the ferry crossing times. The person at the other end just said '*Oui, je comprend,*' and hung up.

★★★★★★★

The four customs officers at Folkestone dock were all fed up with the job. Yes, it was steady, yes, the pay was OK, yes, there was a buzz because of the power and the fear that they put into everyone passing through, even those who had nothing to declare. But mostly it was boring.

Alan was the manager of the section and was coming up towards retirement. Part of him couldn't wait and part of him was scared to death of being at home all day. He got along OK with his wife, although like many relationships theirs had drifted slowly from the fresh and exciting love of youth into a kind of 'rubbing along' relationship. Alan knew that many marriages of their duration had gone the same way but he wished it would just occasionally lurch back and remind him of its previous glory. Alan had had a mini affair many years before – he thought of it as a mini-affair – nothing much had happened. Yes they had 'had sex' but he was the first to admit – and only to himself – that it hadn't been great. He was also pretty sure that she had felt the same. Even after all these years he still wondered if her lack of enthusiasm to continue their meetings was due to some inadequacy in his love making or hers. He had had very little experience with women, apart from his wife. Back in the days when he was a lad, it just wasn't the same. Girls did not drop their knickers on the first date – or even the tenth, well not the girls he went out with. Now he was led to believe from those awful, depressing, television documentaries about holidays in Spain or Greece that everyone got rolling drunk and shagged different people

10

every night. But not in his day.

That was all ten years ago and nearly forgotten. Not forgotten really, it ranked as one of the most fabulous periods in the whole of Alan's life. But the fact it did rank that high was a constant regret in relation to the rest of it, and 'forgotten' could be translated as 'can't really believe it'.

The tedium was getting to Alan more and more; he was just looking for a way out. Maybe if he won the Lottery he could just leave, walk away from his job, his marriage and his life to date. He thought again about getting round to buying a ticket each week. He looked out of the window and thought about the dreadful waste of time, his life, waiting between ferries and the extra waiting when the ferries were late which seemed to be always, and the tackiness of going through people's belongings. It had always reminded Alan of going through racks of clothes in charity shops. There was a particular smell that charity shop clothes had, it didn't matter where is was in the country, nor in what class of charity shop you went into – and the difference between some wealthier suburbs of London and those in the back streets of Manchester was marked – the smell was always the same. Not that he shopped there these days, but in his student days, charity shops were a great source of daft dressing up clothes. His first dinner jacket, which had been far too big, had been bought for a song in one. They had saved him lots of cash and so he had more to spend on the essentials, like drink and maybe even the odd joint.

Alan hated the rummaging, but the job demanded it as people who tried to smuggle stuff through customs always seemed to think that by hiding it in dirty washing wasn't going to be found. Of late though the smuggling game was different, no more the humiliation for travellers when he found that extra bottle of gin under the seat, it was now just the endless search for drugs and, of course, people.

The people trafficking was not for this terminal, all of the freight was sealed containers and so a quick look underneath in the few non-container places that might hold a person was all that was needed. But that was pretty routine. The drug search was more entertaining but seldom were there scores. Alan half-argued with himself that their job was right, worthwhile and stopped some drugs getting through while the other half of him argued that their work was a complete waste of time because the real supply of drugs was coming into the country through other routes by the ton.

Right now Alan sat at his desk pretending to sort through some of the paperwork and began to think about a cigarette again. He had stopped after years of smoking other people's duty frees. The office ban and the unwanted status of leper in the community had forced him to stop. The fact that it killed you did figure as well. But even though it was eight months and five days he wasn't counting the days and felt pretty pleased with himself about stopping. All down to will power he told lesser mortals. 'Nicotine is not an addictive drug, it's all up here', pointing vaguely towards the head. He only really, really wanted a cigarette about three times a day and the desire went away fairly quickly. About thirty seconds and it was gone, as long as he was doing something. Under normal fag-carrying conditions, it would have been alight and inhaled by the time the seconds were up. In pubs was the worst, with a pint in hand a fag still seemed right, he didn't quite know what to do with his hands now.

He wanted a cigarette now because he was bored, and cigarettes were often about boredom. He looked across to Gary's empty desk, he had asked him to work on a load of statistics which was more up his street. Not that he was a computerphobe, far from it, but this week, this month he just couldn't be arsed to work on the stats himself. Gary was young and keen, but he really didn't like him, not a team player, not one of the lads, not quite trustworthy.

Gary was the relative new boy, he was all numbers and whiz, he had come into the section from a government graduate scheme. He thought that the other three in the department were losers, old school, not up to the job. Gary was already frustrated – he wanted the boss's job, Alan's job, he was sure he could do it better, organise things in a more practical way, get things done, make waves. He knew Alan wanted out but he also knew that Alan didn't have the bottle to just leave; it would be a wait for retirement or be given the sack.

Gary was also finding it a bit tough financially. His move to the coast was not going well. He had started out trying to share a flat with a stranger after answering a small ad and it had turned sour. The stranger was too strange, and Gary moved out quickly into a bed and breakfast hotel as a stop gap and found that just too tacky and soulless. So third time lucky into a one-bedroomed flat in which at least he could please himself, but it was expensive and he drank too much. He wanted Alan's job for the money and to get on the promotion path.

Gary disliked the man who sat directly opposite him so much that he squinted his eyes every time he looked at him. Why did he find Geoffrey so obnoxious, he tried to ask himself one day, and found that the list was quite long. Then he stopped thinking about it because even he – the wonderful Gary – couldn't bring himself to admit some fundamental faults in his own character. Jealousy was the biggest stumbling block and his ego couldn't bear the thought of being in anyway jealous of that lump of lard, that acne-speckled out-of-control numb-brain. But he was. Geoffrey knew much more about customs procedures than he did, or indeed would ever know. He knew what to do in just about any situation – probably more than the incompetent Alan – and, he earned much more than Gary did. But, he was almost certainly a virgin. A forty-three- year-old virgin – ha ha ha.

Geoffrey was a forty three year old virgin and hated it. He desperately wanted to have a relationship with a woman, any woman. He knew he was definitely, definitely not gay, despite what the despicable Gary was saying behind his back and he was pretending not to notice. Gary was pretty stupid, he didn't understand the first thing about how the department worked or even the rules and he was so cocksure of himself. He, Geoffrey, knew just about every rule and regulation in the book, because he had read them over and over and could remember and recite them if necessary, like Kryten in the now legendary Red Dwarf series. But he still couldn't get a girlfriend. Why couldn't he? This question he posed every night as he went to bed alone. Even his mother said it most mornings over breakfast. OK, so he was a bit overweight but some women liked big men, and a bit spotty, but fifteen-year-old boys got girlfriends and look at their spots. He knew the Customs rule book by heart that showed he had a good brain. But he still couldn't find anyone to take him on, not even Ali – Alison – and she wasn't a conventional beauty. He thought she was the most wonderful woman in the world and he was in love with her and wanted to marry her. But she thought he was fat and dull even though he knew the Customs rule book by heart, which she accepted was quite handy especially as she was the fourth member of the Customs team.

Ali was falling in love with Gary, or not really 'falling in love' but she wanted to shag him. She knew he was no good, a big head and if she let him do it, it wouldn't last. But 'let him do it' was her fantasy because he wasn't the slightest bit interested in going anywhere near her. She knew that of course, but he was only one in the office who was fanciable. Alan was too old and grumpy and Geoffrey was so ug. She saw the way Geoffrey watched her… yuk.

At that moment Alan and Geoffrey were the only ones in the office, Gary had been sent over to the P&O office to pick up some paperwork for Alan, and Ali was outside being front man for the few cars coming off the ferry from France.

****

The ferry headed for the dock, the usual group of early birds clustered around the top of the stairs. Julie was at the other end of that particular idea; she was the one that wanted to stay in her seat until all were in their cars. Not that she had ever held anyone up – well possibly a bit, but generally the game was to stroll down to the car, get in, start-up and drive off. She had always despised those who insisted on starting their cars up too early. Graham wasn't quite as relaxed about the timing of the return to the car, but he always did know exactly where to go – he was the one that always made a note of the deck and the stairwell. Julie didn't always remember and on several occasions panicked a little, especially as she was usually about last down. They got to their car in plenty of time, drove down the ramp and filed out towards the custom bays.

It was a two-hour drive to home and she just wanted to sleep. Driving slowly through the customs bays was a silly tense time. She always felt like a criminal. She never brought stuff through; she never got stopped, until today.

Ali was bored and had just picked a car at random. There were of course guidelines to follow to pick out the most likely smugglers. Statistically young couples or young men on their own. Experienced customs officers were supposed to be able to pick out the guilty by their body language, the fear and tenseness in their eyes. But Ali could never see it; mostly people looked bored and travel weary. From this point all they wanted was to get home to their own beds and were just willing the beady eye of the all-powerful officer to cast on someone else and not be a pain in the arse and delay their journey with a smug I'm-the-Daddy-here-look, and often even worse, that bit about 'only doing my job'. None of that for Alison, she was just really, really bored and decided to just screw someone. She saw Julie, pretty and snuggled down in her seat and pulled them over – sort of spite really.

'Good evening sir, sorry to delay your journey but I would just like to ask you a few questions.'

'Yes certainly,' came the weak response. Julie groaned and snuggled deeper in her seat.

'What was the purpose of your journey, sir?'

'Well part work and part pleasure really,' said Graham with a false smile.

'Did you pack your luggage yourself, sir?'

'Yes.'

'Can I have a quick look in the boot please, sir?'

Graham got out and unlocked the boot. Ali routed around a little down the sides of the boot, without much enthusiasm. She was just going through the motions. She remembered what Alan had told her when she first started – 'It's a deterrent Alison, we have to be seen to be checking some cars, otherwise it would become a free for all. The penalties are so harsh that only the really determined and foolish would try to bring drugs through.'

As Ali brought her hand out from feeling down the side of one of the suitcases a sharp clasp caught her hand and she pulled it quickly away against the case of wine at the back edge of the boot. It tottered and fell out and cracked against the towing pin, there was a muffled sound of glass breaking.

'Shit,' said Ali

'Oh,' said Graham

Ali quickly grabbed the dented box and put it out of the way onto the pavement.

'I am so very sorry sir,' she blurted out and felt herself flushing with embarrassment and self-annoyance and already thinking about what Alan would say to her.

'I can find you another box to put the bottles in as this one is damaged,' and she started to open the case as Graham was saying. 'Really it's no great problem it was pretty cheap wine… .'

Conversation now stopped as Ali opened the box and pulled out the broken bottle by the neck depositing a surprisingly large amount of white powder over the box and the black tarmac. There was hardly any wine in the bottle at all.

Both parties viewed the powder.

Graham said 'What is that?'

The next few minutes were chaotic. Julie had jumped out of the car as the noise level went up and it was obvious that something was horribly wrong and on seeing the powder her mouth dropped and just said 'What the fuck…?'

Ali recovered some composure and shouted into her walkie-talkie 'Code 1, Bay2, Code 1, Bay 2.' Saying it twice was not part of the procedure but she was stressed. Graham just stood on the pavement repeating over and over 'I don't believe it, I don't believe it…' his face was white with anger or shock and he was holding both hands up on top of his head gripping handfuls of hair. Julie had crossed past the mess on the pathway to join Graham and was saying 'what is that stuff?' She knew pretty much what is was, some sort of drug anyway although she had never seen hard drugs before. Yes, cannabis at university but she had never been in the hard drugs brigade, far too scary. Now though they were looking down at a splash of white that was probably cocaine or something that they had brought through customs and they had been caught with.

18

Julie quietly screamed into her hands as the desperate situation unfolded into her consciousness. This is very bad; this is very, very bad. Her heart was thumping and she felt sick.

The men in the office had reacted swiftly to the Code 1. Alan had immediately phoned the police line and called them in. Geoffrey leapt up and looked at Alan who nodded, a nod meant yes, I am calling the police in and holding the fort here, and yes you get your arse down to the bay as quickly as possible, support Ali and sort out the other things. Geoffrey left and was down the stairs very quickly for such a large man. Gary had just got back from P&O. Geoffrey shouted at him from the doorway without looking back or slowing down, 'with me now'. Gary took half a second to react but although his first thought was something like, 'How dare that fat git tell me what to do,' but he dashed after Geoffrey and was amazed how fast the man could move.

On Bay 2, Ali had moved the two shaking travellers a few paces away from the car and the broken bottle. Several passing cars had slowed right down and were rubbernecking and soundlessly saying 'Look at that, look at that…,' to the other passengers in their car.

Once on the scene, Geoffrey took control. He took a quick look at the open wine case, the broken bottle and the white powder and sussed it. He told Gary to get the screens around quickly and spoke to Graham with a firm smile.

'Good evening sir, please will you come to the office with me,' Graham nodded, realising it wasn't a question.

'And perhaps Madam you could join us.' Geoffrey raised his eyebrows and gave a little flick of his head to Ali as a signal to take Julie's arm and escort her.

At that moment, the police arrived. Two uniformed special unit officers, both armed with machine pistols. Julie gave a twitch, her knees gave out a bit and she threw up on the pavement, while Ali supported her. Graham was propelled firmly and efficiently to the office and put into an interview room on his own. It was spartan with just a table and four chairs but with a very good lock on the door. It was a cell. Julie was put in a separate identical cell and the door was locked.

The nightmare had begun.

Chapter 2

As soon as the couple were secured in their respective rooms, Alan dismissed the two armed policemen – whose role was purely security. Drug smugglers could be armed, and could try make a run for it and in the process could put the UK Border staff and fellow travellers at risk.

Graham and Julie sat alone in their respective rooms while outside there was considerable activity. Julie continued to feel sick and, now with a serious headache, she put her head down on the table and tried controlled breathing. Graham just sat rigidly and with a clenched jaw.

★★★★★★★

Two text messages were received by a Paris-based mobile. The first was short and to the point:

Package seems to be delayed – Charlie.

The answer was equally short:

Hold your position and wait – S.

The second call came a little later:

Package discovered. Advise action – Ivan.

The receiver in Paris bit her lip and swore.

★★★★★★★

Alan and Ali first completed the standard forms for each of the detainees, name, address, age and contact details and they were both required to empty their pockets into a plastic tray. The contents were briefly recorded and each signed a form confirming that the list of items was correct.

Next the interrogation started. Julie was first. Alan and Ali sat down opposite her. Alan spoke.

'First I need to advise you of the situation. You are being detained under the legislation laid down by the Customs and Excise Bill 2004. We, the UK Border Agency have the statutory right to detain people who are suspected of committing an offence until such time as the police take over the investigation. They will decide whether a full criminal investigation is required and will take the appropriate action. This may involve continued detainment, arrest and charging and subsequent prosecution. We would like to ask you some initial questions and the interview will be recorded. You do have the right to remain silent and also the right to request legal representation. Do you understand?'

'Yes,' said Julie quietly.

'We would like you to tell us everything you know. The recording of this interview may be used by the police for possible criminal proceedings. I remind you that you do have the right to have a legal representative present. Do you understand?'

'Yes,' replied Julie 'I am happy to tell you everything that happened because clearly we have been set up by some drug smugglers and need to, well show you, that we are totally innocent. I don't need to get a lawyer involved. We have nothing to hide.'

'OK Miss Webb, tell us what happened then.'

While she had been waiting to be interviewed Julie had tried to think back to the lay-by, tried to re-picture the men. Could she pick them out in an identity parade? Probably not, no one really looked that hard at other people – or maybe it was just her? She had often wanted to have a go at an Identikit thing that the police used, because in films the victims could always do it and come up with an image which turned out to be really close to the villain. She was not at all sure that she could do it. She started to think about Graham's face, someone she knew quite well and realised that she probably couldn't even do one that looked like him. She also thought about what she would be asked, and tried to think of everything that had happened in as much detail as possible. The more detail the better the chance of catching the bastards that had set them up. So she was ready.

'I can't tell you much because I didn't take much notice. Graham was worried about being a bit late for the ferry and that we may not have enough time to call in to the supermarket to get the wine. He then saw an advert of some kind at the roadside and pulled into a lay-by, you know, an Aire. I didn't see what it said, I was dozing. I sat up a bit when we stopped. There was a large white van and a table with some wine bottles and glasses and some wine cases as well. There was only one case on the table but several in the van. There were two men. Both in probably their thirties maybe forties, a bit scruffy and looked like farm hands. Graham spoke to them in French – he has very good French – and they gave him a glass to try. He posed around a bit and puffed his cheeks out and obviously thought it was good. Next thing I know he opened the boot and put a case in the back. And we were off. It all took just a few minutes. That's all I can tell you.'

'Tell us all can think of about the van.'

'It was just a plain white van. It was quite dirty. I don't think it had any markings. It was a Transit I guess, or something similar.'

'Describe the men again.'

'I can't think of any more details – I didn't really look, I was trying to sleep. About thirty... maybe mid-thirties. Scruffy. Jeans. Yes, they both wore jeans.'

'Could you pick them out in an identity parade?'

'I don't know, maybe, I'm really not sure, I didn't really take them in.'

'OK well that's all for now. For your own sake do please try to think of anything else that would help identify these two men.'

The customs officers turned off the tape and got up to leave.

'Can we go now then?'

'No,' said Alan almost with a laugh, 'you have just been involved in a very serious offence and we have to investigate this to the fullest extent. Please don't expect to just walk away.'

'Oh God,' said Julie and sank back.

A similar scene unfolded a few minutes later. Graham answered as best he could. He had been the one who had talked to the two men but sadly he could find even less to remember about the situation.

'In your own words, Mr Spelling, will you tell us what happened.'

'There were two men, in their early forties maybe, they... er... spoke French, oh – sorry.'

'Why did you stop?'

'I wanted to buy some wine and we were running a bit late for the ferry.'

'So what time was it?'

'Well I don't know – um, about half an hour before the ferry time.'

'Do you mean the ferry sailing time or the start of the booking-in time?'

'Oh – the booking-in time, I like to get there early.'

'So what made you stop there?'

'Well there was s sign up saying *VIN*, so I pulled in.'

'You mean *VIN*... V.I.N. not VAN... V.A.N... .'

'Yes of course.'

'Can you show me on this map where the lay-by was?'

Alan had produced a large-scale map of the road running

up to the ferry which he then laid out on the table.

Unfortunately, Graham, for all his pedantic tendencies, could not show them on the map exactly.

'Somewhere along this stretch,' he said, indicating a length of road about 10 miles long. The map didn't show the Aires.

'Can you remember anything about the lay-by that might help us identify the spot?'

Graham thought hard.

'Sorry, no, I wasn't looking at the surroundings particularly, I was only thinking about the wine. Oh, there was a toilet.'

'OK tell us exactly what was said and by whom.'

'The short one – oh yes, one was fairly tall and kept back, the other was shorter and did most or all of the talking.'

'He said bonjour – hello.' Graham translated. Alan raised an eyebrow.

'Sorry,' said Graham.

'He just said try this wine – it's good.'

'So I did, and it was good, in fact, I think very good. He kind of just stood there – he wasn't a particularly good salesman. I asked him how much and he told me, it was cheap – about £1.00 a bottle. I have to say I did wonder if it had fallen off the back of a lorry but I'm afraid I didn't care – sorry.'

'Go on.'

'I said I would have a case and he picked one up and gave it to me, I gave him the cash and put the case in the boot – and drove off – that's it.'

'Describe him in detail if you can.'

'He was fairly short – 5 6ish, early forties maybe, stocky, two-day beard, jeans, a brownish jacket of some sort, fairly worn. His French was fairly slovenly, not refined, agricultural worker I would guess.'

'… and the other one?'

'He was just holding back watching – he didn't really say anything. He was a bit taller, probably a bit older, similar clothes.'

'Would you recognise them again?'

'Er – yes I think so but I'm not totally sure – if they were wearing the same clothes yes sure but, you know… .'

'Did you open the case?'

'No.'

'Why not, the wine sample was good, but the sealed case could have contained bottles of water?'

'I didn't think of that – sorry.'

'Please don't keep saying sorry, Mr Spelling,' said Alan starting to get annoyed, 'saying sorry does not change the fact that you are involved in a possible serious offence.'

'Sor… .'

Graham stopped himself halfway through and looked at the table. Alan got up.

'Can I go now?'

'No,' said Alan a little sharply and left the room.

★★★★★★★

Outside in the main customs office Alan called a meeting.

'Well, unfortunately those two have been able to give next to nothing for the police to go on. I suspect the French police will just laugh. But at least we stopped the drugs getting through. We were lucky to catch this one, more by luck than judgement.'

'Well…' Ali started

'Sorry Ali,' Alan cut back in 'I didn't mean to criticise. The point I'm making is that we don't as a rule check cases of wine to see if there is wine in the bottles and I have to say having a look at this particular set-up, I'm not convinced that I would have spotted the inner bottle.

'Me neither,' said Geoffrey

'This was a very sophisticated job. I can't really show you all as I have put the evidence straight into the cage ready for forensic to have a go at it tomorrow. But simply it is a very dark glass bottle with a fancy, expensive-looking label. Inside there is a second bottle containing what we believe is cocaine, we won't know definitely until it's tested – but it looks like coke. Between the two bottles is wine. So, at first glance it looks like a bottle of wine, you can't see the inner bottle at all.'

'Someone has gone to a lot of trouble' commented Geoffrey, 'I've not seen anything like this before. Presumably the other five bottles are the same – have an inner bottle with cocaine.'

'I expect so, I had a quick look, but I'm not 100% sure, the bottle glass is very dark and with red wine in between… it's for the police boys to check over. I didn't want to put my finger prints all over them.'

Ali put her hand up. Alan smiled but didn't comment.

'Yes Ali.'

'This couple have been used as mules then, without their knowledge?'

'Well probably, but until we get a bit more information

tomorrow, we have to hang on to them as they were the ones carrying through and so technically they are the offenders, obviously innocent until proven guilty in a court of law.' Alan rattled this last statement off in a policeman-like monotone.

'If they are innocent – the gang must have had a method to get the stuff back once over here,' suggested Ali.

'Well yes. Unless of course these guys are the gang? Anyway, they stay here tonight; CID take over tomorrow and hopefully it'll be sorted. So, excitement over for today, go home, unless you're on the late shift.'

They went back to their desks and those who were going, did so.

★★★★★★★

A while later a text message appeared on a mobile phone in Paris:

> One unit of the package broken at Customs. Contents revealed. Two punters, man and woman, questioned and held in cells. CID and forensics here tomorrow morning. Car impounded. Will be thoroughly searched tomorrow by police. All evidence in locked cage. Ivan

'*Merde, merde, merde, merde,*' Silvie spat at the message. She hit the intercom.

'Gerard, we have confirmation, come up.'

Gerard appeared a few moments later, sat at the big table opposite Silvie and poured himself a drink from the open bottle.

'OK what do we know?' She slid her iPhone over for him to read.

'How cool is Ivan and what do you have on him?'

Gerard re-read the message before answering. 'I think he is fairly together, but I admit he's never really been tested – he's a sort of sleeper I suppose. The boss hooked him in a while back and I've been the remote contact since.'

'I know very little about this guy, as usual, information only on a need-to-know basis. Do you know why Pierre coded him Ivan – presumably it means something to him?'

'I know nothing about his code name, just a Pierre joke I suppose, you know, Russian spy. Some while back this guy was in deep, had a major habit and built up a serious debt with one of our regular distributors. He couldn't pay and the distributor asked us to get involved – to play the heavy hand. Because of his job at Customs, the boss gave him a get out of jail free card. He was told that most of the debt would be wiped if he were to help us in the future and the mug fell right into it. As an insurance policy we sent a package through and made sure he was the officer in place. We told him it was drugs and filmed the whole event from the car behind. It was really comical; our man actually stopped and said to him something like. "You're Ivan aren't you, I'm the one carrying the drugs – they told me you would let me through". Poor Ivan nearly died on the spot. The whole thing was a set-up, there weren't any drugs in the package – it was cheese, but Ivan didn't know that, and now we have him on film. Technically we can do what we like with him, we own him.'

'Typical Pierre set-up, he always has a back-up plan and then a plan C as well, just in case,' Silvie said this with a smile. She admired his thoroughness but her smile faded as she thought more about the man she loved. He really didn't trust anyone and that included her.

Gerard went on. 'I have been the contact without ever meeting him. All I've done is organise the set-up, you know – with the film scam and I've sent him small retainers direct to his account – all recorded of course and designed to keep hold of him and blackmail him later if we need to.'

Gerard smiled at the gullibility of Ivan.

Silvie was still thinking about how Pierre might react. 'You know Pierre will spit blood when he hears about this and get very, very cross with Ivan, because he should have ensured that it was him on duty to make certain the car got through without a search. You did send that instruction through with the car's details?'

'Yes of course I did. I got the text from Jean-Paul immediately after the wine was on board the guy's car and I have no idea what went wrong at the dock; probably incompetence or maybe just bad luck. Pierre will want to know and well, he may get vindictive, you know what he's like when things go wrong. Ivan's error may help us put extra pressure on him. What you thinking?'

'My first thought is can we get the gear out of their lock up without them knowing?'

'That would be good, but Christ what's the chance of that?'

She went on, 'We're talking about a serious amount of coke in there – and you know it's high quality and only 50% cut.

Charlie is still standing by with the replacement case of wine. Do you think Ivan has the balls and the opportunity to break into the cage and swap the wine out? That way we still get most of the gear back.'

'I think it's worth a shot. We've got nothing to lose except Ivan, and Pierre will probably blow him out of the scene anyway. He can't get back to us as he has no idea who we are. So if he gets caught then no great loss.'

'From what you know about his position in the Border Agency, does he have access?'

'He did tell me that he could get into all areas; it may have been bravado and showing off to boost his credibility. Don't know.'

'I think we should try and sort this before Pierre gets back from his trip, you know what his temper is like, even with me, and he trusts no one.'

'OK, I'll contact Charlie first and have him stand by with the exchange bottles and try to get Ivan on board with some serious threats. I also think it is to our advantage to lead the UK police into thinking that our mark is responsible, it will give us a bit of thinking time and I have an idea.'

★★★★★★★

Ivan's phone vibrated briefly. Alone in the office at that moment, he read the text and blanched. He read the message again just in case he had misunderstood it. He hadn't. The message was clear – he was being asked, no told, that he must do three things, each difficult. He put the phone away and tried to think clearly. The instructions he was being given were explicit as well as the consequences if he didn't comply. His whole dossier, copies of all their conversations and all his payments plus the film of him waving through the drugs would be handed to police. He was screwed.

Ivan sat at his desk in the Customs Office and reviewed his options and not for the first time thought through his past. How could he have been so completely and utterly stupid, first to take the drugs, second to get into massive debt but third to tie in with this crowd, whoever they were? He had never known who these guys were, all communications had been via text, but he knew they didn't take prisoners – they were very nasty people. Now he was being threatened with exposure. That meant jail. Jail meant pain. Jail meant loss of everything, no job, no future. Tears started to form and run down his cheeks. If he went ahead with this crazy scheme he would probably get caught, because you can't just walk in and out of a Customs office with a load of cocaine and not be noticed. It was ridiculous. Either way he was going to end up in jail. The French guys, were ruthless, that was for sure, and they wouldn't think twice about throwing him to the wolves.

If only he had got down to the dock in time to stop Ali from stopping that car, of all cars, why did she have to stop that one. Fuck it, fuck it, fuck it. He had been ready but he hadn't known that the bloody ferry was docking ahead of time, fifteen minutes early. That never happens. Never, fuck it.

He wiped away the tears. Right, think straight, what were the options. OK. Do nothing. Those bastards would lose their drugs, get seriously pissed off and shop him, or worse beat him up or even kill him. Not a good route. Run away. Sounds good. But where to? He had the awful thought that they had fingers in many pies – possibly even government – and would somehow find him and then they would definitely kill him. Third, do what they asked there was a chance that he would get away with it – slim, but a chance.

He would then be OK, he would still have to get out – run away in effect but he could do it a bit later. They couldn't stop him from changing his job could they? He wasn't even sure about that. What if they made him stay there because that was where he was useful to them. Oh God.

Ivan sat there for several more minutes. Luckily no ferry was due for another hour so he did have time to drive out and meet with this Charlie bloke mentioned in the text. He was pretty sure that he could get into the cage. Security was very tight, unless of course you knew where the keys were kept and you also knew where the alarm combination was written down, which of course he did. It was this knowledge that had kept him from getting a couple of fingers removed when he couldn't pay his drug debts. Right now he was thinking a missing couple of fingers looked a good option.

He was the only one in the office until the next ferry came in; he was just holding the fort in case something happened. He checked the window anyway. No one about. The key to the cage was kept in a locked key cupboard; the key to the key cupboard was kept in the locked top drawer of Alan's desk. The key to the desk was in the boss' pocket, but the spare was in an unlocked box in the bottom drawer of the other desk.

The alarm had a very basic six-figure code known only to

the boss, but in case he forgot it, it was written on a Post-it note stuck to the underside of his keyboard. The code was supposed to be changed every week, but hadn't been for a least a month.

Ivan retrieved the Post-it and wrote the number down on another piece of paper. He checked for the key – it was where he expected it to be. Part of him had sort of hoped that the key wouldn't be there – then he couldn't have done it, so no decision to make. OK, maybe he would still end up getting punished, but the decision to do this or not do this was causing him a lot of stress. He sat down and thought through the next set of orders. He had to have a reason for leaving – a sensible one. The security guard might ask and be suspicious about him leaving the site. Then of course when the police looked in the wine case the cocaine bottles would be gone. Oh… the French had thought that one through. They were banking on the fact that no one knew at this point if there were more bottles with cocaine in – it could be just the one. Good. In fact with just one bottle in the case it might even point the finger back at the guy in the cell. Organised gangs would go for the whole case.

He pulled out his untraceable pay-as-you-go mobile and called the number he had been given, Charlie's number.

'Yeah?'

'Ivan here.'

'Yeah?'

'I think we need to meet… yes?'

'Yeah – turn left out of the terminal. Drive three miles west on the A259. Look for a blue Ford Focus in the lay-by with the left-hand indicator flashing. Pull in behind and stay in your car. I'll be here for fifteen minutes only.' And the line went dead.

Ivan clenched his teeth. He had to work fast. There was a 'green' bag hanging on the coat hooks – it had been there for months. No one seemed to own it.

After another quick check out of the window he took the key, tapped in the code on the keypad and was in the cage. The box with the wine was sitting on a table ready for the police to start their checks in the morning. He pulled out each bottle in turn and loaded them into the jute bag.

He was at the door when he thankfully remembered the transmitter. He went back and found it fairly easily tucked between the flaps in the base of the box, held firm with some sort of adhesive. He ripped the box a little pulling it off but tucked the flap back in, replaced the box on the table and locked the cage back up.

He tested the bag; it was heavy and full and didn't look a lot like shopping. In fact it looked a lot like five bottles of wine in a bag. The saving grace was that if this switch worked no one would be looking for bottles being taken in and out, so even if the bottles were spotted there would be no reason to suspect anything untoward. Ivan thought for a minute about whether the security guard might suspect him of taking confiscated wine from travellers, but they didn't do that anymore. It was years since they had had the bonus of free wine. So maybe there was no problem. He was still anxious and had no real reason sorted for taking out such a heavy bag. He hefted it and it clanked – his heart pounded again. He needed something to dampen the sound. He looked around and saw two or three old copies of the local free paper which found their way into the office and they tended to hang about waiting for someone to take on the dreaded responsibility of throwing them away. He quickly wrapped each of them in the newspaper and put them back carefully into the bag.

He checked his watch and started to panic – time was running out and he needed to get going to meet this guy Charlie.

Ivan picked up the bag and put his coat between the handles to cover the open top. He sauntered out trying to look relaxed. He walked down the stairs and out across the yard to the security gates. The security guards changed with the shifts but they were all well known to the crew. This evening it was George.

'Aye aye, had enough of the daily grind of nicking those poor bastards?' called George as he approached.

'I'm running away to sea George, but sadly I have to be back again in about half an hour to screw a few more punters.'

'You'll get your rewards at the Pearly Gates. Ha ha.' George opened the gate without a look at the bag or its contents.

Ivan walked casually to his car resisting the urge to turn around to see if anyone or everyone was following him. They weren't. He drove slowly out of the car park and turned left.

By the time he got to the lay-by it was well past the due time. He pulled up behind Charlie's Focus with its indicator still going. Charlie turned it off and got out of the car quickly. He looked through the driver's window at Ivan to check it was him. His face matched the picture he'd seen. Charlie had a scarf around his lower face and large dark glasses on – even though it was evening. He yanked opened Ivan's door.

'You're late, give me the bag.'

'I'm sorry I got away as fast… .'

Charlie was already back at his car and very quickly swapped the bottles over and returned the bag and its new contents to Ivan.

'Wear gloves when you put these back. Here's the wine and here's the other package – you know what to do.' And he was gone.

Back at the terminal Ivan had to run the gauntlet again, past George.

'What is it you're smuggling in this time eh?' George didn't sound as if he really suspected anything but at the same time he was keen to look in the bag, and did, more out of nosiness than anything to do with security. Ivan didn't feel he could or should resist but managed to continue to play it cool.

George picked up the coat and saw the bottles and made an exaggerated eyebrow-raising enquiry face.

'It's Ali's birthday tomorrow and we're having a little surprise do for her, so shush eh.'

Ivan had put his finger to his lips on the shush bit.

'Mum's the word, no problemo.'

Ivan smiled, partly because he was relieved at coming up with a half plausible reason for taking in the wine, partly because he was through and partly because a very short, very fat guard in his fifties did not much resemble The Terminator.

Back in the office he reversed the process and within minutes had the new bottles in place and the keys and everything back in where it should be.

He wiped the sweat from his face with his handkerchief and was aware that the tension had doubled his underarm wet and now he was uncomfortably smelly. But, he seemingly had got away with the bottle change. There was no reason to link the bottles coming in through the gate with the bottles in the cage. George wouldn't be in the loop as far as what was being investigated in the office nor had he taken that much of a look at the bottles anyway, certainly not enough to recognise or remember the labels.

He blew out his cheeks, 'So far so good,' he thought almost out loud, 'Christ, I might even be off the hook for the time being.'

He still had the other job to do but he was back at his desk ten minutes later, still sweating and in a slightly shocked state when some of the others came in and three of them went out to check the large ferry which had come in dead on time… and that's when he remembered that he hadn't worn gloves.

Chapter 3

Julie and Graham had been moved from their respective rooms immediately after their interviews and transferred to their overnight accommodation – another plain room with just a bed and a table. There was an adjoining toilet and a hand basin which had reasonably hot water, but it was all very bleak. It was seven o'clock. Julie had been awake on the hard bed for about three hours; spending the time going over and over the same little fragment in her mind; a fragment which she could hardly recall, as it was totally insignificant at the time, though not now. She was very aware that her mind was starting to play tricks with her. Was she really recalling those moments in the lay-by, or was she only recalling the last time she thought about it? She had always been aware that when looking at old photographs and imagining being back, say, on the beach as a child, the memories were not real and that there was an element of remembering the last time she had looked at the photographs. It was these 'mind tricks' that led your memories away from the truth. She lay awake feeling sorry for herself again, which was not one of her normal faults, but she pondered on how tiny insignificant decisions in life   like deciding to buy wine at that moment – sped your life off in a completely different direction.

As the dawn light came into the cell she moved from the sorry-for-herself state into anger. Angry with – somebody, anybody. The room was small and smelt of disinfectant but was clean enough, but the smell annoyed her. She had been given a pair of pyjamas to change into and felt angry about that too. She had decided to strip down to her underwear rather than don the rather dodgy and very large night things. The sheets were harsh on her bare skin and part way through the night she had thought about putting the pyjamas on after all, but had fallen back to sleep, and now, cold and feeling the rough sheet, she felt the anger rolling around.

When breakfast turned up she was dressed, albeit in the same clothes as the day before, and despite herself and wanting nothing to do with this whole farce, she thankfully ate the toast and marmalade and drank the surprisingly good mug of tea.

The woman who had brought her breakfast came back after about fifteen minutes and told her that she would only have to wait another few minutes before being called up to the interview room to talk to the police.

She sat on the bed and once again went through the details as she remembered them as she would no doubt be asked the same questions again by the police. There was something she had seen at the lay-by, something that was important. She had almost recalled it in the middle of the night, between dozes, when the brain is relaxed and going through its management sorting routines. It happened to Julie often, something that was important that had been completely forgotten during the waking hours came drifting back to the front of the brain at

3am. Such was this nagging thought now, but she hadn't quite grasped it. Was it important? Was it real? Or was it just her brain playing tricks on her again, teasing her, just because she wanted to remember something that would make a difference – get her and Graham out of this fix.

Three-quarters of an hour later, the door was unlocked by the same woman and Julie was escorted up a flight of concrete steps, along a cream-painted corridor and into one of two interview rooms she had been in the night before, each with a glass door, inside there was just a simple table and four chairs. Two police officers were already seated.

Julie sat opposite the two; they turned on the tape machine and introduced themselves as Detective Inspector Andrew Curry and Detective Constable Saskia Edwards.

Curry went through the same preliminaries as the Customs Officer had the day before and once again Julie answered that she understood the situation and that she didn't need or want any legal representation.

The inspector asked the questions.

'Miss Webb, I know that you have already given a verbal statement to our colleagues at the Border Agency and answered some of these questions but I must ask again, I hope you understand... .'

Julie just gave a resigned nod.

'Where had you and your partner been in France?'

Julie was slightly taken aback, first as she was expecting to have to answer the same questions and tell the same story and second as she had never verbalised the word 'partner' in relation to Graham. The English language for all its richness had a big hole in it when it came to 'partnership'. When introducing people as 'partner' there is no real way of determining whether you meant 'business partner' or 'sexual partner'. When the other party was of the same sex this could cause doubt, concern and embarrassment. There is also the confusion about when the word partner is used in a love relationship, was it when you are just 'going out', when you were 'going out' and having regular sex, or when you are living together?

Therefore Julie started with an 'Err,' which is not a great start when you are being interrogated about a serious crime and you want to be believed.

'Well,' followed by, 'Graham had travelled all over Northern France, I don't know where exactly. I had gone over on Eurostar to see an old school friend in Paris and I met Graham there. We spent the night in a hotel and came home in his car yesterday.'

'Why was Mr Spelling in France?'

'He was working. Graham sells knives... .' She stopped because for the first time she thought that 'selling knives' didn't sound too good, but then carried on.

'He sells, expensive, no, very expensive cook's knives to... cooks. They are very high quality and much sought after – made in Japan. He went over on a sales trip and we just had a kind of day's holiday alongside.'

'I see. How often do you two go across the channel on these sales trips?'

'It's the first time I have been, but Graham goes regularly.'

'How often is regularly?'

'Oh, he's over at least once a month and stays for perhaps two weeks at a time. I don't see an awful lot of him.'

She stopped short at saying more, suddenly aware that they were being accused of drug smuggling and someone who went back and forth across the channel even if 'on business' maybe put thoughts into the 'police mind'.

'I see from the documents here that you have different addresses, so do I conclude that you don't actually live together?'

'No, we don't,' she decided to in future just answer the question and no more – as if in the witness box.

'How long have you known Mr Spelling?'

'About three months, I think.'

'And you met... ?'

She hesitated.

He raised his eyebrows.

'At a golf club do.'

'Why did you hesitate?'

'Well, I think that neither of us are really golf club types. You know.'

'OK, tell me what you know about the wine pick up in the lay-by.'

Julie repeated the story she had told Alan and was not able to add anything more, but then went on, 'I have been thinking a lot overnight about the two guys in the lay-by, they were rough, you know, scruffy and didn't come across as well educated. I only caught scraps of their conversation but they weren't behaving in the way you would expect from someone selling their own wine at the roadside. I am sure they were not the 'owners' of the wine, even if they had stolen it. Do you know what I mean?'

'I think so; do you mean they were just working for someone else?'

'Yes, exactly, they had been told what to say – or in fact what not to say, as they said very little. Someone had 'schooled' them.'

'OK.'

'That's all I can think of.'

'Tell me Miss Webb… '

Julie looked up at Curry, he had moved from a very friendly style of questioning to a bit more focussed and a bit harsher. She thought of the good cop bad cop scenario.

'Have you ever been a drug user?'

'No, of course not,' She looked him straight in the eye and he stared back; she looked away and folded a little.

'Well, apart from the odd joint at university.'

'So that's a 'yes', is it Miss Webb?'

'No, that's a 'no', Inspector, I don't count a couple of spliffs fifteen years ago as relevant to today's problem and I don't believe you do either. I have never taken any hard drugs, full stop.'

'OK, what about Mr Spelling?'

'He doesn't either, I am not even sure he would have done as a student.'

'Where did he study?'

'Oh, he has said, but I can't remember. He read French I think. Sorry, I can't recall, ask him, again I can't think that it's at all relevant.'

'We will be the judge of that Miss Webb.'

Julie felt told off and decided to keep quiet again, even though that was difficult for her.

Detective Inspector Curry leaned forward to the tape recorder and said, 'interview stopped at 9.08am,' and then looked up at Julie and said, 'could you please stay here for a few minutes.' Curry and the constable got up and closed the door behind them but stood in the hallway. Julie could see them through the glass door. They were nodding at each other. After about a minute, Curry open the opened the door and sat down again.

'This may sound a little formal, but technically you have been arrested on suspicion of smuggling drugs although we are not charging you on current evidence. We are releasing you but on bail. This means that we can insist on certain conditions relating to your release.'

'OK, what conditions?'

'First, we may need to speak to you again in the next day or so while we try to get more information about what has gone on here and it would make sense if you stay locally   is that possible?'

'Well yes, I suppose so, my sister lives about half an hour from here. We can stay there for a while I'm sure.'

'Good.'

'Oh, OK. Can we go straight away?'

'Only you for the time being."

'Should I wait for Graham?'

'We still need some more time with Mr Spelling. I will have a car drop you at your sister's as the Scene of Crime Officers people need to check out your car, or rather Mr Spelling's car.'

Julie frowned and just said, 'Oh.'

'Nothing to worry about, it'd just be easy for you to go now rather than hanging about.'

He had her passport in his hand and had been flicking through the empty pages while talking. He closed the little book and said, 'and the second condition of your bail is that I will hang on to your passport.' Julie again said 'Oh,' and pulled a face at him.

'You don't want me to travel abroad then?'

'I think that would be inappropriate right now.'

'Can I see Graham before I go?'

'I think not, sorry. Here's my card, if you think of anything else, call me'

Curry stood, so she did as well and they walked together with no further conversation to the front desk. Julie was left to sign some forms and give her sister's address and telephone number to the desk sergeant who then called the number for her.

'Maddie, it's Julie. Graham and I have run into a bit of a problem at the port and I need your help, can I come and stay the night? I will tell all when I get there.'

'Of course, my love, are you OK? Is there anything else you need?'

'No, I'll be there in an hour or so.'

'Fine, I'll be here.'

'Bye.'

****

47

Back in Curry's office, the two detectives sat on the edge of their desks.

'What do you think Saskia?'

'Look Andy, it's your call, she comes across absolutely clean, but Spelling, I don't know, this going back and forth across the channel, hell, with knives, makes you feel uneasy, doesn't it?'

'I had a quick look in the car and what she says checks out; those knives are superb things, just like the ones you see someone like Jamie Oliver using, or some of the other celebrity chefs, except of course they don't buy them.'

'Even so, it would be a good cover if you wanted to regularly bring in drugs; if stopped, the guys at Customs would be taking more interest in the knives rather than anything else.'

'Yeah, a bit far-fetched I think. This has got all the hallmarks of a sophisticated organised crime as those bottles aren't cheap to make. I reckon these two are both legit and they have been 'muled', just as they say. But we should hang on to him a bit longer and check him out – just to be sure. I'm happy to see her go – she can't tell us anymore and she can't go far, if we need to talk more.'

****

The Scene of Crime Officers arrived early, had a quick look around inside the car, wrapped it up in plastic film and pulled it by winch onto their flatbed. They put the wine box into a large plastic bag and put that in the cab of the truck and drove off. The SOCO unit was based in Ashford so was close to the Kent ports and close enough to London where The

Met sometimes needed a hand with analysis. The site was in a nondescript building at the back of the main police station in the centre of town. Although the building was old it had been completely rebuilt inside and was now exceptionally 'clean'.

Once in Ashford, the team unloaded Graham's car and pushed it into the large well-lit garage space. The wine box was taken through double doors into the main laboratory and placed on a stainless steel table similar to those found in autopsy rooms. Two gloved-up civilian scientists carefully removed the plastic bag from the cardboard box took out each bottle and stood them alongside the box. Every part of the broken bottle was laid out and photographs were taken of everything. Much of the white powder from inside the broken bottle had ended up inside the box, now stained red from the wine that had leaked out from the space surrounding the inner bottle. Every grain was picked up using brushes and tweezers.

The powder would be analysed and the outside of the bottles screened for fingerprints and DNA material. The box would be taken apart and minutely examined. Another two scientists would go through the car.

★★★★★★★

Detective Inspector Curry decided that it would be a lot easier for him to be back at the police station for the interview with Graham. He was also thinking that almost certainly he would be releasing him later on and by then the car would have been checked out, and so Spelling would be able to drive it away and pick up his partner from her sister's.

When told of the move to Ashford, Graham was not pleased and saw it as a negative move, but when told that Julie had been released and was waiting for him at her sister's, he thought that was a positive sign and maybe this was going to end soon and they could get back home. Curry told him that his car was at the police station in Ashford and so it made sense.

Back in Ashford, the two detectives sat down opposite Graham and went through the same procedure as before with Julie. They turned on the tape and started the interview.

'The time is 11.03am, present are Detective Inspector Curry, Detective Constable Edwards and Mr Graham Spelling.'

'Mr Spelling you have agreed to come to this police station to answer questions relating to the alleged offence at the Folkestone Channel-crossing port.'

Graham frowned a little at the statement Curry had made, 'agreed to come,' he wasn't at all sure that he'd had a choice, but he said nothing.

'We are arresting you in connection with the offence and you are now requested to answer our questions.'

Graham was even more annoyed at the idea of his being 'arrested' but again kept quiet.

'Mr Spelling, how often do you travel across to mainland Europe?'

Like Julie, Graham was surprised to be asked that question; he had thought the police would be running through the same story that he had told the Border Agency.

'Oh, um, quite often I suppose, I sell knives all across Europe and go over most months. It's where the majority of my customers are.'

'And when did you travel to France on this occasion?

'About a week ago, yes, a week, last Wednesday.'

'And when was your previous trip to France?'

Graham was not comfortable, 'Look, Inspector, I get the distinct feeling that you do not believe me when I say these drugs were planted on me. I have told the Custom's people exactly what happened and no doubt you have seen the transcript of that interview. Have you seen it?'

'Yes we have Mr Spelling, and now we are asking you some more questions in order to establish whether we need to detain you longer.'

'Um,' said Graham, unconvinced.

'Now, we need to know exactly who you visited on this latest trip, names, addresses and telephone numbers.'

Graham jumped up, red in the face and suddenly fuming, 'What! You are joking, these are my customers, you can't go phoning them all up and telling them I'm being accused of drug smuggling.'

'Sit down please Mr Spelling… .'

'I'm not answering any more of your questions, I want my lawyer here, do you hear me?'

'Sit down please Mr Spelling, NOW.'

He sat. The officers kept their cool, but both were taken aback. The mild- mannered man had suddenly seen red and shocked them with his response.

'It is of course your right to have a lawyer with you when answering questions. Do you have a lawyer, near here?'

Graham had calmed quickly, 'Well, not really,' he said quietly, 'but I know of one here in Ashford and I would like to call him.'

'Certainly sir, interview terminated at 11.12am.'

The two police officers stood up and left the room. Graham sat quietly fuming.

Outside in the corridor Saskia Edwards gave a soft whistle, 'That was a surprise; I didn't think he had it in him. Do you really think he had anything to do with this?'

'Not really, the guy's under a lot of pressure and even law-abiding people get pissed off with the police when they ask penetrating questions. As I said earlier, we do have to check his story, at least now we have a bit more time before we let him go, well, until his lawyer gets here and then I expect he will walk. I was going to let him go straight away, like his lady friend. Oh well.'

★★★★★★★

Although Graham had stood firm about his rights, he had got it wrong – he had read the situation poorly. He thought that the police were trying to 'fit him up' in that they were asking questions about his past that he didn't want to answer – these were not in any way relevant to the situation that he was in and so he had decided that his best route was to get a duty solicitor on board that way he could be released as quickly as possible. What he misread was that Curry didn't really suspect him of anything much and had been at the point of letting him go.

He knew of a local solicitor but had never used him and so

he asked to see the list of local and available duty solicitors. The desk sergeant gave him the short list. He scanned down and took the number of an Ashford firm, Sprake and Gilmot. When the phone rang he asked to speak to Sprake, but only got as far as his secretary and was transferred to Aariz Al Amir, British-born of Pakistani parents.

Al Amir was the designated duty solicitor. Graham briefly explained the situation and asked if it was possible for him to come over immediately.

'Mr Spelling, I just need to ask you a couple of questions in order to prepare a little. Can you tell me what you think has happened here, I am assuming that the drugs found in your car are not yours?'

'Well, the 'drugs in the wine' was obviously a way to get the stuff through Customs with impunity. In England they must have had some plan or other to recover the coke – or whatever it is – and we were just unlucky to be picked.'

'And do you, or the police, have any idea who these people might be?'

'I don't think they know anything and the French police will do nothing. To be honest, I don't think there's a cat in hell's chance of these people being caught; there just aren't any leads as far as I can see.'

'OK, thank you, I have to make a few phone calls right now but I'll be down there in about twenty minutes.'

'Thank you.'

Al Amir made one phone call, made a quick check on some points of law and walked down to the central police station in Tufton Street.

Becoming a lawyer had always been his aim; he worked hard at school and had planned it early on, choosing the right A levels, English, History, Economics and French – he was advised against taking Law at A Level, because universities hated it. He took all four through to A2, with straight A*s – and cruised into a place at the LSE.

The Ashford firm of solicitors Sprake and Gilmot had readily taken Aariz on, first as an intern in his vacations and then they gave him a bursary to help him financially. It was realised early on that Aariz was exceptionally bright and also that the firm needed to have a presence in the ethnic community. At the end of the course which Aariz came through in the top five in his year – he was taken on as a junior associate.

James Sprake was his mentor in the firm and Aariz got along well with him. Rumour had it that Sprake had been an enfant terrible in his youth, having played in a rock band and apparently even had a record in the top ten, with a one-hit-wonder band that Aariz had never heard of – along with most of the population. Now Sprake was the epitome of respectability with his very handsome salary, his very grand ex-debutant wife who came from a very well-heeled 'old' family and a ridiculously large house in Willesborough, just outside Ashford. Aariz had been to the house once and had been bowled over by its size and the stuff inside – the paintings on the walls, the extent of the wine investment in the cellars and the cars in the garages.

Aariz had an older brother, Mohammed, who was bright

and 'easily led', he had hung about with the wrong lot, a group of disaffected young Muslims bent on causing waves in the community with their own brand of anarchy. Most of the group were just kids, going through a delayed adolescence; some, however, took it more seriously. There had long been aggro between Asian youths and their mirror group of extreme right-wing idiots who thought that their support of the English Defence League – the EDL gave them the right to throw stones in the street at whoever was there, and more often than not the opposition was Mohammed's gang.

In the spring of Aariz's first year at the firm, violence broke out in the streets of Ashford, following an argument in a take-away. This had led to the owner, a Turkish Kurd, breaking the nose of a shaved-headed bully who was being abusive to the owner's cousin. A group of the bloodied-youth's friends threw bricks through the window of the restaurant, smashing some of the equipment and injuring two of the staff. News of the incident travelled fast and within half an hour there was a running battle between the AJs – Ashford Jihadists – and the EDL supporters.

The Asian boys were better organised and had greater numbers of members and managed to rout the opposing gang, who broke up and disappeared before the police could get on to the street in force. While the victors were congratulating themselves in the town centre and being kettled by the police, the rump of the EDLs took their revenge on one of the 'known' members of the AJs – Mohammed. Mr Al Amir ran a very successful business selling cloth   silks, fine cottons, linen, all high quality and many were specialist lines. He sent material all over the country and more and more into mainland Europe.

The fire bomb through the letterbox of his warehouse caught the inflammable stock in minutes. Aariz's house adjoined the warehouse and the family were lucky to get out alive. All suffered from smoke inhalation, especially Mr Al Amir. Their business, their belongings, everything, was destroyed. Al Amir senior was never to fully recover or work again. Mohammed ran away, partly through fear for his life and partly through his shame at bringing disaster to the family. He turned up in Pakistan some weeks later and was given a place to stay by his uncle.

Aariz was suddenly, in effect, the head of the household and there was much to sort out. The family needed to be rehoused, the insurances sorted, the endless talking to the police and to just be there for his mother and father. Sprake was brilliant. 'Take as much time off as you need Aariz, and I will help where I can on any legal matters.'

A month or so later when family things had mostly been sorted and Aariz returned to work full time he went to see Sprake.

'Thank you Mr Sprake, I could not have worked full time and supported my family over the last month without your generous agreement to this leave of absence. I am indebted to you.'

'Think nothing of it old chap. Glad to be of help.'

'I will obviously try to make up as much time over the next few months, or any other way to show my gratitude.'

'Well good. There is one small favour that I might pull in.

As you may know, I am a founder member of the Kent Duty Solicitor Scheme covering the Folkestone Port and surrounding district. For my sins I carry the label of an 'accredited criminal defence specialist', which is really a load of old hooey. But, it's good for the firm; in that we get called if there is an arrest or 'detention' by the police and they need a solicitor quickly. It sometimes leads to some significant billing. The truth is at my age I can't be doing with it and it usually gets passed down to some junior – like yourself. So, I would appreciate it if you would 'volunteer' for this task, suffice to say there is a quite generous fee payable to you directly for any time you spend – especially if it is unsociable hours, and I expect that you and your family could do with some extra cash right now. Um, what do you say?'

'Thank you very much sir, I would be pleased to help out and obviously any extra cash would be very useful.'

Aariz was trying not to sound too excited – but he was – because he had only recently started to think seriously about moving out of the family house and into a flat with his girlfriend; the extra cash would be a godsend and make it financially possible.

'Excellent, I will put your name on the list. Just one small thing, I would very much like to keep tabs on any visits that you make – not that I am trying to keep a check on you, but in my role as founder of this scheme I need to know how it's working, yes?'

'Of course, I'll keep you in the loop anytime I get called out, and thank you again for this opportunity.'

Aariz left the office feeling good; he saw this as a great

feather in his cap and it wouldn't do any harm at all to his future prospects.

When he had gone, Sprake leaned back in his leather office chair and thought about the keen young man and how in an odd way he was reminded of himself at that age, desperate to get on in life. He had come out of university with a first-class law degree and a great future. In his last few weeks at college he had met the beautiful and exciting Christina in a jazz club and had fallen immediately and madly in love. She was in her first year at LSE, was clever, vibrant and French. They laughed a lot, all night sometimes, and then as suddenly as it had started it was over. She left and went back to her parents in France. She never gave him any plausible reason for leaving and he was heartbroken. He tried to contact her but failed, and time went by. Sprake met and married his present wife, whose family contacts projected him into a significant law firm very quickly, and he mostly forgot about Christina. But about two years before, a strikingly beautiful and tall young woman turned up at his office. She brought the sad news that her mother, Christina, had died and on her death bed had told her the name of her real father in England and a little about him. She was Sprake's daughter. He was surprised, and then delighted, and then a little concerned that she might be a carpet bagger, but she wasn't Christina had left her comfortably off. Christina had died a full year before and the daughter had had no particular need to track him down and make contact. She did now because his name had appeared on a document at the Paris company where she worked. Pierre had sold Sprake some fake vintage wine.

Two years later and several months after Aariz had been appointed duty solicitor, the office received the call from a man called Graham Spelling who had just been detained at Folkestone docks for smuggling drugs through the port. Aariz took the call and then, as requested, he called Sprake on the internal phone system.

'Ah,' said Sprake, 'wine bottles over from France eh, tell me all you know Aariz.' And so Aariz outlined what Graham had told him on the phone.

'Um, sounds interesting, fine, go on over to the police station and we'll speak again when you get back.'

Sprake put the phone down and rubbed his temples. 'Oh hell, let's hope not,' he said to no one.

Text received in Paris:

Packages in place. Car gone. Woman released without charge. Man taken to Ashford police station for further questioning – Ivan

Chapter 4

Maddie, Julie's sister, lived in a post-war ex-council house in the village of Broomfield, two miles from Hamstreet in the Romney Marshes. The house was large, well built with a huge back garden. Maddie lived alone now; her marriage to a merchant seaman had lasted only as long as it took Maddie to realise that he would never settle down on land, nor settle for one woman in his life. She was happy on her own, with her cats and a group of good friends who provided all of her social needs. She was very close to her sister, as was normal with twins, although as Maddie was 20 minutes the older she did at times fall into the role of 'older sister', much to the annoyance of Julie. When they were younger, Maddie had been the impetuous one, particularly in her teens. Julie the more studious, although later on Julie had spells of being wild as well. Maddie was bright, but had left school at sixteen with a fistful of GCSEs and got a job in a local clothes shop. Her reasoning at the time was that she was bored with school and hated the teachers and that she wanted to get some money and have fun. And she did. There was a string of not-particularly-suitable boyfriends, all much older, with cars and the normal range of sexual demands.

By the time she was 22 years old she was manager of the shop, and at 24, manager of the large town centre branch and married to the mostly-absent seaman Alex. Julie in the meantime had gone off to university and had fun in her own, but rather more controlled way. When Maddie's marriage reached the actual break point, Julie dropped what she was doing and stayed with Maddie who had been trying to put on a brave face but at the time was very low. Julie stayed for a month and looked after her older sister until she was strong enough to put things behind her.

By 30, Maddie had got fed up with the politics of the chain stores, had long ago got over Alex and had started her own 'boutique' for fashionable, middle-class ladies. That was now her life and she loved it.

Maddie employed an assistant who looked after her shop when she needed to go off buying or when she just wanted a break. The assistant was very flexible and keen to earn as much as possible. Immediately following Julie's call from the police station, Maddie had called her helper, suspecting that today she needed to be 'big sis' at home with Julie.

The police car dropped Julie off at 10.30am. The sisters hugged on the doorstep and Julie burst into tears and could not start telling Maddie about the events of the previous day until part-way through a mug of coffee. She carefully told her everything. Maddie sat with hand over mouth, with just the occasional 'oh no'.

'On the journey here I have had time to carefully think about my best course of action… .'

'What do you mean – course of action – what on earth can

you do except sit and wait until Graham has been cleared, surely the police will let him go later this morning and this will all be behind you?'

'I am not at all sure of that – we were carrying drugs through customs, they take all this very seriously, look at what happened in Peru and Bali to those tourists who were caught smuggling.'

'Yes, but in most of those cases they knew that they had stuff on them, even if they didn't know exactly what it was; they took chances and had to pay the consequences. You on the other hand knew nothing about this, there's a massive difference.'

'Yes, maybe, but I still feel that I need to do something, something positive to help Graham. I am certain now that if I saw either of the two French guys again I would recognise them.'

'Can't you do an Identikit thing?'

'No, I can't get my head around the actual features enough to describe them or even visualise them. Do you know what I mean? I am sure that I would recognise them if they were in a line up for instance. The problem is that the French will do nothing to help. You know what they're like, "Not our problem".'

'So what do you think you can do that will help then?'

'I can only think that I need to be there. I reckon that those two are local men and so, if I could spot them, then Graham would be in the clear, so I thought… .'

'Don't even say it Julie. You can't go back to France,' interrupted Maddie.

'Why not?'

'Well first, the police have told you not to, second it could be dangerous, third, the police have got your passport.'

'Well I can look after myself, I speak French fluently, and no one would know I was there.'

'And the passport?'

'Well, I thought as we are identical twins… .'

'No, never, what are you thinking of? No, I'm not going to, oh Julie… .'

'Look I know it sounds daft, but if I went over this lunchtime, had a look around, I could be back tomorrow easy. Couldn't I? No one would know and I just might get lucky… .'

'The chance of you "getting lucky" as you put it is almost nil, and, as you have told me and the police, the van was white and unmarked and so you wouldn't be able to identify it against the 5 million other white vans driving around. Anyway – where would you look? The likelihood is that these guys came out of Paris, or maybe Calais, or anywhere in between, or you could even try Brussels as that's quite close. You're bonkers Julie if you think you can track these people down.'

Julie had sat quietly through Maddie's tirade and then said 'I think I know where they came from at least. There was a sticker in the back window of the van, I didn't take any notice at the time and had forgotten about it when talking to the police. I still can't quite get it, but I think I would recognise the name if I saw it. Have you got a French map handy?'

'Oh Julie this is a wild goose chase… .' She looked at Julie's face. 'Alright, alright, I'll get a map'. She brought one from the bookcase and gave it to Julie.

'I can't quite see the name in my mind, but it was on a green and yellow decal. It was an ad for something like a florist and it had a town name on it.' Julie found the page and drew her finger down the A26/A1 corridor between Paris and Calais.

'Oh, that's it I think, Querchamps-les-Ardres, yes, I'm fairly sure that was it. Some sort of florist in that town. It had the Interflora logo on it.'

'OK Julie, let's get real now. You saw a sticker in the rear window of the van that might have said "Querchamps". That might mean that the van owner lived somewhere near there, but only might. They could be delivery drivers for the whole region, couldn't they?'

'Yes, they could, but it is something.'

'OK, I accept it is something   not a lot   but yes, it is a clue to their identity. So phone up the police and tell them and let them pass it on the French or whatever they do.'

'Well, that's exactly the problem isn't it? Any information will be passed on to the French, but what have they got from Graham and I? Almost nothing – a few sketchy descriptions of the men and the van and even with the possibility that the van does come from this town, Querchamps, the French police will laugh long and loud. They may go and look at the lay-bys and they will find nothing and it will take them three weeks to find that nothing. You know that, as well as I do Maddie.'

'Well maybe so, but that still doesn't mean that you should go and think that you can solve this   you've been watching too much Poirot. Look Julie, my love, these people are drug smugglers   they don't take prisoners. Look what's happening in Mexico... .'

'This is not Mexico.'

'Anyway, this seems a bit over the top, you planning to do this crazy stuff to get this bloke Graham out of trouble, you hardly know him… .'

'That's an awful thing to say Maddie, I am "with him" and he is in trouble, and so am I still. If I can help I will, and should.'

'I thought you said he was dull.'

'That's got nothing to do with anything. He may not be Mr Dynamic, but he is pleasant.'

Maddie laughed.

'OK, I know, very funny. Look Maddie I'm 34 and I need to think about what I do next. It may be that Graham, or someone like him is what I need and well, I haven't given up on the idea of children… .'

'Oh I'm sorry Julie that was very unkind of me.' She gave her a hug. 'I'll help if I can, of course, but I still think it's daft.'

'Thanks Maddie. I can go over on the two o'clock ferry from Folkestone as a foot passenger, hire a car and be in Querchamps-les-Ardres by tea-time.'

'But you have no clothes and, of course… .'

'Maddie, we are the same dress size, aren't we… ?'

★★★★★★★

Julie stepped onto the ramp a minute before the doors closed for the 2.00pm ferry. She carried her sister's suitcase through to the lounge area, sat down and smiled. After the trauma of the last day she was actually doing something and as a bonus she felt more alive, more excited, than she had done in a long time.

★★★★★★★

As Julie was boarding the ferry, Aariz was walking into the police station in Tufton Street to see Graham. He was made to wait in the reception area for a few minutes and then escorted to Interview Room 3. Graham was already there.

'Good afternoon Mr Spelling my name is Aariz Al Arim and I have been assigned to you as your duty solicitor. Here is my card.'

Graham looked at the card, 'Sprake and Gilmot. Whom do you report to Mr Al Arim?'

'On a day-to-day basis I report to Mr Jackson, who is one of the junior partners, but as far as my work as duty solicitor I report directly to one of the senior partners, Mr Sprake.'

'How come?'

'Only that Mr Sprake was instrumental in setting up the duty solicitor programme in Kent and so he likes to keep a close eye on how things are working. Is that a problem?'

'No, not at all. OK, when can I get out of here?'

'Soon I hope. You were detained by the UK Border Agency at 7.54pm last evening I understand from the information I was given at the front desk and you arrived here in Ashford at 10.36 this morning. The police are only able to detain you in custody for 24 hours without charge, so at the very latest they must release you by 7.54 this evening, if not before.'

'Good, because this is a complete farce. Obviously, I am not a drug smuggler, someone had planted this stuff in my car and I have unwittingly taken it through Customs. Clearly I had nothing to do with it.'

'May I ask, why did you call us in, if you thought that there was no evidence against you?'

'The police started asking all kinds of questions about my business and implied that they were going to make calls to my clients to check my story, well, I just don't want that to happen. It could ruin my business, Christ, think about it. I can just imagine some fourteen-year-old constable phoning around telling my people about my being arrested on drugs charges.'

'To be pedantic, you haven't actually been charged with anything and you can't be forced at any stage to give them information that you consider confidential.'

'OK.'

'I take it Mr Spelling that you are telling me that you thought you had bought wine and nothing more and had no knowledge of any other substances that might have been hidden inside.'

'Yes.'

'And are you also telling me that your companion Miss Webb also had no knowledge of any other substances that might have been in the wine bottles?'

'Yes, as far as I know.'

'Is it possible that Miss Webb is involved?' said Aariz with some surprise.

'Well no, I don't think that at all.'

'OK. I am now going to speak to the officers involved in

this case and I expect that we will be able leave within the hour. Bear with me.'

★★★★★★★

As the ferry got further away from England Julie's resolve began to desert her. She had moved to the front saloon, facing out to sea and now huddled down in her seat so as not to be seen. She was frightened that someone might recognise her. Someone might see her and realise that she was travelling on someone else's passport and supposedly therefore some kind of fugitive. She knew it was ridiculous but she kept looking behind her. Every time someone new appeared in the room she had a mini fright. She looked for tell-tale signs that would show them to be a detective in plain clothes, and found herself re-running old film scenes where the criminal's best laid plans were cocked up because of some chance encounter.

The crossing seemed to take forever. She was tired and anxious and woke with a start when the ferry docked. She had drifted off. She hadn't been caught by the police and the ferry had docked. She quickly gathered her bags and panicked for a moment about how to get off. This was the first time she had ever been on a ferry alone and as a foot passenger.

She followed the few other passengers that had large bags and rucksacks, who were obviously travelling on foot, and all who seemed to know where they were going. She saw the signs for the foot passengers to exit, and felt a little calmer. Next, the ordeal of passport control.

Going through the English customs had been easier than

expected. The Border Control inspection of her passport was cursory to say the least. Not really surprising, who wants to escape good old GB – all the important traffic was going the other way. Entering France might be a little more difficult.

Julie knew all about body language and how Customs and Border control people could apparently see right through any subterfuge. Putting on a bored and a frankly-dear-I couldn't-give-a-damn expression was what all good criminals could obviously do and ordinary folk tried to do – just to be cool. But when you were, in essence – a criminal – not so easy, and Julie was aware that her relaxed smile to the French Border official was so false and through clenched teeth that they were sure to haul her away just because she was hiding something. The daft idea that she could pass unnoticed past these clever and observant professionals was plain ludicrous. And then she was through. The Frenchwoman on the gate had given her picture a long look and her long look and pretended to scrutinise the two images. Her expression didn't change at all. It didn't say to Julie 'You look a bit different in this picture', or, 'you've got a lot more wrinkles since this picture was taken', or 'ha ha! I look younger than you do'. In fact, the uniformed lady did not look at the picture at all. Her actions were purely mechanical. She treated each person the same, five seconds looking at the passport, four seconds looking at the person, two seconds looking again at the passport, seven seconds flicking aimlessly through the pages, another two seconds looking at the person, then hand back the passport with a slight flick of the head and no change of expression. She could do this all day while composing her shopping list or, more interestingly, as on this occasion, working out exactly what to say to her boyfriend later to try to get him to spend more time on getting her to an orgasm.

Julie pushed through the door to the Hertz office and established that even the smaller cars were overly priced, and then on top of that she had to decide on what insurance cover to buy. How much excess to have? Too many decisions in her state of mind. She went for the very expensive option rather than the ridiculous-do-you-think-I'm-a-total-dork option and told herself that this was not a great deal of money when you looked at the greater picture. The greater picture being… she was doing the right thing and was doing it to help prove that Graham was not an international drug dealer but really was a kitchen knife salesman.

As she signed her life away on about a hundred forms she did start to think that carrying a bag full of kitchen knives through customs was a bit odd. Did the Customs people think that carrying knives – albeit kitchen knives – made Graham more likely to be a drug smuggler? She put the idea away, took the keys to her little car and followed the instructions to the car pound.

Like most English people abroad she went to the passenger side of the car, opened the door and stood for a moment wondering where the steering wheel was. She looked about hoping no one had seen, placed her bag on the seat – her intention all along of course – went around the car, sat in, adjusted the seat, played with gears with the unusual hand and reversed out of the space. There was that moment of slight panic pulling up to the gate – not remembering which side to drive on, but then it was OK. If in doubt, follow another car, easy. A moment's pause while she tried to change gear with the window switches in the door and then away and out of town.

She knew exactly where she was going. Querchamps-les-Ardres was just two miles or so west of the Paris Autoroute and equidistant between two exits. The Aire where the wine was bought also lay between those two exits.

★★★★★★★

Inspector Andrew Curry sat in his office looking at the pile of paper on his desk. 'So much for the paperless society,' he said more to himself. Saskia, sitting at the other desk, picked up his comments and added, '…they say that since computers have become commonplace in the office, paper usage has tripled.'

She had been looking into Graham's knife business – Cooks Supersharp UK Ltd – 'Spelling's company looks OK,' she said in an apologetic kind of tone as though disappointed that no signs of malpractice had come to light.

'Can't say I'm surprised,' Curry replied without looking up from a report about the rise of the Eastern European mafia. 'I can't really see him as any kind of criminal, although he has got a bit of a temper on him.'

His phone rang, he looked at it, willing it to stop, and debated briefly about ignoring it and letting the answer phone kick in, but he didn't. 'Yup, Curry.'

Saskia looked up and watched his face which had adopted its serious frown, a look he kept only for bad things. He listened for several minutes to the caller, then said, 'Oh, well shit, I wasn't expecting that, OK thanks Brian, let me know soonest about anything else you find, cheers.'

Curry put his head in his hands and Saskia knew that it was politic to wait before asking him any questions. He just sat there for a few minutes and then looked up and said to Saskia, 'The 24 hour detention period started this morning when he got here. Tell the solicitor.'

'Right, sir.'

****

Aariz left the interview room and returned to the front desk and asked to see Inspector Curry. He had waited for ten minutes when Detective Constable Saskia Edwards came out instead, shook Aariz's hand and introduced herself in a slightly too loud voice, such that the desk sergeant looked up and pulled a face.

Aariz smiled and said 'Detective Constable Edwards, you have my client here and I would like to request his release before 7.54pm this evening, that being 24 hours since his detainment at Folkestone dock, unless of course you charge him.'

'Mr Al Arim, your client, Mr Spelling, agreed to come to the police station this morning and is being held in custody. The custody period was therefore deemed to have commenced at 10.36am and so we will either charge him or release him by 10.36 tomorrow morning.'

'Detective, you know that is not correct, the detainment

by the UK Border agency must be considered as part of the custody period.'

'That decision has been made by the inspector handling the case, based on new evidence. Mr Spelling has already been escorted back to his cell and we have scheduled another meeting for 9.00am tomorrow morning which you are invited to attend. That is all I am able to say this evening.'

'What new evidence is that Detective Constable?'

'I am unable to divulge that Mr Al Arim, at this stage.'

Aariz looked at her and gave her a frustrated smile and threw up his hands. 'Thanks,' he said sarcastically, and left.

★★★★★★★

Paris – text message:

Five bottles distributed as normal – Charlie

'Excellent news,' Silvie passed the iPhone to Gerard, 'one bottle is no great loss, around 16,000 street value so we are maybe 8,000 out of pocket – better than expected.'

Gerard slid the phone back, 'When does Pierre get back?'

'Should be sometime tomorrow, but he doesn't always stick to schedule.'

'I think you are right to stop shipments for a while, it's likely that the Customs guys will be checking some wine cases for a while; we can wait a few weeks until they get fed up with it and then it can be fired up again. The only problem I see is that we are sitting on quite a lot of stuff at the moment. I would have preferred to ship it all out, however, right call. I am sure Pierre will say the same tomorrow.'

'Gerard, has Pierre talked to you much about the losses, or apparent losses from these shipments to England?'

'A little, he thinks that someone in the network is nicking some of the coke, as the final cut is always somewhat less than we have expected.'

'So where or who could be taking it?'

'We don't know, but the bottles are handled by several people en route to the end user so it could be any one of them. Look, it's not a massive loss and we can cope with it, it may even be just down to slight variations in the quantities, it's just that Pierre hates the idea that anyone is ripping him off and he's got a bit manic about it.'

'OK, we can start again filling the bottles up in a couple of weeks, so just sit tight. We can talk it all through tomorrow when Pierre gets here.'

Chapter 5

'What did his duty solicitor say, when you said we were hanging on to him?'

'Well, not surprisingly sir, he wasn't happy and seemed to think that the 24 hours should run from when he was detained at Folkestone.'

'Fine, let him stew on that one.'

'So, do we have more evidence? Something Brian has found over in SOCO?'

Curry looked up and shook his head, 'This job, eh, constantly takes you by surprise. The SOCO boys have just found a stash of cannabis in Spelling's car.'

'Shit.'

'Yes, exactly,' Curry smiled at her unintended pun. They both sat for a few moments, thinking through the different possible scenarios. Saskia spoke first. 'Presumably the fact that the cannabis was found in the car... where was it, by the way?'

'Under the back seat.'

'...um that makes it impossible that the two guys in the lay-by – if they existed at all – could have planted the stuff under the seat. Spelling didn't say anything like – 'Oh they put the wine on the back seat for me', he told us that he had put it in the boot himself. Both of them said that, didn't they?'

'Yes, they did.'

'So Spelling must have put the cannabis under the seat, yes?'

'It seems so.'

'Well it looks like Spelling is back in the frame then? Or of course Julie Webb.'

'This isn't right somehow though Saskia, why go to all the trouble of getting special bottles made, only put one in the case and then be so stupid to stash some pot under the seat. If the Customs boys had had a dog out there, they would have picked it up immediately and all the careful preparations with the coke would have been in vain. '

'Yes, but sir, they don't usually have dogs checking the cars do they, any dogs around are sniffing out the illegals in the trucks.'

'Umm, well I think we need another little chat to our Mr Spelling, but we can let him stew until the morning when his man comes back. What time did we say?'

'9 am.'

'OK good, in the meantime can you go back into the computer files and check again just to make sure that neither of them have had anything to do with drugs.'

'Right,' said Saskia jumping up.

'I think I'll have a word with Miss Julie Webb,' said Curry picking up his phone.

****

Detective Inspector Curry had started his career with the police force straight from school. He would have left school at sixteen and joined up then if he had been able to, but they weren't interested looking at young men before eighteen. When he was fifteen he had tried to get work experience during the standard two-week session through school and to his surprise there were no openings. He and the school organiser were frustrated not to be able to get him in somewhere, given that at the time the force were advertising heavily for recruits. The reason given was all about the 'confidential nature of the work'. He thought it was more about the fact that they didn't want nosey kids poking about.

With no other route planned he stayed on at school, finished his A levels – with mediocre results – and joined up immediately on leaving sixth form. There was some talk of him being sponsored to go to university, but he didn't want to do that, partly because he wanted to start to being a policeman straight away and partly because he didn't think he was bright enough to go on to university. There were many times later in life that he thought about what college life would have been like, and there was an element of regret at his decision. But he usually pulled himself out of that way of thinking, Curry was definitely a man not to dwell down the 'if only' thought process.

He had spent eight years an ordinary copper, but he showed himself to be a bit brighter than the norm. Because of his interest, he was seconded to the local CID unit on a particularly difficult murder inquiry and, at the successful conclusion of that investigation – the murderer was caught and sentenced to life imprisonment – he applied for a post in CID and was accepted. Fifteen years later he had risen to Inspector, not exactly a meteoric rise through the ranks, but calm and steady was his way. He had gained the nickname of 'Korma', because it was a near pun on Karma, plus the obvious. He was liked and trusted.

The business over Graham Spelling was worrying him, he didn't often get people wrong, that is, he could usually tell when people told the truth – or not. He had been pretty sure that Spelling and the girl were straight; he totally believed Julie and 'almost totally' went along with what he was saying as well. The fact that Spelling had blown up was not of great concern, he'd seen it happen many times before, but the new information – finding the cannabis   was a worry. He definitely hadn't got him down as a smoker – let alone one who smoked weed. He could of course be taking it through for a friend, but the risks were high and he didn't come across as a risk taker at all, far from it, he didn't even like being late for the ferry. But the fact that even he had told them that the two Frenchmen with the wine had not gone anywhere near the car meant that the stash under the seat was a mystery.

He therefore went back to thinking about Julie. She seemed straight, a school teacher, although that in itself meant little. Many young teachers had been pretty lefty in the early days, and yes, quite a lot smoked pot. But Julie was now 'mature' and seemingly responsible, but a risk taker – maybe. Had she stashed the cannabis under the back seat – unbeknown even to Spelling? He didn't know. But the next step was obviously to re-interview them both.

He thought briefly about getting Saskia to call Julie at her sister's, but decided that he would prefer to hear her reaction himself, so he got the number from the front desk and phoned it.

The house phone rang and Maddie picked up.

'Yes?'

'Is that Miss Webb?'

'Yes,' she said with some guard and expected yet another unsolicited call, selling God-knows what. She always tried to be civil. When the caller started with something like 'Hello is that Madeline Webb', or Madeline McWalters – her married name – she knew it was a cold sales call, because no one in the world called her Madeline, not even her mother. All of her personal dealings were carried out using 'Maddie'. The problems of using a nickname had caused her considerable hassle a few times. A while back she had decided to change her credit card company because her previous one had started making annual charges, which she objected to. She completed the forms and sent them off for her credit 'worthiness' to be checked, which was not a problem having never defaulted on anything, including her twenty-year mortgage and healthy business accounts. She was rejected, with no explanation. Enraged, she contacted the card company to find out the reason and they refused to divulge anything and so she was forced to 'buy' a credit check. It was finally realised that all of her previous applications, mortgages and cards were in her 'proper' name – Madeline – and the computer systems had been unable to work out that it was the same person, regardless of the fact that they lived at the same address.

'This is Detective Inspector Curry at Ashford and we would like to have a further discussion with you about your ferry crossing.'

'Right,' said Maddie.

'Good, I will send a car to pick you up tomorrow morning at 8.00am.'

'Right,' said Maddie again, and Curry put the phone down before she had a chance to change her mind.

'Oh shit,' she said to the buzzing phone.

She replaced the receiver and sat down heavily, and tried to think clearly about the situation that she now found herself in – and that her sister was in. If the police knew that Julie had skipped the country then that would cause them to think – wrongly – that she was implicated in the drug smuggling and had done a runner. That also brought the fact back to her in that she had given Julie her passport – well, Julie could have stolen it – um, not easy to believe. So if she didn't tell the police that Julie was in France – where was she when the car turned up? Down the shops? Ill in bed? Not very satisfactory. Again, if she had known that the police were coming why had she gone out, and of course the police think they had just spoken to her.

Maddie had to talk to Julie and try to get her back into England for the next morning. She hadn't got her sister's mobile number written down anywhere and so she found her mobile, picked off the number from the contacts list and phone it from the house phone. Julies' phone was switched off. She swore, redialled from her mobile and left a message.

An alternative drifted into Maddie's head, she pushed it out, but when the idea re-presented itself it made her shudder. She sat for a few more minutes and then ran upstairs to prepare for the morning.

Maddie was Julie's older sister, by two hours, an identical twin. They had gone through school with no teachers and hardly any friends being able to tell the difference between them. Almost always it was a pain, people guessed which one they were and not surprisingly 50% of the time it was wrong and each of them corrected the other person with a quiet resigned voice. Both of them loved being a twin but hated being identical. When they were older they had obviously had fun, tricking boyfriends and even their parents at times. As they matured and needed to be seen as individuals, they went to great lengths to make sure they wore different clothes and hairstyles so that most people knew who was who.

Julie had left all of the clothes she had been wearing the day before at Maddie's. They were now freshly laundered and hanging in the spare room awaiting her return. Their hair, although quite different styles, was of similar length, and Maddie now set about trying to practise a reconstruction of Julie's hairstyle.

★★★★★★★

Querchamps-les-Ardres was about as typical a little French town as you could get. The traffic on the main road was slowed down by parked cars and newly created chicanes up to the central cross roads which had very elegant town houses on each corner, most had little balconettes on the upper floors. At ground level there was cluster of cafes, flower shops and bakeries.

Julie drove in to a wide street with cars parked in the

middle and past a gravelled boules park under plane trees. She smiled at the scene – almost too much. Some town planner had obviously read the manual. She drove on looking for the Hotel du Pont where she had booked a room on the Internet.

She was expecting a bit tatty and she wasn't disappointed, as it was indeed a bit tatty. There were several small metal tables and chairs outside and the regulation pair of elderly Frenchmen with a drink. She parked almost outside, a little beyond the drinkers as, being British; she didn't feel quite right parking right next to them so as to block their view of... well, the cars. They watched her intently as though her arrival was the most interesting thing that had happened all day and it may well have been.

Once out of the car she took in the smells of France and was immediately transported back to the wonderful times she had been in Normandy – three formative years, travelling, working, playing at being young, relaxed and carefree. The smell took her back to a town just like this one, Livarot, where she had met Philipe, become hopelessly infatuated, had lots of fun, grew up a bit and then moved on to live in Annecy for a further four years.

As she passed the two elderly men she gave them the customary 'Bonjour messieurs' and they responded with a 'Mam'selle'. Once again she wondered how French people always seemed to get it right. Madam or Mademoiselle – even knowing nothing about their marital status.

The interior of the hotel was dingy, but not unclean. There was an empty bar with tables and benches around. The counter was apparently the hotel reception–cum– serving bar and the hit-me-if-you-dare bell was much too loud and made Julie jump.

There was a long pause, long enough to start thinking that no one was coming and to consider the dilemma of a second belling. Before that awful moment arrived, a very pretty young lady with Eastern European features and a very strong German/Czech/Polish or whatever accent appeared and went through the formal registration. Julie's French was perfect but even she found the girl's accent difficult to follow and it was clear that she was still learning the language. Key in hand she as last started up the stairs. At the first turn she came face-to-face with a well-built, moustached man who stepped back and gestured for her to pass with a broad smile, an eye twinkle and a deep '*Bonjour Mam'selle*'.

Julie '*mercied*', smiled back and was astonished to feel a flush on her cheeks and neck. She hurried up the stairs in embarrassment.

Julie pushed open the room door, it was dark, she found the light switch and dropped her sister's case on the bed. Larger than most hotel rooms, there was a double casement window up high on one wall, with the shutters closed. There was a slight musty smell to the room – a sign of low occupancy she concluded. She had to stand on a chair to reach the latch on the window then pulled the casements inward and pushed the shutters out. A warm but disappearing late afternoon light filtered in. There was no real view. Directly opposite stood the blank wall of another building, she leaned out and could see some view to the left of roofs and fields and trees beyond.

Directly below on the first floor there was a small elegant wrought-iron balcony with a table and two chairs. French doors were open from the bedroom below.

She sat on the bed and gave it the obligatory bounce test. It squeaked a little. She took off her shoes and felt very alone and a bit silly. She was here because... the answer was not immediate. She was angry mostly, angry at the situation. Some bastard had dumped drugs on them and they were taking the rap. She wanted them caught and strung up as well as getting Graham out of jail. She felt tired and travel weary – time to test the shower and flush away the blues.

★★★★★★★

Henri, the hotel proprietor, had been pleasantly surprised to see Julie on the stairs. Single female travellers were usually older and far less attractive. He reached the bar, poured himself a sensibly large brandy and went back upstairs to the linen cupboard.

There were two keys for the cupboard, the external one, a copy of which was held by several others – primarily the maids, for the linen. The second key was just for him. It opened the inner door. The lock for this door hid behind a block of wood which swivelled. The inner door was in fact the back wall of the cupboard on which sat a series of shelves complete with sheets and towels. Henri closed the first door behind him and in the dark moved the block of wood aside and slotted in his key. The well-oiled lock moved silently and the door swung forward leaving just enough room for him to squeeze himself around. The inner room was very small but had a high stool and a narrow shelf for the brandy, next to the box of tissues. With the inner door safely closed it was totally dark.

Henri carefully slid aside the black curtain which covered the mirror and waited.

★★★★★★★

The phone rang again on Curry's desk and he reluctantly picked it up.

'Hi Andy, Brian.'

'Hello Brian, don't tell me, you found a nuclear bomb in the boot.'

'Not quite, but something of equal interest. Do you want to pop over and I'll explain?'

A few minutes later Detective Inspector Curry was sitting in Brian's office which was like an ante-room to the laboratory.

'Several things I want to show you, first, the broken bottle does contain cocaine, which was no surprise, good quality as far as I can determine and about 50% cut. I haven't tried to analyse it but my best guess is South American, probably Columbia. The inner bottle is really quite simple.' Brian held up the remains of the inner tube for Curry to see. 'It's like a large test tube made from dark red glass, it's 2.6cms across and 30cms long. This means that it will slip neatly into the neck of the bottle and when flush with the top is still off the bottom of the bottle. They have glued around the top of the inner tube so that it doesn't drop inside. What I suspect, I don't know for sure of course, is that they have very accurately drawn out the right amount of wine, so that when the tube is dropped in, the wine completely fills the gap between. I bet you they used a calibrated syringe, that's what I would use.'

'Brian, you're enjoying this too much.'

'Oh, yes, sorry Andy, but it is quite clever.'

'Umm, do go on.'

'By making sure the wine fills the gap and using the dark red glass means that it's almost impossible to see the inner tube, unless you unscrew the cap. The top of the inner tube has been blocked off with some sort of wax. I have roughly calculated that there was 310grams of cocaine in the tube and at a 50% cut I reckon that's worth about £14,000 on the street.'

'OK, thanks for confirming that Brian... .'

'Hold on Andy, that's not the interesting bit. The unbroken five bottles in the case do not contain cocaine they are just wine, same outer bottles, no inner bottle of course, same label, but nothing inside apart from wine.'

'Oh, right, that is a surprise. I would have thought anyone going to that extent would have gone the whole hog and put through all six bottles.'

'Yes, I agree, not really logical, but that's not all. The fingerprints on the broken bits of bottle are consistent with multiple handling, several sets are showing up. Probably the Customs people and maybe even the two travellers, who may have picked up bits themselves, people do that. I can check all those prints later. But the other bottles, the five still in the box, are clinically clean, they have been scrubbed, there is no DNA or any other signs of handling apart from one very clear set of prints on every bottle.'

'Sorry, Brian, what are you saying, that someone has gone to great lengths to remove all traces of fingerprints and DNA but then one person has left their prints all over the bottles?'

'Exactly, the pattern of prints is regular and I am pretty sure suggests that the prints were from someone putting the bottles into the case.'

'Christ, Brian that doesn't make any sense does it?'

'No, not yet. I have already checked them out on the system and no match came up.'

'I'm getting too long in the tooth for these conundrums, Brian. My best guess at the moment is that the coke and the cannabis are two completely different events. Right now, I reckon that one of the two occupants in the car is responsible for the hash and someone else has stitched them up with carrying the coke through the port. This double-skinned bottle is quite sophisticated and points to organised crime, so I start to get out of my depth. But the fingerprints thing is odd, it almost seems like someone has deliberately screwed someone else in the organisation. But that's going to be over in France and again out of my reach. OK Brian, many thanks for that, whizz me the prints and I'll get them sent over to France for the police to check out. If these prints are from someone in the drugs business in France they should have them on record. In the meantime I'll cross check those we took from the two in the car and I suppose I had better rule out the Customs people at Folkestone.

'I've already checked the bloke from the car as your guys took his prints this morning when he got to the nick. He's clear, but I can't see any record of prints from the girl yesterday, well they're not showing up on the system anyway.'

'Right, OK Brian that's great. I'd better get back, keep me posted on anything else, bye.'

Curry walked back across the yard to the main police station and quietly reprimanded himself for not taking Julie's fingerprints at Folkestone.

Chapter 6

It was getting late into the afternoon when Curry picked up the phone to call the UK Border Agency in Folkestone. He had known the head of the department there, Alan Protheroe, for some years but there hadn't ever been much call to talk, as very little crime from the dock came his way. Most of the problems these days were caused by illegal immigrants which was not his business, thank goodness. But drugs were and there had been the occasional incident, but not enough for Curry to have spent a lot of time with Protheroe.

'Could I speak to Alan Protheroe, please?'

'Yes, speaking, who is this?'

'Detective Inspector Curry,' he announced in a rather formal way, because he was used to doing it, 'Hello Alan, how are you?' he added

'Oh hi Andy, sorry to give you more work yesterday, how are our two "drug smugglers", did you get anywhere with them?'

'Well, it's about them I'm phoning. It's all got a bit confusing really.'

'Oh yeah, why. It looked to us like a pretty open and shut case, those two having got used by some drug people.'

'Yes, that's what we first thought but some other information

89

has come to light which means we have to check on a few things.' Curry would have normally shared information with people like Protheroe, but he was now being a bit more cautious and so he was telling him the absolute minimum.

'OK, ask away,' said Alan, who was only glad to help.

Curry continued, 'When you took control of the case of wine, only one bottle was broken and part of that fell out in the road, yes?'

'Yes, one of my staff had opened the box and pulled out part of the bottle and spilt the contents.'

'OK, what happened to the box after that?'

'The two travellers were escorted up here to the interview rooms while another staff member put a screen around the car and mess on the ground, to prevent people rubbernecking in the kiosk areas and running into each other. Err, then, one of them brought the box up here and put it on my desk.'

'Right, did he open the box further?'

'No, I was still here and I gave instructions to leave the box alone.'

'OK, then what?'

'Um, we left the man and woman in the interview rooms and all went down to clear up and pick up the evidence from the road. We had to because the car and the glass and stuff on the floor was blocking one of our check points and would have caused a bottleneck. I have to keep it clear Andy, we had another two ferries coming in within the hour.'

'It's OK I wasn't criticising. Did you all glove up when clearing?'

'Yes of course, standard procedure.'

'OK, back to the box on your desk. Did anyone pull any of the bottles out when it was still in the office?'

'No, definitely not. Alison – she was the officer who caught them   only tore open a corner of the top of the box to get the broken one out. The rest were still in there, you know it's difficult to pull bottles out of the box unless you open the whole of the top. So no, no one took any bottles out. Why are you asking Andy, what's the problem?

'It's nothing, the SOCO boys have picked up some prints on the bottles and I just wanted to make sure that none of you lot had put your dirty fingers all over it.'

'No, no dirty fingers here my friend, leave that to the Frenchies eh?'

'You presumably then caged the box.'

'Yup, when we all came back up here, I immediately put all the bits we had picked up and the box of wine into the lock-up cage and it was there until your SOCO boys arrived and removed them.'

'…and the cage was securely locked during that time?'

'Yes, of course.'

'OK, thanks for your help Alan, if this goes any further we may have to take all of your prints to eliminate yours from the bad guys.'

'Yeah, fine, no problem.'

'Thanks, goodnight.'

When Alan had finished the call, he sat and thought about the conversation he had just had with Curry. The set of fingerprints on the bottles would be passed back to the French police to try to track down the guys that had set up the two travellers. Alan was just a little concerned about the final question Curry had asked about security. He was well aware that he hadn't changed the alarm code that protected the cage for some time and that it really wasn't terribly bright to keep that copy of the code underneath his keyboard. But he was comforted by the fact that no one knew he kept it there. He changed the code anyway and put the Post-it note with the new code on in his wallet.

★★★★★★★

The hotel bedroom was en-suite, but not quite the normal suite. It had the standard loo and hand basin but instead of a conventional bath or shower cubicle there was an 'upright bath'. She let out a little gasp and giggled at this throw back, a rather sweet piece of Victoriana. The bather sat in the bath on a raised area, which had a wooden seat a bit like a toilet seat. Legs and feet half stretched out into the lower part. The sides were quite high, such that when full of water the seat was just below the surface. On one side at shoulder height was a shower faucet hanging on a hook. The hot and cold taps sat at waist level to one side and there was a switching device to send the water up to the shower head. Soap sat in an indent in the roll of the enamel side. The idea was that the bather sat only just in the water and washed by playing the shower head over the body trying to keep the water inside the bath.

There was a large mirror on the wall directly next to the bath. Julie looked at herself in it. She took a side view and appraised her bum.

'Well,' she said out loud 'not bad'. She was wearing a sweatshirt over a tee shirt and a pair of M&S jeans that hugged her hips quite well considering they belonged to her sister, but gapped a bit at the waist. She ran her thumbs around the band. 'Yes, a smaller waist on these jeans... or possibly a smaller bum on the person?'

She stood facing the mirror, crossed her arms and hauled up the sweatshirt taking the tee shirt up as well and so getting knotted up around the neck. She pulled down the shirt and pinged the sweatshirt over her head then with the same action pulled over the shirt and dropped it on the floor.

She now looked again at her boobs in their not particularly sexy bra. She was a 34C ish, that's what she always went for anyway but was constantly being told by 'sensible' older women's magazines – that she occasionally bought but mostly read in the dentists – that 67% of women were wearing the wrong sized bra. She cupped her boobs and pushed them up into a better cleavage and pouted at the mirror.

She breathed in and popped the top jean button out of its slit and dropped the zip. The jeans were a bit tight on her across the hips and so to pull them down she moved from side to side easing them as she went. It was a bit of a ritual, getting out of tight jeans, you couldn't help but move to some distant beat as they gradually crept down the thighs and finally off the tight bit and down to her knees. She sat on the chair still facing the bath and in turn pulled each leg out.

With just her bra and pants on she leaned forward and turned on the two taps at the side of the bath. Hot water appeared quickly and started to fill up the lower part of the slipper bath. She reached around her back, unhooked the bra strap and shook it off. Then in a single movement, thumbs in the side she swept down her pants and flicked them off her foot.

She faced the mirror once more and liked what she saw. Front view, side view and over-the-shoulder back view. Yes, she agreed not bad at all. The bath water was steaming and she realised that the mirror had not steamed up. That was odd. She leant right over across the bath to the mirror and realised that there was a thin light running across the base that presumably worked off the room light. She felt the bottom edge and it was warm, just warm enough to heat up the mirror to stop the condensation. Very clever of someone she thought.

She tested the water and gently eased herself on to the wooden seat, dropping her legs into the warm water. She popped the lever over to stream the water through the shower head, leaned back and let the water run over her bare breasts. She lay there for several minutes playing the water over her hair, her neck, her stomach, her crotch, her thighs. She put the shower head down into the foot well and ran the soap over the whole of her body, building up a fragrant foam. She lay back into the rear of the bath and continued to rather aimlessly let the soap glide over her stomach and down into her pubic hair and then back up and around her nipples. Her nipples were quite small relative to her actual boobs, which were quite large, but they protruded and this had given her some problems on cold nights with tight tops. Julie was not in the least prudish but never felt relaxed or happy with prominent 'coat hooks' and had even on occasion used nipple pads inside her bra to hide them and, of course, to hide the embarrassment of others. Men did find it impossible to look a girl in the face when confronted with a pair of sticky-out nipples.

On a little shelf next to the mirror was a line of shampoos and conditioner bottles; she took one, leant forward and thoroughly lathered up her hair and then with soapy hands took the foam down her body, across her breasts, and then her pubic hair, spending quite a long time making sure these parts were especially cleansed, and enjoying the process.

After a few minutes she took up the shower head again and rinsed off, still sitting on the wooden seat, then standing and facing away from the mirror she soaped her bottom and hosed that down. With the water turned off she then flicked the surplus drops from her whole body using her fingers – another ritual – and stepped out onto the mat, wrapped one towel around her waist and then rigorously dried her hair. She pulled the plug and walked out to the bedroom.

★★★★★★★

Henri had sat transfixed just a few inches from this stunning, naked woman. He was very, very turned on. He quietly and quickly slipped out of his viewing cupboard and down the stairs.

Finding the viewing room while doing some structural alterations had been quite a shock to Henri. He knew the elderly previous owner and his wife quite well and didn't see him as a pervy voyeur. He had intended to remove the false wall of the linen cupboard, board over the two-way mirror and put more shelves up, but hadn't got around to it. Sometime later when a very attractive woman had booked in to that room, he was tempted. Henri had always seen himself as an alpha male and a peeping Tom was not his style and he did feel guilty. But he had also reasoned with himself that any man given the opportunity of watching a beautiful woman undress – with impunity – would do the same. Watching Julie was only the fourth time he had used the cupboard, and although there was a small measure of self-loathing, there was also a large measure of enjoyment.

★★★★★★★

Julie felt much better for her session, she had thought that the funny old bath was a joke but she thought better now, it had been strangely exhilarating; to sit upright and bathe had somehow seemed erotic, sensual. Now she lay on the bed in the evening gloom, warm and sleepy. The anxiety of the last day had temporarily slipped away but the reason for her being there was ever present. She felt a little guilty at having enjoyed her bath and tried to imagine Graham stuck in his cell in England.

The window and shutters were still open from earlier and she was aware of voices below. Still naked, she jumped up on to the chair and peered over the edge of the sill down to the balcony a floor below. Light flooded out of the room. The East European girl from reception was laughing quietly; she came out into view and with a flowing movement jumped up and sat on the iron balcony edge, wrapping her feet through the uprights so as not to fall backwards. She was wearing little, a very short skirt that flicked out such that you could easily see up to where a knicker line should be. Her top was a baggy tee shirt, several sizes too large, the arm holes hanging down baring much of her side and had you been standing alongside her, much of her chest would have shown too. She gripped the rail on either side and adjusted her legs to a wider position, again wrapping her feet through the wrought iron. She pouted and blew a kiss back into the room and cocked her head to one side. To Julie, a scholar of body language, it was the strongest come on possible. Henri came out wearing a long tee shirt and no obvious other clothes. He kissed her hard on the mouth and whipped both hands up her shirt onto her bare breasts; she folded her arms around his neck and kissed him back.

Julie was holding her breath and flushing. Part of her wanted to turn away but most of her wanted to be down there sitting on the rail. Her left hand held on tight to the window sill, her right slipped down to the warm patch between her legs.

Henri had moved in closer and with a fluid motion he thrust himself inside the girl. She broke away from the kiss and gave a guttural moan and threw her head back, at the same time started to gently rotate her hips. There was hardly any movement at all. Henri stood perfectly still. She was a professional; she was using a technique few ordinary women are able to perform, using just her pelvic muscles she was massaging his erection up and down. The perfect masturbation.

Upstairs, Julie watched, mouth open; she wanted to drag herself away but was held by her first 'dogging' experience, and was finding it, not just absorbing, but totally erotic. She dare not breathe or move a muscle to give away her position, but was able to move her hand and massage herself. Her fingers slid up and down alongside her labia, first slowly and then speeding up as the fluid flowed. Her eyes were glued to the scene below where, although there was little movement, it was apparent that Henri was rapidly progressing towards an almighty orgasm – the expression on his face, his open mouth, his closed eyes and continuous low growl. The girl watched him closely and was matching the speed of her pelvic muscle ripples to his muscle build up.

Julie was working up on the same schedule. Her speed of movement was also increasing to a furious tempo, and absolutely together, Henri and Julie came, he with a great roar, she with a more sedate and muffled gasp.

Neither of the pair on the balcony heard or would have cared what Julie was doing. The girl had also seemingly come to an orgasm with just a simple 'Woo'.

Henri and the girl held the position for several minutes before he slipped his hands under her bare bottom, lifted her off the rail and carried her – still connected, back into the bedroom.

Julie stepped from the chair still holding one very wet hand in place and flopped backwards on to the bed, exhausted and confused. She had really enjoyed the last minutes and it put her recent sex life into perspective. Of late it had fallen on to a plateau rather lower than it had been, certainly at a lower level when compared to her time in France. When she had returned to England she had 'settled down'. She winced at the word even though it was just a thought in her head. But it was true; she had taken the job as French teacher in the school and had slipped into the role of respectable, safe, school 'ma'am'. Meeting and going out with Graham had cemented the creation of the new Julie and now she was experiencing a bit of a fling-back. The idea that being with someone who was steady and had a good mind had prevailed, Graham was sexually very competent but lacked the impulsive, the emotion... the love. She lay back on the bed in a solo after-glow and tried to think about her relationship with Graham as she fell into a luxurious sleep.

Chapter 7

Aariz and his girlfriend had moved in together after a fairly brief relationship. The extra cash that Aariz was receiving for his duty solicitor role from Sprake and Gilmot was useful and made the financial jump from family home to independence a little easier. They were from very different backgrounds – but got on well – and even though both had stressful jobs which demanded unsociable hours, when they were together they enjoyed themselves.

The fact that Aariz was of Pakistani decent and his girlfriend was white Caucasian had raised some issues with both families. Parents always want their children to avoid extra complications and know that life is tough enough without adding racial tension. In the end, after meeting up with their prospective partner's families, all were resigned to the inevitable – parents are not going to be able to influence their children when it comes to matters of the heart, and so with some reservations the match was accepted and each family gave as much assistance as they could for the couple to move in together.

There was no way that they could yet think in terms of a purchase and a mortgage, financially the gathering of the necessary deposit was way off the radar and anyway, this was testing the water. Better to check out whether they could make it work before the great commitment of a mortgage.

Aariz had been at the police station that day and had been frustrated by the reaction of Detective Inspector Curry, which had not gone down well with his mentor, James Sprake, when he had reported back as obliged. Sprake had indicated, although not stated, that Curry was well out of order and that he Aariz should have been more insistent and demanded to see Curry face to face rather than be fobbed off with a junior detective. Aariz felt angry at the situation as he had lost brownie points with Sprake, which was the exact opposite to what he had intended when he agreed to take on the duty solicitor role. His anger was being directed at Detective Constable Saskia Edwards as he paced around the empty flat. She was not to blame of course, she had only been directed to say that by that bastard Curry but she had smiled or even smirked at him – that made it worse.

His girlfriend finally came home and as soon as she appeared he jumped at her.

'Are you trying to get me into trouble with that game at the station today Saskia, or what?'

'Keep your turban on Aariz, you know what Curry's like, he plays games with you guys all the time.'

'I really got a roasting today from Sprake, he thinks I'm a wimp because I haven't stood up to Curry and you just stand there and laugh at me.'

'I'm not laughing at you, my love, I am smiling at the man I love because you are so fanciable when you put on your angry-bird face.'

'No, no that's not fair, who can't get round me that easy... .'

'Yes I can,' and she kissed him hard on the lips and that was the end of the conversation.

★★★★★★★

When the doorbell rang at 8.00 o'clock the following morning, Maddie was still in front of the mirror, in Julie's clothes, making the final touches to her makeup and looking as good as damn it like Julie. She stood up, took a deep breath and stubbed out her third cigarette of the day. Julie had not called back and her mobile was still turned off. The police driver was polite, opening the rear door for her, but he was non-communicative and she definitely felt like a criminal sitting in the back of a police car.

On the journey back to Ashford Maddie started to get the jitters but there was no going back now – she was some sort of accessory to some sort of crime, although she was a bit woolly over the exact crime she was committing, only that she knew it was a crime and there was a very good chance that she was going to be caught.

Maddie was shown into the interview room and after a few minutes Curry and Saskia came in. Curry switched on the recorder and started,

'Good morning Miss Webb, thank you for coming in again. We need to ask you a few more questions as we now have some extra information.'

'Right,' said Maddie, petrified.

'Can you tell us again, exactly how the wine got into the car?'

Maddie felt this was some kind of trick question and stalled a little, partly to give herself a little thinking time and partly to try to get to the point they were making, 'I'm sorry, I thought we had already talked about that, how can it be different?'

'Please, just tell us again, exactly what happened?'

'Um, Graham bought the wine and put it in the car.'

'Are you absolutely sure that he put the box in the car? Did you actually see him do it?'

'Well, yes, he picked it up and put it in the car.'

'Where did he put it?'

'In the boot I think, yes, in the boot.'

'Did the Frenchman come over to the car at all?'

'No, I don't think so.'

'OK.'

'You told us last time that you had smoked cannabis at university... .'

'Did I?' Maddie said with rather too much tone. She had slipped back into Maddie and was in fact showing surprise that her goodie goodie sister had actually smoked pot. Luckily Curry saw it as a lack of memory.

'Yes, you told us that yesterday.'

'Oh yes, I did, then.' She felt a little silly adding 'then' as it didn't quite make sense and she saw that Curry had pulled a little frown, but he continued. 'Do you smoke cigarettes?'

'Um...' Maddie was caught in a slight dilemma, in that she knew Julie did not smoke cigarettes at all and hadn't since being a teenager, while she had continued with the habit. She wasn't at all sure whether she should admit to smoking when pretending to be Julie. She carefully let her hands drop into her lap, aware that her fingers were always a little nicotine stained. She couldn't lie about that now.

'Yes I do smoke cigarettes occasionally,' hoping that would sort of sit on the fence, and carried on trying to keep her hands covered.

'Do you occasionally smoke cannabis, then?' continued Curry

She hesitated again, because occasionally she did.

'No, of course not,' she tried to sound indignant and the mere suggestion that she might be doing that. Curry and Saskia exchanged a quick glance.

'When was the last time then that you did smoke cannabis?'

'Oh, not since well, as you said, at university.'

'That is what you said, I only repeated it... .'

'Look,' said Maddie sitting up and striking a pose, 'What is this all about? We all know that Graham and I were used as unwitting mules to carry drugs of some kind through Customs, what is all of this stuff about pot, for Christ's sake?'

Curry paused for effect. 'Can you explain how a kilo of cannabis found itself under the back seat of your car?'

Maddie sat and opened her mouth. Several thoughts rushed through her mind. First, the police have planted this. Second the smugglers must have somehow put it there. Third, oh no, they didn't get into the car. Fourth, oh shit, Graham and Julie were smuggling dope under the seat and fifth, oh shit, maybe they were smuggling the coke as well. Maddie sat and said nothing. The two police officers were waiting in silence. She had to say something, her silence was an admission of some kind of guilt, but she didn't know what to say. All three sat there for what seemed to Maddie like an hour or two and finally with pain she said in a small voice, 'I don't know anything about any drugs, coke or pot, nothing. I have no idea how the stuff was there, nothing, nothing.'

They sat there for a few more moments and finally Curry stood and said, 'interview terminated at 13.06am.'

'It will be necessary for you to stay here Miss Webb we will want to ask you more questions a little later, and the two officers left the room.

★★★★★★★

Graham sat opposite the two detectives, alongside him was Aariz Al Amir. On arriving at the police station, the solicitor had spent ten minutes alone with Graham, going through again what had happened at the Aire on the A26 Autoroute to Paris. It seemed like an open and shut case to Aariz and he was confident that he would be able to have Graham released very quickly.

'Tell us again Mr Spelling – do you smoke cigarettes?' opened Curry.

'What?' said Graham, again starting to get angry with the officer.

'Just answer the question please Mr Spelling.'

Graham looked at Aariz, who nodded in agreement – that he should answer. He pulled a face, and said 'I do not smoke cigarettes nor anything else.'

'OK. Can you tell us if Miss Webb smokes cigarettes – or anything else?'

'Yes, I can tell you. She doesn't smoke cigarettes or anything else.'

'That's interesting. Miss Webb just admitted that she does have the occasional cigarette – her exact words in fact… .'

'What kind of nonsense is this? I don't know what game you are trying to play here, but I can tell you categorically that Julie does not smoke, in fact she is more anti-smoking that I am. You are talking nonsense and I would like you to stop right now and let me leave.'

Aariz spoke up. 'Detective Inspector, my client is being accused of smuggling what we all believe to be cocaine. Has that been established?'

'Yes is has.' replied Curry. The fact that the coke was only in the one bottle he kept quiet about, for the moment.

Aariz continued. 'Your line of questioning seems a little unorthodox, that is, whether Miss Webb is a smoker or not has no relevance to the apparent offence to which my client is answering questions to the best of his knowledge.'

'What I am trying to establish here Mr Al Amir…' said Curry calmly after glancing at the solicitor's business card, '… is the truth. You see, when some apparently insignificant fact – like smoking or not smoking – is inconsistent then, being a determined and hopefully conscientious policeman, I will follow it up until I am satisfied that all parties are if fact telling me the truth. Is that OK with you Mr Al Amir?'

'Yes, please continue Inspector.'

'Thank you.'

'Mr Spelling, can you explain to me how about one kilogram of cannabis resin was found in your car, under the back seat?'

'What, no, what, cannabis, in the car, when?'

Aariz broke in again. 'Inspector, may I have a word with my client in private please?'

'Certainly, interview postponed at 9.29am.'

Graham was calm but red in the face when they were alone and Aariz said, 'What do you know about this Mr Spelling. I can't advise you on your best route if you keep things from me – especially information that the police are bound to find out.'

'I know absolutely nothing about any cannabis, I don't smoke the stuff and I wouldn't be stupid enough to bring it through Customs, would I?'

'If you didn't, do you think it possible that Miss Webb hid it there?'

'No, I don't think so. I didn't put it there and well, I don't see how she could have done it either. I've been driving around northern France for a week, and Julie only joined me yesterday, it's not very likely that she would or could have popped out somewhere and tracked down some pot. Anyway she doesn't smoke.'

'OK. Could the French guys in the lay-by have planted it there?'

'No, they didn't go anywhere near the car. I put the wine in the boot.'

'Could they have slipped into the car when you were doing that?'

'No, Julie was in the car anyway and they just stood back

and watched me load up.'

'Detective Inspector Curry was pretty sure that Miss Webb was a smoker, of cigarettes. Can you explain that?'

'No, I can't. Look, she doesn't smoke, full stop.'

Aariz was unsure how to proceed. He certainly believed what Graham was telling him, although of course all lawyers had a duty to defend their clients in this sort of situation, based on what they said, rather than what the solicitor thought was true. However, Graham was either a very good liar or he was telling the truth. What confused Aariz was the fact that, if Graham was lying, then he had not come up with any convincing story about how the cannabis had appeared in the car, had he been a covert smuggler then he would have told the investigators that the Frenchmen had got into the back of the car on some pretext. But he hadn't, and so there was no obvious answer, apart from a rather unlikely scenario which involved two sets of drugs being independently placed in the car, the first having been prior to the lay-by incident, when the car was unattended at some time. By far the most likely explanation was now looking like the unseen Miss Webb was in fact the perpetrator and Spelling was in some way trying to cover her tracks.

Outside the room Curry and Saskia were again in close conversation. 'I don't get this, why would Spelling try to lie about Webb not smoking. It was bloody obvious that she smoked, her fingers were nicotine stained and I could smell the smoke on her clothes as soon as she came in.'

'Could she just have chain smoked in the last 24 hours since she got home?'

'I suppose so, but he reckons she's a committed non-smoker; yes a smoker might go off and chain smoke when under pressure but it's not really likely that she would, is it? But possible I suppose. It just bothers me. When something like this doesn't fit then it bugs me and I have to get to the bottom of it before I let them go again. It may have absolutely nothing to do with the drugs in the wine bottles... .'

'Look,' said Saskia, 'one of them is telling porkies. They have to be. No one else went near the car. Is it possible that someone got into their car when it was parked on the ferry deck?'

'Well again, it's possible, but highly unlikely. That someone would have to break into the car very quickly before the decks were closed – no one's allowed on the car decks when sailing.'

'What about a deck hand?'

'That doesn't make sense either. Ferry workers have all kinds of simpler ways of smuggling stuff through without breaking into a car on the deck. Remember they would have to reclaim it once the car's gone through.'

'I'm stumped.'

'Me to, let's get them in together, see what happens.'

Graham was sitting still and calmly concentrating on the far wall when the two CID officers came back in, but this time with Maddie in tow.

'Come in Miss Webb and sit over there please,' indicating a chair to the side of the interview table.

'Hello Graham,' said Maddie.

'Hello,' said Graham and he then looked down at the table.

There was an awkward silence in the room until Curry spoke into the recorder and announced those present.

'Now, Miss Webb, could you tell us again, do you smoke cigarettes?'

Maddie drew a breath and said, 'Yes, I do occasionally smoke cigarettes.'

'Have you kept this secret from Mr Spelling here?'

'Er, Yes.'

'Mr Spelling, do you think that it likely that you have been mistaken about the cigarette smoking habits of Miss Webb?'

Graham looked at Maddie who was still looking at the floor. 'Yes, it may be that Miss Webb here is in fact a smoker.'

'Good, at least we have sorted that out. Miss Webb, would you be so kind as to hold out your hands, and show them to Mr Spelling.'

Maddie hesitated a moment and then held them out.

'Please note Mr Spelling, that Miss Webb's fingers show the signs of significant nicotine staining; I would guess that she is in fact quite a heavy smoker and indeed has been for some time, and yet even though we are led to believe that you are 'good friends' having just spent some time travelling together in France, and I dare say, sharing a bed at night, you hadn't noticed that she was in fact a committed, heavy smoker.'

Graham looked at the floor and said nothing.

'I can't help but think that there is something a bit odd going on here and it would be helpful if one of you, either of you, would save us all a lot of time by explaining.'

Silence.

'Right. I believe that one of you was trying to smuggle a

kilo of cannabis through customs into this country, which is an offence. Could you, Miss Webb, tell me if it was you?'

'I know absolutely nothing about any drugs, cannabis or cocaine. I did not, categorically not, put any drugs in the car.'

'Do you then, Miss Webb, believe that Mr Spelling here was the person that did it?'

'I object to this kind of questioning Inspector,' interrupted Aariz.

'Tough. Well Miss Webb?'

'I don't know if Mr Spelling put it there, all I know is that I didn't.'

'Mr Spelling, did you put the cannabis in the car?'

'No, definitely not.'

'Well someone did. Do you have any thoughts on who?'

Graham sat quietly for a moment and then looked up at Maddie and said, 'How's your sister getting on, Miss Webb?'

Maddie clenched her lips and said 'Fine, as far as I know Mr Spelling.'

The other three in the room all looked puzzled by this exchange.

Saskia leaned over to Curry and said 'Could I have a word outside sir?'

'Detective Inspector Curry and Detective Constable Edwards are leaving the room at 9.41am'

Outside Saskia spoke, looking back through the glass door. 'Andy, do you think it possible that Julie Webb has an identical twin sister?'

'Oh, oh, oh Saskia, that is a very interesting thought. Let's find out shall we.'

Back in the room, Curry started again with Maddie. 'Miss Webb, could you please tell us your full name?'

Maddie dropped her head and then looked up, glared at Graham and said in a clear voice, 'It's Madeline Susan Webb.'

Aariz sat amazed at the turn of events and wrote down her name on his pad. Curry went on.

'Could you please tell us all where Julie Isabelle Webb is right now?'

'She's in France, she went over on the ferry to try to find the two Frenchmen that sold them the wine.'

'When did she go?'

'She went yesterday as a foot passenger – on the two o'clock ferry.'

'Thank you.'

'Mr Spelling, when did you notice that this was not your 'friend' Julie Webb?'

'As soon as she walked through the door.'

'I am certain that whatever else comes of this investigation that both of you will be charged with obstructing the police and before you ask, Mr Al Amir, no, I am not releasing either of them until I get full statements from them both and have finished my investigation,' and with that he stormed out.

Saskia stayed behind and took Maddie, who was now in tears, to a different room leaving Graham with his solicitor.

As soon as they were alone, Aariz spoke. 'So, Mr Spelling, do you now think that Julie Webb put the cannabis under the seat?'

'Yes, I suppose I do.'

'Do you think that she had anything to do with the cocaine in the car?'

'I suppose I now think that it must be possible.'

★★★★★★★

Detective Inspector Curry was not a happy man. He had just been made to look a fool. Identical twins, who would have thought it, and to make matters worse, it was Saskia, his rookie detective that spotted it. Something to do with women's intuition he supposed. He couldn't dwell on it, thank goodness she did spot it sooner rather than later. At least that sorted out the 'who smokes – who doesn't, conundrum. He now had a firm favourite for the cannabis – Julie Webb, who had 'run off' to France, seemingly to 'find the French wine blokes'. Would she really have gone back over to do that for Spelling? If she seriously thought that Spelling was going to be arrested and charged then yes, I suppose she might try and do something really stupid like that. Saskia Edwards came back into the office.

'Well done Saskia for spotting the twin with the perm.'

'What, she had a perm…?'

'No, sorry that was a blast from the past. Well done for getting to the bottom of that. I had missed it.'

'Well not really, it was you that picked up on the smoking thing.'

'Yes, well anyway, we now seem to have a prime suspect, certainly for the cannabis, but I am still not convinced about her involvement in the cocaine. What do you think?'

'I have to say sir, I'm still confused about who's done what.'

'Yes, so am I, look, I may regret this, but I'm going to hang on them both for the day at least so that we can check this out a bit more.'

'Don't we have to let Spelling go this morning, it's 24 hours since we took him in?'

'Yes you are right I can only detain him for the 24 hours on the original matter of the cocaine in the wine bottle, but I can now detain him for another 24 hours because of the cannabis under the back seat – different offence. His solicitor will have a fit but so be it. Is his solicitor still here?'

'Yes, he is expecting to have him released any moment.'

'OK, I'd better go and break the news to them both, this will be fun.'

'Can I do it sir?'

'Err, yes I suppose so, if you feel up to it.'

'Yes, I'm fine.'

The phone rang on Curry's desk. It was the head of SOCO again.

'Oh hello, Brian, any more revelations?'

'Well more interesting things I suppose Andy, do you want to come over as soon as you're free for a chat about it?'

'Yeah, why not, I need to sort some paperwork first I have to write up my report on that bank job on the Nat West last week for "Herr Commander" who must be obeyed. I'll be over after lunch, OK with you?'

'Fine, see you then,' said Brian.

'Right, Saskia, you can go and break the news to Mr Spelling and his solicitor and then check out the ferry arrival times and talk to the car hire companies at Calais. She went over as a foot passenger and so would probably hire a car – hey just a minute, I've got her passport. Oh right, of course. First check with a sister, I'll bet she's using her sister's passport.'

'OK sir, will do.'

'Blimey Saskia, the charge sheet's getting longer and longer.'

Chapter 8

Julie woke up slowly and much later than she had planned. She looked up at the ceiling directly above her where there was a large crack running diagonally across one corner. She wondered what had caused it. She thought briefly about the odd and unfamiliar smell of the room. This all happened in the first five seconds by which time she had remembered where she was. It took another ten seconds or so to remember why she was there. This was now the difficult bit… many more seconds passed before she had come to terms with the answer.

She then recalled the events of the previous evening and was inwardly a little embarrassed, then not. She was lying diagonally across the double bed pretty much where she had fallen back from the window exercise and had obviously dragged some of the bed covers across herself. She pulled back the covers, had a quick check of the under sheet and tottered into the bathroom.

Fifteen minutes later she was dressed and resolute and felt like a slug of caffeine. The hotel was room only which was fine as there were plenty of very French spots to have breakfast just up the road.

She passed through the empty bar and was relieved not to

see either the proprietor or the receptionist for fear she may blush because then surely they would be able to guess exactly why.

Sitting outside the café with a bowl of great coffee and a fresh roll, she wondered once again why she had not returned to France after helping her sister, when you could sit outside a café like this one in most towns and villages and drink coffee this good and feel this relaxed.

Julie had gone through several periods of 'change' in her life. At university, overall, she been pretty conventional, drinking too much at times, occasionally smoking dope (but never cigarettes – 'far too dangerous'), some bedding of the wrong men, but nothing terrible. Her somewhat muted behaviour had been influenced by her sister, who, when away from the limitations meted out by loving parents, had gone a little over the top. Maddie had got into some quite serious scrapes through drink, drugs and unsuitable companions. Julie, who had witnessed her sister's fall from grace, pulled up short of self-destruction, had moderated her behaviour and worked hard. She had let things slide a little during her 'year out' in France – as part of her French degree; there she had been a bit wilder when her place at university was not on the line. She worked in the language faculty at Jean Moulin University in Lyon as a language assistant. Her hours were short, but gave her enough money to live on and flexible enough to have a good social life. Her boyfriend for most of that year had been a very bright techy from the IT department called Edouard, who was an accomplished computer hacker. It had started out as great fun, hacking into other people's lives and

then company files and then financial institutions, and then…
it had been great fun to actually take some of their money.
Julie had not known what was going on but neither had she
asked too many questions, telling herself that his day job was
very well paid. The cars and the restaurant dining and the
weekends in five-star hotels were all left behind when she had
to return to England back to normality and her finals. She left
at just the right time and so was not implicated when Edouard
was arrested and subsequently jailed.

After her finals – she got a first – Julie returned to France to
work for a small local advertising agency in Livarot, Normandy,
and then moved on to a larger firm in Annecy, the beautiful
Haute Savoir town in the Alps. Skiing became her main
winter occupation and she quickly and happily became part
of the well-heeled social scene. Her Englishness and her now
perfect French meant that she was enthusiastically accepted
and once again she adopted a somewhat wild existence; there
was a certain amount of the sex and drugs and rock and roll,
although not so much of the drugs, keeping it to just the odd
spliff, as she had done at university. She became even more
popular following an epic ski from the top of Mont du Vallon,
above Mottaret, all the way down to Meribel Village   topless.

Maddie's call for help drew Julie back to England. Her sister's
marriage to a totally unsuitable merchant seaman had finally
come to a head and although Maddie had seen it coming she
was still in need of sisterly TLC. So Julie abandoned the Alps
temporarily to be with her sister, but when back in England
realised that she was growing out of her hedonistic lifestyle
and was keen to move on. To everyone's surprise she spent a

year in teacher training and then gained a position in a private girls' school in Berkshire.

As the coffee disappeared so did her elated mood – she was here on a mission, to find out what had happened, to find out who had stitched them up and to get Graham cleared. Easy. A flood of despair, lack of confidence, bags of self-doubt and once again the nagging thought that this was probably – no – definitely a really stupid idea. A rush of acid came up from her stomach to her throat and stopped her from breathing for a moment.

Cup down, she took some deep breaths and got back control. Just about at that point a short rather scruffy man in his thirties came out of the café, laughing and calling back some unheard friendly abuse to the café owner. He jumped into the driver's seat of a dirty white van and drove off.

Julie sat stiffly immobile, oh my God, oh my God. That was him, that was the van, what do I do, what do I do? She turned to see the van turn off to the left and disappear. It was far too late to run down the road, get her keys which, damn it, were back in the room anyway and drive after him… and then what… ?

The proprietor had followed the man out of the café and was clearing away cups from the next table. Julie's head cleared. She put on her best smile and said in her best, and almost without accent, French…

'Excuse me sir, but the man that just left is very familiar – I think I know him from somewhere… .'

'You mean Louis, Louis Montard, he's a local, lives out at

Ferme de Bray, he and his brother Victor run a stall at the market each week, you've probably seen him there.'

'Ah yes,' said Julie.

She paid for the breakfast and walked quickly back to the hotel. By the time she had reached her room several plans were emerging, daft plans, but a plan was a plan.

She had reasoned with herself that there would be no sign of the van or its contents out on the lay-by. The French police possibly had a message by now from the UK police and maybe they had checked it out, maybe they hadn't bothered. Either way there were unlikely to be any clues left. Would the police have looked for tyre tracks? Did they even know where the lay-by was? Certainly her recollection and description of the place was dodgy, maybe Graham's memory would have been better. But it was pretty unlikely that anyone would have taken the events very seriously. Back at the Customs Office she had sat in her cell and fantasized that the French authorities were running about and sleuth-like taking finger-prints, putting up road blocks with stingers, and generally doing everything possible to catch the criminals. The reality of the situation was that nothing would have been done, they may have sent a car out to look at the several lay-bys along this stretch of road, but what could they possibly find?

She hadn't even been able to give a good description of the van saying 'a bit like a Transit, I think' was hardly worthy of an APB, whatever that stood for – and probably only in America anyway. The recognition of the driver at the café had focused her mind. She was 100 per cent sure it was the shorter of the men in the lay-by. This was helped by the fact he was wearing the same clothes, but also his accent and then there was the van. Subconsciously she had seen and remembered things about the van that she hadn't recalled when being interviewed. Not only had she seen again the green decal in the back window, but the dirt up one side had been cleaned off a bit by someone brushing against it as they got in. There was also a long scrape down the side which had started to rust. Somewhere deep in her memory she now recalled that she had thought 'You ought to get that repainted because it will carry on rusting and ruin the vehicle'. It was only when she saw the scratch again that it came back to her.

She now believed she knew who the drug dealers were and where they lived. A first thought was to call the police... .

'I am an Englishwomen who was arrested for taking drugs through customs and I have been let out on bail pending further investigations on the strict instruction not to travel. I have taken my sister's passport and travelled illegally into France and now think that I have seen the real criminals. Oh, by the way, I have no evidence that makes any sense, but I think you people should go around to their house, arrest them, search their house and jolly well lock them up... .'

Next idea. Go round to their house, sneak in, search the place and find loads of bottles stuffed with drugs, then call the police in, anonymously... .

Next. Go round to their house, knock on the door, pretend to be a... double glazing salesman, Jehovah's Witness, a carpet cleaner, a mad person, a tramp wanting a drink of water. Get invited into the house and when their backs are turned find the drugs etc.

Next. A woman with a broken-down car... mmm maybe. Get invited in, ask for a drink of water, ask to use the loo, ask to do a pole dance... and while their backs are turned... oh no, they wouldn't be.

Next. Give up, cry a bit and go home.

Next. Drive to the house and make something up when there. Good plan.

What to wear was now confronting her. If she was going to get into the house she needed to be... professional looking... smart... sexy... vulnerable... mad? She needed to be careful in any case, take precautions. Take a gun, knife, penknife, hammer... what was in her handbag. Umm, hit them with a sharp comb, thrust a Tampax in their eye, smother them with a hankie or just whack them with your handbag, Maggie style, yeh.

OK, just dress normally and find the place – then think of something, or just drive back again and then think of something. Possibly just phone the police with some story which would interest them enough to drive out there and have a look. Maybe, 'I heard a gunshot' or 'I heard a woman screaming... . '

Julie went downstairs to the public phone which sat by a table at the bottom of the stairs. It had coating of dust, testament to the rise of the mobile. There was a local phone book under the table and she quickly found Montard and Ferme de Bray. It gave the address as Le Haut, Querchamps-les-Ardres. Henri had been quietly watching her for a few moments from the door marked Privee that just opened into the area behind the bar. He looked her up and down, noted the tight jeans, her rounded arse and remembered the view he had had the night before. It started to arouse him. He broke the silence and made her jump about two feet in the air.

'*Mam'selle…* pardon, I didn't mean to make you jump.' She had turned to face him and he thought of a startled rabbit. He smiled and said 'It's OK you are allowed to use the phone but it only takes a phone card. No one much uses it these days.'

'Thank you, no,' she stammered trying to regain some composure, partly due to her jumping and partly due to sudden recall of the night before.

'Can you tell me how to get to Le Haut, please?'

He furrowed a little. 'It's very easy, but there is very little to see there, just a couple of houses… .'

She didn't try to give him a reason for going, just raised an eyebrow. He gave a Gallic shrug and pointed down the road.

'Take the first left, go about 2 kilometres, and at the 'T' junction turn right, and you are there. There are a few farm houses and a derelict chapel. That's all.'

'Thank you,' she said and walked out to her car.

She felt his eyes on her as she left and as she pulled away from the kerb, he was standing in the doorway of the hotel watching her go.

Her feelings were very mixed at this point   she was pushing herself forward with bravado plus there was an odd bit of showing off. 'I am a confident woman who knows her mind and will not be intimidated by you Monsieur Patron, and remember I know that you have sex with your receptionist and that can't be right, and just because I find you rather attractive there is no reason for you to patronise me, so there.'

She turned left and drove out of town as suggested and found… almost nothing. La Ferme de Bray stood alone, not even in sight of the other few buildings. It was a beautiful old building in the 'uncared for, peeling paint, rather tatty, very French, like my parents used to salivate over' style. But it really was tatty. There was a front yard, which should have been shingled with large pots of flowering shrubs and a few hens pecking about; there were a few hens pecking about in fact, but they were very scraggy. There was also a lot of mud, two dead-looking cars, an old car trailer, and an assortment junk but no sign of life and no dirty white Transit-like van.

Julie sat in her car just up the lane from the farm house. She had been there for an hour and no one had appeared at the farm. She started the car and drove past the house and on for about half a mile. The road gradually narrowed and the grass in the middle of the lane grew longer until it was a muddy track in a field. The path probably went somewhere but only if you had a tractor or at least a 4x4. The rental Peugeot 208 was not made for the job and she feared for the underside. Her hassle at the car rental office in Calais had resulted in a vast insurance fee, also combined with a ridiculously large excess and she had no wish to pay any more to them. She stopped the car, turned around with a spin of mud and drove back down the lane past the house to resume her wait. After another hour all she had seen was one rusty tractor crossing a field ahead of her and an elderly lady who had hobbled passed pulling one of those two-wheeled shopping baskets which always seemed to use tartan material, even in France. The woman had passed right by the car without showing any signs of noticing Julie's presence. Goodness knows where she had come from or where she was going, for it was a long walk back to the relative civilisation of the main town. For a moment Julie had thought she might jump out and ask after the Montard brothers, but decided against it. The doubts about her ridiculous adventure welled up again and after a few more minutes she gave up, started the car and drove back slowly to the hotel.

★★★★★★★

Maddie had sat alone in tears in the interview room, feeling silly and sorry for herself at ever getting mixed up with her sister's reckless trip to France. Now she was in the firing line and her sister was in worse trouble. The lady police officer had been very understanding and gave her the impression that her boss, the Inspector, was actually not as bad as his bite. She helped Maddie make a full statement, even though she did realise that it was self-incriminating, but by now Maddie didn't care, she just wanted to tell the truth, clear the air and help her sister stay safe.

'Has your sister been in touch since she left?'

'Yes, she is texting me and keeping me in the loop.'

'What has she told you so far?'

'Only that she has landed and driven to some little town which I think is near where the thing happened.'

'Look Miss Webb, you do realise that Julie is in quite a lot of danger, don't you? She is out there, on her own, trying to track down drug smugglers who may well be nasty people. She needs to come back and leave the policing to the police.'

'I know, I know, I tried to stop her but she can be very determined when she gets the bit between her teeth. I couldn't stop her.'

'Well you did hand over your passport; if you hadn't then she couldn't have got through passport control.'

'I know I did, I shouldn't have done. It was stupid, but she was so determined to go that in the end, as her sister, I had to help her. Stupid I know, but there it. Twin sister bond I suppose.'

'May I see the text messages?'

'Yes, I suppose so,' and she handed Saskia her phone. Saskia called up the text log and wrote down the two short messages that Julie had sent.

'maddie landed at calais hired car all ok j'
'at hotel in town all ok j'

'Have you actually spoken to her since she was in France?'

'No, just these text messages.'

'We should have the car details soon from Calais and we have contacted the police in the region where she is, so hopefully they find her, will arrest her, and send her back. That's our best option.'

'Do you think we should phone her and tell her to come home?'

'Possibly. You know her, if the police phoned her now and said that, what do you think she would do?'

'I think she would ignore you and carry on; as I said, she can be very determined when it takes her, which is a euphemism for bull-headed or just bloody stubborn.'

'And she would react in the same way to you asking her to come back?'

'Yes, I think so.'

'OK, let's not phone just yet then, but maybe we can at least monitor what she's doing and try to help her until the French police can pick her up.'

'I suppose you're right.'

'Yes, we need to find because her first there are several unanswered questions, and second, assuming that her explanation to you was true, then she is swanning around in dangerous company and therefore we have a duty to get her back safely.'

'Do you still think she put the hash in the back of the car?'

'I really don't know, I couldn't say, but we do need to talk to her about it, to eliminate her from our enquiries at least. Look, Miss Webb, I think the best route forward is for us to keep the phone so that we know where she is and is coming to no harm.'

'Yes, yes I suppose so. I just want her back and no harm to come to her. Whatever you say.'

'OK, I'll keep it then, you just need to sign your statement and this form which is in effect a receipt for the phone. Sign here and here.'

'Thank you.'

★★★★★★★

Saskia was pleased with herself and couldn't wait to show Curry. She dropped the phone on his desk with a flourish and a 'ta-da!'. Curry raised an eyebrow.

'It's Maddie Webb's phone   she's been texting Julie.'

'Ooooo, clever girl.'

'Look at the texts so far,' and she opened up the recently sent texts to show him.

'OK we should be able to find her if she's switched on, get the number off the contacts list and use that techno stuff you know all about to try and track her down.'

'Will do sir. I also talked to Calais. She hired a Peugeot 208 at 4.10pm our time, the registration number is here,' she said pointing at the typed sheet.

'Great, I'll get this through to the French guys; you try to find out where she is on that tracking thing.'

Curry was very aware of his lack of understanding of the new-fangled techy things that made up quite a lot of police work these days. He consoled himself with the fact that he did know most of what could be done but, he neither understood the technology nor how to actually do it, although he knew a man who could, in this case a woman, so that was alright.

He could do email though, and he went through his contacts and reached the number for his French counterpart in Calais with whom he had had a few contacts. He typed out the details – Julie's name plus the name on her passport, her brief description and the details of the car. He also added that he believed she might be travelling to the area near the lay-by where the alleged drug 'placement' happened. He asked the French police to detain her and contact him to arrange transfer back to England. He was very aware that the request was somewhat ambiguous in that he was saying to the French he believed that she was somehow involved in drug smuggling and had done a runner, but she might also be just going back to where she said that a drug smuggling gang had placed the drugs on them. Both couldn't be right except he still had the notion that she and Spelling were not guilty of the cocaine business but were somehow guilty of the stashing of the cannabis in the car.

He had written the email in English. His reasoning was that they all spoke fluent English over there, which was just as well as his French was at the 'O' level fail standard.

By the time he had written and sent the email, Saskia had gone into the police system, put in Julie's mobile number and tried to track it. Julie's phone was still turned off and so her exact whereabouts remained unknown.

★★★★★★★

'Hi Brian, what have you got for me?'

'Come into the lab.'

Brian led the way through the door at the back of his office directly into the lab ante-room. Curry wasn't allowed into the full lab for fear of contamination, but the ante-room was a kind of half-way house. Brian had finished his examination of the car and the wine case which was now on the counter.

'First the bottles, I told you yesterday about the print patterns, so just to repeat what I said. Someone had placed them into the wine carton, using as you would expect, mostly thumb on one side and fore finger with a trace of other fingers, like this...' and he picked up a plastic water bottle to demonstrate. 'There were some smudges around the neck made by someone wearing gloves.'

'So,' said Curry, 'as we were saying yesterday the final person handling them had moved them from one box to another. The previous person had put them in the first box using gloves.'

'Yes, but I think we can go a little further, if it's any use.'

'Go on, everything is potentially useful.'

'Well I'm pretty sure that the bottles were picked up by the final handler from a container, which was not a wine box.'

'OK, clever clogs how do you work that one out?'

'Well the prints are also around the main part of the bottle. The person must have picked them up when they were lying on their side. They used the right hand to pick up the bottle, then used the left to position it better and then the right hand again with the thumb and forefinger.' Again Brian showed how the print patterns matched the handling of the bottle.

'I see, got it, it may be relevant, I have no idea at the moment.'

'Next, the carton. The cardboard was quite clean with evidence of many smudged prints and some minor DNA material but all inconclusive for any kind of analysis. From what you told me there were several people who would have handled this. The French guys, your man, the Customs people, and us when we picked it up. The other thing Andy is that something was torn out of the underside; by the indentations around it and the size, I would guess that it was some kind of electronic device, like a transmitter, which, if I am right would indicate that there was a means of tracking the box but it's been taken out. Now the really interesting thing is I am pretty sure that it was taken out after the wine was spilt.'

'Um, how can you tell?'

Brian showed him the patch of torn cardboard, 'Look here, where the tear has been pulled across the corrugations. You can see the wine has penetrated into the board and the tear cuts right through it.'

'Yes, I see, I think you're right. That means that someone tore this out after the wine was spilt and before it got to you. That points to someone in Customs, doesn't it?'

'Well yes, or of course in here, in the labs.'

'OK, to be pure, yes it could be you... thanks Brian, you're a star as usual.'

****

Alison walked through the security gate at the back of the Folkestone Customs building and showed her pass to George who said,

'Did you enjoy your little birthday surprise yesterday Miss?'

'Sorry George?' said Alison.

'I know everything that goes on around here you know.'

'What?'

'You know, your birthday, yesterday... all that wine.'

'It wasn't my birthday yesterday George, my birthday is in December.'

'Oh,' said George with a worried look. His recall wasn't as good as it had been but he was pretty sure that that other Custom's bloke had said it was her birthday that they were celebrating; he must have heard it wrong.

Alison raised an eyebrow and walked on in. In the office she greeted Alan.

'Hi boss, I think it's about time George hung up his keys, he's starting to lose it out there. He reckoned it was my birthday yesterday and kept mumbling something about drinking wine in the office. You haven't been having parties in here without me have you?'

'I assure you Ali, if we had an office party in here you would be the first one I would invite, especially as you are the only woman and I don't fancy the other two.' He stopped himself as what he had said wasn't very bright. Alison had turned and had given him 'a look'.

'Sorry, sorry, what I meant was… .'

'It's OK Alan, I know you're an MCP and that you secretly ogle me every time I walk into the room.'

'I don't Ali, I… .'

'Joke, Alan, joke.'

'OK, sorry anyway.'

Andy felt a bit silly. He really didn't in any way fancy Ali, she was, well, not his type. He was of course totally aware that Geoffrey did ogle her and she that didn't like it. As manager of the unit he often thought he should confront him about it, because it really was a form of sexual abuse these days. But then she couldn't keep her eyes off Gary, and could often be seen undressing him across the room, so that was no different. He found it all too much and so he did nothing and hoped that it would blow over. Relationships or non-relationships in the office were always very difficult to handle. His thoughts slipped to his own behaviour with Emily.

A few years back, in a low period when he felt that his life had not really panned out quite as he thought it should, an opportunity was presented to him on a plate, and he just had to either take it or walk away. He was fifty then, but looked younger, his wife was the same age and looked older.

'Not bloody fair,' she used to say, '…that men seem to carry their years better than women.'

'…and how come older men can always get younger women and not the other way around?'

Alan had always thought, but never dared say, that women had the advantage of makeup – but only if they bothered to wear any these days… .

A VAT-trained employee had come into his office on secondment, which was all a bit daft, what were accountants going to do in the Customs Office? But, as both sections were managed through the same government department at that time, in order to progress up the ladder all prospective senior folk had to do the Custom's bit, much to their chagrin and everyone else's.

So one day came Emily, just turned 40 but passing for 32, recently divorced and loving it.

She saw Alan as the font of all knowledge, much better to get it all from the man who was doing it rather than the text book that wasn't. Or at least that's what Alan thought she thought. Emily took the opportunity to talk to Alan whenever she could. She was attractive, no, very attractive and he was flattered that anyone, especially one so gorgeous, would want to talk to him even about work, let alone flirt with him, and oh yes – she did.

Alan started paying more attention to his appearance, even using a little of that aftershave that had lain in his man-drawer, unused for years. He bought some new shirts and trendier shoes. His wife didn't seem to notice – or didn't care.

They went for a drink a few times after work, at her behest, in order to ask him more questions... he often stayed late and as the shifts constantly moved around depending on the ferry times, it wasn't in any way unusual to be late home.

She was staying in a neat little B&B hotel, a short walk from Customs, and one evening in the pub she looked him straight in the eye and said, 'So, shall we go back to my place and make love?'

Alan had fantasised about this for weeks, could he, would he, should he, take her to bed? How would he ask her? What would she say? Would she be shocked, embarrassed, offended? He worried about all of that, and had still not had the balls to ask her, and now she had asked him. He was shocked, embarrassed and not offended. But did find himself tongue tied and red in the face. He said nothing for a moment and looked around the pub in a kind of check – was anyone watching, overhearing? He turned back to her, smiled and just nodded, like a naughty boy. She smiled back and got her coat.

They walked down the road side by side. Alan felt it would have been right to hold her hand but didn't. She didn't seem in the least bit anxious or in any way different (unlike him) and asked a question about some procedural matter he couldn't think of the answer as his head was so full of other things, like guilt and would he be actually, really – no really, able to do 'it' with her when he had only done 'it' with his wife for the past

25 years. There was panic inside, his heart was pounding, his mouth was dry and he definitely could do with another drink.

Emily got all this just from the way he walked. Once inside her room she kissed him gently on the lips and got him a Scotch and they sat on the sofa. She cuddled up to him and said, 'I wonder what Geoffrey would say if he could see us,' and they both laughed, and their laughter broke the tension and within a few minutes they had moved to the bed, clothes were removed and they had made love. It was over fairly quickly. He apologised. She said it was fine and snuggled up again.

Alan lay there thinking about whether he should try again, but decided against it – nothing worse than a failed attempt. After about an hour and some unconvincing small talk he said that he had better be going, very self-consciously dressed, while she pretended not to look, gave her a quick kiss and was gone.

Back in the office the next morning, Alan remained in a kind of semi-trance; the others kept asking if he was alright and was he coming down with something. He found reasons to get out of the office more than usual. Emily was totally at ease and behaved in exactly the same way as the previous day although spent less time with Alan and more time with Geoffrey.

Towards the end of the day Emily went up to Alan's desk and said in quite a loud voice, 'Alan, it's nearly knocking off time, is there anything I can do for you?' She smiled just a little but still faced him so no one else saw her face.

Alan kept his cool this time, 'Oh yes, Emily, if you don't

mind hanging on and run your eye down this column' and he held up the department's account's read-out.

She nearly 'corpsed' but managed a very controlled. 'Of course Alan, I'd be happy to do that for you.'

When the others had gone the two of them went directly to Emily's room in the guest house. Alan was a lot less anxious and by his own standards, performed pretty well; yes, he was a little disappointed that Emily had not called out in some way, not necessarily 'Oh God Oh God, yes yes yes,' kind of response like they seemed to always do in those videos, but a little bit of moaning or perhaps an 'Oh Alan,' would have been polite.

Once again he left after a while and went home. Part of him wanted to stay the night and then he would have definitely attempted a second go. But he went home.

Emily came in late the next day and brought little wrapped presents for each of the staff in the office as it was her last day. Alan was speechless, he had been given the dates of her secondment right at the start, but he had forgotten all about it. A taxi had been ordered to take her to the station, and that was almost immediately.

'Can I get hold of you in London.'

'That's going to be quite difficult Alan as I will be moving around quite a bit over the next six months; bye, and thank you for all your help.'

She kissed him cheek to cheek and was gone.

Alan sat back in his chair and stared at the window and then took in the others in the room. None of them were happy, none of them really wanted to be stuck here. He wanted to shout at them and tell them to run away and do something more meaningful before it was too late. But he didn't. He instead remembered that there was a ferry due in and that he was also expecting Detective Inspector Curry from Ashford nick to look at their fingerprints. He had forgotten to tell the staff.

'Can I have your attention please guys,' he said to the room all three of them were in as there were several ferries expected that day. 'Following on from Alison's cocaine find on Tuesday, the Ashford boys need to take our fingerprints to exclude them from their investigations, normal practice. You'll all need to pass your lilywhites through the scanner here. They'll be here soon. OK.'

'Ye-es,' came back a resigned collective groan from the room. While he had their attention, he added, 'George reckoned we had a party in here yesterday, any of you been singing and dancing more than usual? No, fine. Carry on then. If you see a couple of men in white coats walking him off, let me know. I'll send flowers.'

When Detective Inspector Curry and Detective Constable Edwards arrived, Alison showed then into Alan's office and the door was closed. The two other men, Gary and Geoffrey were out on the dock as a ferry from Calais had come in.

Chapter 9

Julie walked from the hotel down to the bakery in the centre of Querchamps-les-Ardres, bought her lunch, and sat on one of the benches just across the road from the shop alongside the ubiquitous boules parc. She was pretty sure that she had seen the right man in the café that morning and again sure that the farm she had sat outside was where the brothers lived. But she couldn't just sit outside their house hoping they would turn up without any good reason to be there, let alone find a reason to talk to them and miraculously get them to incriminate themselves enough to get Graham off the hook. On the other hand, she had come this far and had achieved what the French police probably wouldn't have done – identify the culprits. She still hadn't a shred of evidence to link these guys to the events on the lay-by apart from her slightly dodgy memory. She decided to have one more drive up to the farm house, if there was no one there she would go home and somehow feed the information she had into the police system.

A plan at last, she finished the pastry, dumped the wrapper in a bin and set off back to Le Haut.

Once again she parked in the lane just up the road from the

house, where she could see most of the building but they couldn't really see her. A dirty white van was parked in front. She took out her mobile and snapped a couple of pictures, without any real purpose. Suddenly a figure loomed at her side and banged on the window. She jumped and her heart pounded in her head. A man was standing right next to the car peering in. She smiled at him even though still shaking, and wound the window down half way.

'*Bonjour*,' she said brightly.

The man was fierce looking, wearing shabby clothes and definitely unpleasant. He was the second man from the lay-by the one who had stood back and by his looks Julie suspected he was Louis's brother.

For some peculiar reason she dropped her perfect French with its passable accent and adopted very poor French with an American accent.

'The house, is it you,' as she pointed at the farm house. He said nothing but just looked even fiercer.

'What?' he grunted.

'Your house is it, yes?'

'Why do you want to know?' he said without really opening his mouth.

She decided to get out of the car and be more forward – like an American. He stepped back and watched her slide out, and didn't avert his eyes when her skirt rode up her thighs. But he still managed to hold on to his grim face.

Her mind was working overtime and making up a story just a fraction before the words came out of her mouth. She pulled down her skirt a little and held out her hand to shake his. He was a little taken aback by this and carefully and lightly shook her hand.

'The name is Megan Pullman, and I am worked for a company of films.' He looked puzzled.

'I search for houses for the film, to make a film with and the house here is good for a film.'

'What?' he said again.

Julie's bad French was confusing him so she changed tack a little and started speaking in better French but still with a strong and slightly ridiculous American accent.

'I work for an American film company and we plan to make a film in this part of France and I am looking for suitable locations for some of the scenes. Right now I am searching for an old farm house, just like yours. We would pay you well for the use of your house – for just a few hours.'

'I am not sure about that.' The mention of money had changed his facial expression a bit; he looked over at the house to see his brother walking towards the car.

'*Bonjour Mademoiselle,*' said the younger brother with a certain amount of charm in his voice while at the same time unashamedly sweeping his eyes over her whole body.

'How can I help you?'

Julie felt a shiver run through her as she had the distinct feeling that part of him expected her to say 'Well yes, you could help me, I'd very much like to be dragged into your house and rogered senseless for a couple of hours.' Instead she just repeated what she had said to the other brother.

He turned to look at the house and said 'Yes, it is beautiful isn't it, it needs a little tidying up here and there but I am sure we can sort that. What kind of payment do you think we would get?'

'Well,' said Julie with a smile, desperately trying to think of a number that would be tempting and not silly.

'It's not my call of course, it would depend on how many hours, or days the film crew would work here. But the normal rate for this kind of work is around 1000 euros a day.'

The brothers said nothing but they all carried on looking at the wreck of a house.

She carried on. 'It would be more, of course, if the director decided to use the inside for scenes as well.'

The younger man raised his eyebrows and held out his hand again and said 'My name is Louis and this is my brother Victor. Let's go inside.'

'Why thank you Louis, lead the way.'

Louis walked in front. Victor watched her arse.

Inside the farm house, Julie cast her 'professional' location eye over the tip that confronted her and tried not to gag over the smell.

'Mmm,' she said 'very interesting.'

They all stood around again nodding at the obvious charms of the hovel.

'This is exactly the sort of house that I am looking for – perfect.'

Julie wandered through the mess that was La Ferme de Bray. It smelt of cabbage, dogs, sewer and unwashed men. Louis was getting excited talking to Julie – a woman – which was not something he did a lot of, being uncouth, without any redeeming features and yes, smelly too. Victor was similar although taller and quieter; he had some of the same unpleasant characteristics as Louis but was a lot grumpier. Louis's excitement stemmed from the fact that in his mind he was getting somewhere – scoring – because she seemingly was taking an interest in him. This was only because it was relative to the total lack of success he had ever had with women. Both of the boys had been dominated by their mother even when she was invalided. They just did as they were told and it had only been since she had died that they had to make any decisions on their own. They were incompetent and they argued about everything. They had drifted into petty crime, stealing a few things when the opportunity arose, buying things that fell off lorries, selling it on making a few euros from their market stall. They did odd jobs around the town; they were mostly harmless, but pretty stupid.

They had been particularly stupid getting involved with the drugs racket. They didn't really know what they were doing. They knew the gig out on the main road was illegal, that the box they passed to the English guy had something in it, like drugs. Jean-Paul had paid them well and used them because they were stupid, but he also knew that they wouldn't talk if they got caught. Jean-Paul was a family friend who had helped them out when they fell on hard times, so they owed him big time. The family had owned the warehouse in the centre of town that now was his wine store and shop front. He had bought it from them at a much inflated price – to help them out and so they had remained in his debt.

Jean-Paul had actually paid a bit less than a fair and reasonable price for the building – and would have paid significantly more. His very good friend the estate agent had vastly undervalued the property and it only seemed like he overpaid. They didn't ever understand the true value of the property and to this day saw him as a benefactor. No, they would never grass on Jean-Paul.

Louis and Victor were out of their depth, they had this attractive and confident American woman with the significant '*balcon*' and short skirt, talking about using their house on a film set and they hadn't the skills to negotiate. They hadn't even got the skills to stop looking at her legs. Along with Julie, they didn't know whether €1000 a day was a good or bad price.

'Please, *Mademoiselle*, have a seat.' indicating a dark red thing which she presumed had once been a sofa. It was worn out, low, and without sound stuffing. Julie sat and sank deeply into it and her legs went up in the air. The boys had an unrestricted view of her slightly insubstantial knickers. They stood wonder-struck, mouths ajar and close to dribble. Julie composed herself quickly yanked at her skirt, cursed her sister's fashion and smiled sweetly at the sweating pair. They both sat down opposite her on kitchen chairs, alert.

Louis smiled back and said to Victor at machine gun speed – so Megan wouldn't follow with her poor French comprehension –

'What the fuck do we do now, do we do this – is this a good price?'

'We shouldn't do it,' was the retort.

143

'Why the fuck not – this is easy money – you moron.'

'Don't call me that you fuckwit.'

They were both aware that Megan was looking at them and smiling in an American way.

'Would you like a drink?' said Louis.

'Oh please sir, thank you,' said the American.

Louis jumped up and crossed over to the table, poured out two glasses of red wine from a bottle that was already open and brought them back. Victor glared – he wasn't part of the party. He got up with a huff and poured himself a glass from the same bottle.

'What is the name of the film company?' he said from the table, still holding the bottle. Julie turned to him to answer and caught her breath. He was holding a bottle of red wine which was almost black in colour with a faded-looking label. It was the same bottle and the same label as the drug-filled bottles that had dramatically changed her life just two days before.

'Oh gee, you won't have heard of it – it's only a small affair.' She stalled for a chance to think of a name – any name.

'Uh-uh,' said the bottle holder.

'Kremlin Films,' she said – where the hell did that come from? Kremlin, was that really the only name you could think of… she said to herself.

'Never heard of it,' said Louis.

'Me neither,' said Victor

'As I said, it's very small, we are based in California.'

'What's the film about?'

'Well – (oh shit) – it's all about a London- based financier who inherits a vineyard from his eccentric uncle and as he has no particular interest in wine, he tries to sell it, and then he goes there, meets a girl and falls in love and ends up staying.'

Julie bit her lip because a) she had used some fairly sophisticated French and b) she had just described the plot of a film called 'A Good Year' starring Russell Crowe. Maybe they hadn't had it in France, maybe they hadn't seen it… .

Victor gave his version of a Gallic shrug. Louis pulled a face which was fairly non-committal. There was a silence. She had seemingly got away with it; they didn't recognise the film and certainly hadn't noticed her perfect French leaking out.

'Great wine guys, is this local?' Victor pulled another fierce face. 'This is not a wine region miss.'

'Oh right, still, great wine, can I get buy some around here? This is a 25 buck bottle of wine where I come from.' They looked blank. 'About 25 euros,' she translated.

Louis pulled another face this time approving and looked at the glass of wine he was holding. Louis tapped the side of his nose with a grimy finger and gave a kind of wink with a twist of his head which he intended to convey a complex idea, namely – I am a resourceful man with hidden depths and this includes a sure way of securing as much of this elegant and rather expensive wine at a price which will astound you and would surely buy me a place in your bed. What it really said to Julie was – 'I am an especially stupid man.'

However Julie actually said 'Can you possibly get a few cases of this – I would be really grateful and I am happy to pay the 25 euros.'

'We-ll,' said the idiot.

'What are you doing you stupid bastard?' said Victor in staccato French.

'Shut up,' said Louis out of the side of his mouth.

'I will phone a very good contact of mine – he's a local wine dealer, and see if we can find you're a few bottles,' cooed the younger brother.

He swaggered over to the phone, pointed a stubby finger at the hand-written phone list above the phone and dialled.

Jean-Paul picked up.

'Yes.'

'Ah hello, my friend.'

'Who is this?'

'It's Louis.'

'Louis who – is that Louis Montard – I told you never to phone me.'

'Ha ha ha,' said Louis.

Julie tried to keep an expectant look on her face – she had good hearing and could hear pretty much everything the other end was saying.

'I have a beautiful young American girl here who is very keen to buy some of your excellent Château du Pape Village and she… .'

Jean-Paul was not amused and interrupted him with a very curt, 'Not in a million years you stupid bastard,' and slammed the phone down.

Louis was undeterred and continued the conversation to the burring dead phone.

'Oh I see – a limited vintage and we had the last of the batch – oh what a shame – never mind, thanks anyway,' and he gently replaced the receiver.

He gave yet another shrug with arms out.

'I am devastated – there is no more to be had. Jean-Paul is a very good family friend and the best wine dealer in town and if he can't get any more then there is none.'

'Pillock,' said the brother under his breath.

★★★★★★

Jean-Paul was furious. He walked up and down in his office and aimed a string of the worst swear words he knew at the phone. He sat down head in hands and thought about what might happen if those two idiot brothers started talking to God-knows-who. Paris would be unforgiving. The whole operation could be compromised and his own position made untenable. He had to do something, but he didn't know what for the best. With some trepidation he picked up the phone and dialled a Paris number.

★★★★★★★

'Oh what a shame,' said Julie and eased herself out of the sofa with as much dignity as the sofa would allow, and stood. Louis was blocking her exit.

'What about the deal – for the film company?'

Julie was a lot less interested in following that line as she now had another lead – the wine had been supplied by a certain 'Jean-Paul, the best wine dealer in town'. She wanted to get out of this grimy house as quickly as possible. Louis had a more ugly face on him now that the money seemed to be disappearing and she suddenly started to feel uncomfortable or even a little scared.

She recovered.

'Of course, we are still interested in the house, just write down your name and full address and my boss will write to you with the terms and a contract.'

'Yeah but how much will you pay us?' snapped Louis, now closer and even Victor had moved in.

She side stepped over to the table where the phone was, picked up a scrap piece of paper and wrote 'Kremlin Films Ltd, 4027 Front Street, Santa Barbara, California 23097 Telephone 001 484 2323'.

She had no idea even how many digits the American postcodes had, nor what the international dialling code for the US was, and she guessed and hoped they wouldn't either.

She wanted to write down her made-up name but had completely forgotten what she had said, Megan something. So she just wrote 'Ask for Megan', and then added 'or Roger'. She handed the slip of paper to the nearest brother Victor. Louis snatched it out of his hand and read it slowly. They seemed satisfied. She picked up another piece of paper from the table and gave it to Victor for him to write their address down. He just held it and said nothing.

'Oh no,' she thought, 'He can't read and write'. She turned to make one final sweep of the house in order to break the tension in the air and managed to read the name on the phone list – J-P Capaut.

She turned, took the paper from Victor and said, 'It's OK, I know the address. Well guys, thanks for the drink' and stuck out her hand. Louis took it and held on.

'When will you contact us then?' still holding her hand – a little too tightly.

'I will be back in the States in two days so I will contact you then, OK?'

She pulled her hand away and half pushed him aside and made it to the door. They were both right behind her. She opened the door and walked out trying very hard not to run but just strode purposefully across the yard and out to her car.

The two men stood in the doorway and watched her arse.

When she got back to her car she was completely out of breath as she had been holding it all the way across the yard. She started to shake and gripped the wheel hard and drove slowly down the track with her teeth clamped together.

By the time she arrived back at the hotel she was calm again and drove around to the rear into the hotel's little car park, which she hadn't seen when she first arrived.

Chapter 10

All modern Customs offices in Great Britain have electronic fingerprint scanners so in fact there was no real need for Curry and Saskia to have made the journey down to Folkestone, but Curry had insisted that they went in person. Saskia had queried Curry on the need to go in person and had been told quite firmly that it was necessary to be there. She was a bit put out and spent much of the journey thinking that it was really about the old-fashioned Curry not being able to keep up with technology. In her mind she prepared a speech about modern police methods, one that would never be voiced.

Curry had not shared his new-found knowledge about the tear in the box which he had gleaned from Brian in SOCO, he wasn't sure why he hadn't told Saskia. Deep down he knew really and was trying very hard not to come to terms with that thought. As he drove he was regretting not telling her and now it would be awkward because it was ridiculous, a man of his experience wanting to show off to a junior officer. He decided to bring it up now and pretend that it was a learning exercise for her.

'Brian showed me that there had been something fixed inside the box – possibly something electronic… .'

'Oh, like a transmitter of some kind, so that they could track the box and somehow get it back.'

'Yes, and more, there was a tear in the cardboard where it was taken out, which had a wine stain across it. It indicated that the tear in the cardboard was made after the wine was spilt. What do you make of that?'

Saskia thought for a moment. 'OK if the transmitter or whatever was taken out after the wine was spilt then either the wine was leaking earlier, not likely but possible, and the transmitter must have been in the box at Calais. That means that it must have been ripped out after Spelling was taken into custody. That means that someone in Customs has had a go at it. Oh, shit, that's not good. Right, that's why we are driving down there. The fingerprints are probably from one of them. Smart thinking boss.'

'Not really, or rather, you are just as smart. What puzzles me still is that someone along the line has been careless or stupid enough not to put gloves on. Or were they being set up?'

'You're right, that doesn't really fit. The indications are that these guys know what they are doing, in that the inner bottles are almost undetectable and they've cleaned the bottles properly but then they've screwed up right at the end. I suppose it is possible that the French guys at the roadside may have opened up the box. Do we know if the box was still sealed when the Custom's girl opened it on the dock?'

'She said it was sealed, Alison, the Custom's girl that found it.' Curry replied. He was still thinking through the other options. He was again slightly taken aback because he hadn't thought that the roadside men might have handled them. Curry picked up the threads again. 'We can only assume that this person is part of the gang and decided or was instructed to remove the transmitter. But why risk it, the chances are that after a few hours Spelling would be found to be innocent and we would presume that the drugs were planted on him as he claimed. What's more, if there was a good reason to take the transmitter out, why didn't they remove it from underneath instead of taking all the bottles out, one by one and yanking the transmitter out from inside?'

'Maybe the inside man didn't know where to find the transmitter. He was told to remove it and thought it must be inside the box and so he took all the bottles out unnecessarily.'

'Umm,' said Curry, 'Brian also said something about the patterns of prints on the bottles. He thought that they had been picked up from the laid-down position.'

'I don't understand.'

'Well, what he was saying was that if you imagine taking a bottle out of the box, you would grab hold of the neck of the bottle, stand it aside and then again grab the neck of the bottle to replace it. You would leave in fact two sets of prints on the neck, he reckons that there are two on the neck bit but others on the sides of the bottles. This could mean that the person was picking up the bottles from a laid down position and then holding the neck to put it into the box.'

'So that seems to be saying that he or she took the bottles out of the box, to get at the transmitter, and laid them down rather than stood them up. That all sounds a bit far-fetched doesn't it? Surely people would pick up and hold bottles in lots of different ways when taking them in and out of a wine box?'

'Yes, you're right, but Brian doesn't get many of these kinds of things wrong, and for the life of me I can't get my head around the fingerprint patterns.'

'So sir, what do you expect to find this morning?'

'I expect to find the person with a set of fingerprints that match those found on the bottles.'

They had arrived at the Customs building in Folkestone, they got out and walked to the security gate and showed their badges to George, who phoned up to the office. Alison came straight out and took them through.

'Hello Andy,' said Alan shaking his hand, 'and hello again, Detective Constable Edwards isn't it?'

'Yes, hello Mr Protheroe.'

'Come into my office.'

Alan had taken scans of each of his staff as well as his own. The scans were on a disc, which he gave to Curry.

'I could have just whizzed them down to you Andy, saved you the bother of driving down.'

'It's no problem. Good to get out of the office sometimes. Is it OK if I talk to your staff about this again? There are one or two odd little things that I just need to check on.'

'Of course, use this office; I need to go over to the P&O office for a while anyway. The lads will be back in a couple of minutes.'

When he had gone Saskia put the disc into the computer by Protheroe's desk and called up the scans. Curry had a hard copy of the prints in his pocket. They didn't need to spend long checking – the prints made clear, they had their man.

A few minutes later the two Customs men returned and Gary was asked to step into the office. By the time he sat down he was sweating.

'Gary, we need to clear up an anomaly that we've uncovered. It's why we asked for all of your fingerprints to be taken.'

'I know what you are going to ask me and yes I did touch the bottles. I don't really know why. It was stupid of me and I know that this is going to get me into trouble, I'm very sorry.'

Curry continued in a slow but deliberate voice. 'Can you tell us what happened then? Alan didn't think that anyone had touched them once they had got up here into the office.'

'Well, it was all a bit confusing, people rushing about and the two people in the car being taken into the cells and all. I was left alone for a few minutes and curiosity got the better of me, I just wanted to look I suppose. Look at the bottles in the box, sort of check them out. No one saw me.'

'Could you just show us exactly what you did? On the book shelf there was a box of permanent markers in a small box, the top corner had been torn off in order to get pens out. Most were still in there standing upright. We can use this as a sort of dummy wine box.' He gave the box to Gary. 'Show us how you took them out.'

Gary hesitated, he hadn't a clue what they were thinking but he had to go along with it. He picked out one of the pens with his thumb and forefinger and put it down on the desk. 'I just took it out like that and then put it back, Curry stopped him.

'Did you stand the bottle up or lay it down?'

Gary frowned as he still had no idea what was going on. 'I stood it up of course.'

'Show me,' said Curry.

Once again Gary carefully picked the pen out of the box and stood it upright on the desk. Curry nodded at him and Gary picked it up with his thumb and forefinger and put it back in the box.

'And did you take them all out of the box and have all five bottles standing on the desk and then put them all back or did you take them out and put them back one at a time?'

Gary was sweating more now for he had the distinct feeling that he was missing something; this charade with the pen box was very significant and he was losing and he still didn't understand why. He just answered, 'Yes'.

'OK, was there anything else in the box that you took out?'

Gary pulled a face and gave a huff and said, 'No, just wine,' and wanted to say 'of course, it's only wine in a wine box you dummy,' but didn't.

'You see Gary, I know that you are telling me lies. I know what you did. I know exactly what you did and I can prove it. So much better if you tell me now. You are already up to your eyes in this and it would be sad if you drowned alone in this shit wouldn't it lad?'

Gary sat still for a moment trying to work out whether this cop really did know everything or was bluffing. Or... he couldn't think anymore. The tears started rolling down his face. He wiped them away with the back of his hand and sniffed.

'Start from the beginning lad.' And he did. He told them

everything. Saskia had clicked on her recorder and Curry told him his rights. It came out in a rush. When Gary got to the bit about switching the bottles Curry just nodded in agreement as though he knew all along about that as well. Then came the revelation about placing the bag of cannabis under the seat. Again Curry and now Saskia, both nodded and gave that 'ah yes' kind of expression which told Gary that there had been no point in keeping anything back as these two police officers knew everything already. He didn't know how they knew but they obviously did. Twenty minutes later the case was pretty much wrapped up on their side of the Channel. They had no information about the perpetrators and would never know from Gary, because he didn't know. They formally arrested him and took him back to Ashford.

★★★★★★★

Gerard had worked for Pierre for five years although they still knew very little about each other. The business was very structured. Gerard looked after the wine warehouse at the Paris site, the packing and the shipments. He was also the muscle. Pierre was the boss, the money man and the salesman. He also sorted the supplies of cocaine – their main money maker. Silvie bought the wine, looked after the paperwork, was the face of the business and stood in for Pierre when he was away on either sales or buying trips, and, shared his bed when he was home. He was due back any day from a trip. Ethan was the young man who worked in the warehouse under Gerard.

The initial operation was simple and successful. They bought fairly decent wines in and decanted it into fake bottles with fake labels from the best vineyards. The labels were distressed and resold as the real article. Wine snobbery was such that few of the bottles ever got drunk, but languished in a cellar for years   partly as an investment and partly as a way of showing off to other moneyed people.

Most of the original bottles for the Châteaux brands were made in small factories around the wine growing regions. To pull off the scam the fake bottles had to be perfect. It transpired that the bottle makers of Poland were the experts so Pierre had tracked down the right factory and paid the right money and he had counterfeit bottles made that were indistinguishable from the originals.

This business went well for Pierre for a few years but limited. There were only so many people prepared to pay ridiculous amounts of money for rare bottles of old wine. However, he realised that the very careful and secure handling of these precious bottles by the security couriers meant that there was no great check on the actual contents at any of the ports. No one actually saw or got close to bottles, no one was ever likely to try to check the contents.

Pierre was a lateral thinker and mostly dishonest, so his thoughts eventually led him into drugs smuggling.

He had the Poles make an insert for the bottles. He found a rare brand of wine that used a very dark green glass and so, with the cocaine inside the inner bottle and any old red wine in the outer skin, to the casual inspection, nothing was amiss.

Further, the care in distribution was strengthened. The

wines were always couriered with maximum security, worthy of a precious cargo, with strict instructions not to shake, disturb or even look hard at the bottles for fear of ruining the contents. This was now taken to extreme with security guards accompanying the cargo as you would works of art. The paperwork was always perfect and so far no one had even hinted at inspecting the boxes.

Pierre and Gerard had run this nice little earner for about a year. Gerard made absolutely sure that the bottles were filled correctly; the outsides were perfectly clean with no hint of even a molecule of powder. No one outside of the Paris warehouse had any idea of the real contents, bar of course the clients who were very carefully selected by Pierre.

His client list for the distressed wine started from the original 'old school' list, mostly made up from daft and very rich people who wanted to show off their wealth. Gradually some of the nouveau riche started to be added to the list, those who were not from the old families but from the new generation of pop stars and media celebs. They were not only filthy rich, but into social drugs, and cocaine was the habit of choice.

A courier arriving with a special consignment of a few very, very, expensive wines was not unusual and it all worked well.

Over the years Gerard had become Pierre's right-hand man. Not only was he in total control of the distribution but he collected insurance policies – people he came across who he could trust, sleepers that might be called upon in an emergency, people that had great allegiance to Gerard because he had something on them, usually this something being drug related. He could ruin their lives with a single phone call and if that was not enough leverage to remain loyal, he could always threaten to kill them.

Gerard was not a criminal who used idle threats to get what he needed; he used serious and very real threats to get what he wanted. His upbringing had slid him into a murky world. When a teenager, his father had died following a knifing in a bar brawl and as he had never seen eye to eye with his mother he had joined the army as soon as he could. Neither wrote and so when, years later, he went back to the family house, it was no surprise that his mother had gone, with no forwarding address. The army became his life where he learnt to look after himself, to fire guns and kill people with his bare hands.

After the army Gerard had picked up a few lucrative security commissions in Africa, mostly supporting the oil and gas exploration companies. During a space between overseas assignments, he was helping a friend out – bouncing outside a club – when he met Pierre. Pierre was there with Silvie who, as usual, was wearing an outrageous costume, exposing many parts of the body that are normally hidden. A drunken reveller tried to make out with her and went over the top. Pierre intervened, and punched the guy, who responded with a broken bottle. Gerard got there first, floored the man without any fuss and without anyone else getting hurt. Pierre was very grateful and offered him a job.

It was Gerard who had set up the logistics for the latest drug smuggling route. Jean-Paul was a man with a past which unfortunately for him, had got to the ears of Gerard. Many years before, Jean-Paul had had a fling with a girl who looked

24 years old but sadly was only fourteen. The girl's family were neighbours of Gerard and he knew them fairly well. They came to him for advice. Essentially the question was whether to go to the police or not. Gerard convinced them that he would sort it out, without them having to go to the police. He told the girl and her parent's to write down everything that had happened, in detail. There was a substantial amount of evidence, certainly enough to send Jean-Paul to jail for a long while. Jean-Paul had been seen plying her with drinks, seen getting into his car with her and again seen coming out of his house with her in the morning. A month or so later she also found that she was pregnant. Gerard had the full set of signed statements from the family plus a number of independent witnesses – the evidence against Jean-Paul was just as thorough and complete as the police might have collected. Then, armed with the facts, he confronted Jean-Paul, and Gerard made him pay – handsomely. The girl's pregnancy was terminated, the girl and her mother were paid off and Gerard took his commission. He also kept all of the documentation.

Now, years later, Jean-Paul was obliged to work for Gerard to sort his part of the distribution chain. To refuse could mean a lengthy stretch at the Republic's pleasure.

Jean-Paul had no choice but tried to distance himself as much as possible from the actual act, hoping that if caught, the finger would be pointing at Louis and Victor– who were loyal – and at not at him, the respectable wine merchant.

Things were now turning bad because Jean-Paul had underestimated the stupidity of his hired hands. Not only had they seemingly stolen a case of his wine but they had now linked him in directly with the very special wine consignment in front of some passing American woman.

He had paced up and down working out whether better to ignore it and hope it goes away, or to tell Gerard about it and hope he somehow made it go away. If Gerard found out that there was even the faintest chance of a leak in the system he would go mad and who knows what might happen. Perhaps then it was better to pass the problem up the management chain for someone else to sort it out. He had made the call.

Gerard was calm on the phone – he asked several questions of Jean-Paul, thanked him for his candour and told him to sit tight.

Three hours later Gerard stood outside the farm house of the Montard brothers. He watched the house, the road, the doors, the windows and the back fencing until he was satisfied.

He walked to front door and knocked.

Chapter 11

When Julie got back to the hotel it was very quiet, there didn't seem to any other guests and even the proprietor and the receptionist seemed to be absent. Perhaps they were 'at it' again. In her room she felt confident once more and was now 'certain' that the brothers were the two in the lay-by and the fact that the wine she drank at the farm was from an identical bottle to the ones Graham had bought made her sure that it had been supplied by this Jean-Paul. It now seemed likely that he was in fact the drug dealer behind her and Graham's demise. Next then, she had to get to speak to the wine dealer, but how, and under what pretext? The idea of reprising the American film location person seemed a bit weak and she didn't think it a good idea to link the 'chance meeting' at the farm with another 'chance meeting' with Jean-Paul.

He was however a wine dealer and she reasoned that he would be interested in selling wine; although not perhaps the 'special' wine that she had seen and tasted at the farm.

It was 'goutez' time, a bit like the old English 'tea time', in the mid afternoon when most French people sit down with tea or coffee and eat fabulous cakes and pastries   the fashion that keeps the huge number of patisseries profitable right across

France – and so Julie went back downstairs with the thought of walking into the town centre for food. As she reached the ground floor she saw that the proprietor was perched at the bar drinking a late lunchtime beer. He looked up as she approached

'Please,' he said, indicating the bar stool beside him, 'let me buy you a drink.' Before she could answer he held out his hand and said, 'Henri,' she took it and said 'Julie,' and she sat down where he had suggested.

'We don't get many customers and so it is a pleasure to welcome you at least I can eat this week, what can I get you to drink?'

'Well, that's kind; I'll join you in a beer.' She had been looking forward to a coffee and a cake but the opportunity to get information about the town's wine merchant was presenting itself and so she took it.

He nodded his approval, walked around the end of the bar and poured her a pression beer from the tap, and rejoined her on the customer side.

'So, Julie, what brings you to our wonderful little town?' He looked her straight in the eye, with a pleasant smile, but somehow his directness was not intimidating, in fact she found his approach rather welcome. Julie had of course just been thinking upstairs about what she might say to Jean-Paul if she were to knock on his door, and so now she had the opportunity to practise – to make up some plausible story for this guy Henri.

'I work for Sainsburys… .'

'Oh, yes, the big supermarket chain, doing what?'

'I have a very nice job; I drive around Europe, mostly France, looking for new products and lines that might work for us.' She looked him straight back into his eyes, and he didn't look away but continued to ask questions.

'And what is it that you would like to buy from us here in Querchamps?'

'Oh, nothing specifically, I am really just stopping off on my way back home.'

'What is it that you have looked at in the last few days then that inspires you?'

Julie wasn't quite ready for that question and so she had to stall.

'I really can't divulge my interests, who knows you could be working for Waitrose.'

'In other words, Henri, mind your own business,' and he laughed. Julie just smiled.

He changed the subject and they chatted for a few minutes about the weather and French politics. He was easy to talk to and she felt safe and so she pushed ahead with her own agenda.

'It's not my field, but I know that one of the other departments in Sainsbury is looking to introduce new wines into our range, but exclusive. Our research shows us that because there are so many different and confusingly labelled wines for sale, no one can really keep track of what they buy. So, we thought a Sainsbury's own brand might work well. What do you think?'

Henri gave her a '*boff*,' and a shrug, 'I know that the British drink a lot of poor wine, they buy on price don't they, and I also know that sales of French wine into UK have fallen dramatically as other regions have come on line, America, Australia even the Eastern block countries now produce OK wine, none as good as the French, of course… ,' and he creased his eyes at her.

'*Mais, bien sur,*' she replied, 'are there any people in town who know their wines that I can talk too, there's a dealer called Jean-Paul something, do you know him?'

'Of course, I know everyone in town, yes, Jean-Paul Chaput seems to know his stuff, and he always has plenty of money so I guess he is doing something right.'

'Do you think he would see me if I contact him?'

'Well yes. I'm sure you realise that this is not a wine producing region but no doubt he would be happy to talk to you if you tell him you are looking to buy for Sainsbury's, I'll phone him if you like.'

'That would be great, thank you.'

★★★★★★★

Two hours after Gerard had been to Ferme de Bray, a local debt-collector called to try to get the Montard boys to pay their long-overdue bills from the hardware store, only to find the door open and much of the downstairs furniture turned over during what had obviously been a terrible brawl. The two brothers who had repeatedly fought each other in public had now managed to kill each other. Victor had a kitchen knife up to the handle in his chest but had had enough time to shoot Louis at close range with an old service revolver, which was still in his hand. They lay locked together in a great pool of blood.

★★★★★★★

Half an hour after her chat with Henri, Julie was walking down the road to the wine warehouse. She had changed into her 'best' outfit, which was one of her sister's suits, a dark blue jacket with a white shirt, a pencil skirt and highish heals. It wasn't really her style but she did look quite professional in it.

She had her small shoulder bag, which didn't quite match but hey ho. She walked slowly and felt very, very nervous – very much like she was walking into the lion's den.

She stopped directly opposite the warehouse. It was an elegant building considering it was large and industrial. The front was dominated by two large wooden doors, large enough to drive a truck through, painted green and slightly flaking – but elegantly so. Julie was reminded of journeys through northern France as a child with her parents who constantly oohed and aahed at the peeling paintwork on the doors and windows of seemingly all the houses they passed. As a girl she had often wondered way the French didn't ever seem to paint their houses and second, why her parents thought that peeling paintwork was so wonderful. Their own house was always perfectly painted. Julie now stood thinking that the peeling paintwork was rather attractive. How did that happen? She brought herself back to the present and the task ahead of her. She bit a lip and reminded herself of the fact that Graham was still holed up in a cell and could be there for a very long time. Once again she wondered what the hell she was doing and was she being plain bloody stupid. It was overcast and thinking about it getting dark, she took a breath and crossed the empty street.

She pressed the bell beside a small green door, with peeling paint, which had a very shiny brass plate announcing 'Le Societé du Vin – Pas de Calais' and in smaller letters Jean-Paul Chaput. She heard a distant ring.

She stood waiting, nervous and trying very hard not to look over her shoulder at the thousands of people watching her, and wondering why this smart-looking woman was ringing the doorbell of M. Chaput. The door opened with a squeak and a slight but dapper man in his early fifties stood there. He gave a quick but not very subtle up and down assessment of Julie and then gave her a plastic, but somewhat charming smile.

'*Bonjour Mademoiselle?*' he said raising an eyebrow and putting a very large question mark into his voice.

'*Bonjour, Monsieur Chapu*t,' she replied with an equal smile. 'Julie Kranmer.' She had decided on the walk down to use a different name, for fear of something… she didn't really know what. Ruth Kranmer was the name of the head teacher at the school where she worked and when Henri had phoned to make the appointment he had just said 'friend' and not used her name.

'Please come in, any friend of Henri's… .' he said immediately in English keen to show off his command. Julie followed Jean-Paul through a small-shop front area then through another door which opened out immediately into the warehouse. It was decked out with shelving and was about half full with cardboard wine boxes. She was slightly surprised – expecting racks with dusty wine bottles lying on their sides 'to keep the corks damp'. He turned to the left and up a steel stairway to a wooden framed office on a mezzanine. The front part was a comfortable office with an antique pedestal desk, some filing cabinets and a couple of chairs. Jean-Paul led through another door into a small sitting room with a two-seater settee, an armchair and several small tables.

'Please,' he said indicating the armchair.

There was a Carrefour supermarket plastic bag on the table next to the chair, which he quickly swept up and Julie just caught his eye which had dropped its smile and replaced by a touch of something else. Whatever was in the bag he wanted it out of sight and she didn't think it was embarrassment over having gone to a down-market supermarchée.

'May I give you a glass of a splendid wine?' and before she had answered he had produced an open bottle and poured her a glass of the light red wine.

He turned back to her and added 'I am pleased to hear that Sainsbury's are thinking about increasing their wine sales, but I have no idea how I could help. Please enjoy this wine here and excuse me for one moment,' and held the plastic bag behind his back and went down the stairs into the warehouse. Julie jumped up, looked out through the glass windows overlooking the shelving and just caught him going through a door at the back. She thought for a moment that he was leaving, doing a runner, but he just partly closed the door and seemed to get down on the floor.

He was definitely behaving a bit oddly, but she now had a few moments alone to look for… she didn't know. Any clues would more likely be back in the office area, but she didn't have the nerve to go back there and risk being caught – with no reason to be there. He, in fact, returned very quickly to find her sitting in a suitably relaxed pose sipping the wine. It was not the same wine as she had sampled at the farm house but equally as good.

He had a bunch of keys in his hand which he dropped onto the side table and sat opposite without a drink.

'Now,' he said, 'What do you think of this wine, it's from a small vineyard near Beaune and very good.'

'I like it' she nodded 'it's light and I think would go down well in the UK.' Julie had formed a bit more of the 'plausible story'.

'*Monsieur Chaput*, we are considering looking seriously at own-branding a range of French wines – sold in our stores as 'Sainsbury's' rather than the vineyard name, and I am heading up a small team to look into this. As a start I would like find several local experts whom we could use as consultants who… .'

The front doorbell rang and Julie stopped talking.

'Forgive me, I will get rid of whoever it is and return – my apologies… .'

He looked towards the front door as people always seem to do as if they could see through it.

'*Excuse moi encore,*' and went out through the office leaving both doors open and clanked quickly down the metal stair.

Again, Julie jumped up to watch but this time she had his keys. He disappeared through the first door into the shop area and she heard the front door open to the visitor while she studied the bunch of keys. She shook her head – to herself – at the plain ridiculousness of the situation. She was behaving like James Bond, pretending, believing, that she could solve the crime in some way by, what, breaking into his desk drawers and finding incriminating evidence to help Graham? 'Get real Julie,' she said to herself.

She broke out of her reverie suddenly by a raised voice in the room downstairs and then heard a shout '*Non*'. There was a 'spit', not a sound she recognised, and then Jean-Paul came backwards out of the doorway and fell heavily. Julie stood in horror, shock, her mouth open. A second later the visitor stepped through the doorway, in his hand was a gun with a very long barrel.

Instinctively, Julie dropped down out of sight and crawled across the floor to the back of the sitting room. There was another door. She just wanted to get away from the scene below. Still on the floor, she reached up and pulled the handle, pushed open the door and scampered through. She pushed the door closed behind her hoping there had been no noise. It was a small bedroom dominated by a double bed, with just a small wardrobe and a bedside table below a Velux window in the roof.

She could feel her heart pounding and felt ready to throw up. She dropped down on the far side of the bed and pushed herself under it. It was only just high enough but she squeezed in and tried to pull the bedspread neatly down and then lay there holding her breath.

There was noise below – which sounded like a sack being pulled along the floor, then after a couple of minutes she heard the clank of feet on the metal stair. The gunman was coming up. Julie had held her breath so long that she was near fainting but she turned her head to look out under the bed to see a pair of legs in the sitting room. The man was looking around – he picked up her glass and put it down again. He walked into the bedroom, had a cursory look around and left.

Julie stayed where she was for several more minutes to make sure he had gone then rolled out from under the bed, and froze again as she heard noises downstairs. She strained to hear, ready to roll back under the bed if he came back up. She lay on her back looking up at the Velux above and once again thought about her adventure which had now brought her face-to-face with death, for she was sure that Jean-Paul was lying dead downstairs.

She lay there trying to make sense of what had just happened. Someone, a professional hit man, God, a professional hit man, had just knocked on the door and shot this man without a word being said. He had come to the door with the definite intension of killing this man. This was not some kind of accident as part of a robbery, it was an execution. The man, the executioner, had obviously thought he was alone, otherwise he would have checked properly. He looked at the glass – a single glass. Jean-Paul's glass he must have thought.

But now what? Was the man now going to search for something, some evidence, some hidden documents that he needed. If so, he would return to the bedroom and find her. Could she get out of the Velux window without being seen? Could she even reach it? If the man was standing below he might spot her when she stood on the bed. Oh God, she was starting to panic and hyperventilate, She felt sick again. How stupid, how stupid, how stupid.

She kept low behind the bed but still watched out underneath it and through the open door into the sitting room. She strained to listen for the sound of the man's footsteps up the metal stairway. She could hear other noises below and her heart bumping, but no footsteps. Did she dare to get up and peep of out the window? No, not yet.

Julie lay there for maybe five minutes before she heard a different sound, an odd crackling from below, and then suddenly there was a massive blast – blistering heat and noise and light and flame and thousands of bits of glass. The windows that overlooked the warehouse had all exploded in across the sitting room and then blown in and through the bedroom door showering the bed and Julie. In an instant the room was full of choking acrid smoke. Burning pieces of something had landed on the bed starting little black-flamed fires and there was a great overpowering choking stench.

Julie leapt up from her hiding place, forgetting about being seen from below, she was now focused totally on staying alive and getting out. There was no way back down even across the sitting room as it was thick with black smoke and through the smoke she could see flames streaking up fifteen feet into the air from the main warehouse floor. The Velux window was high on the roof and the glass still intact. Julie picked up the bedside table, throwing off the phone and a glass of water, and stood it on the smouldering bed. She started to cough from deep in her lungs, painful, searing retch-like coughs. Her feet were burning and being cut by the glass shards but she jumped up onto the wobbling bedside table and was able to reach the roof window which she yanked open. It pivoted about its centre point and she managed to pull herself up through the narrow lower side of the window kicking her legs out into the air to help propel her through. She got her top half through, her legs were hot below and smoke was swirling around her making her eyes smart and run. At last she wriggled out onto the roof and slid face down on the tiles to the gutter. The tiles were green and slimy, her clothes were being torn to shreds but she was out of the building.

The roar from the fire was steadily increasing and smoke and sparks were pouring out of the Velux window even as she went through and smoke was now starting to leak out through other parts of the roof. It was getting dark but she was able to see enough to realise it was a long drop to the ground and she couldn't wait for rescue. She swung herself around and slid along the roof with one hand and one foot in the gutter and painfully reached the end of the roof where it joined a lower one. She swung down with a small drop on to that roof and got to the ground via a lean-to shed. She was now at the far end of the building in a narrow lane. She could hear shouts from the other side of the building, from the main road, but she hobbled away shoeless from the building out into a dark lane that turned back in the direction of the hotel.

★★★★★★★

A stocky man stood beside his Mercedes about 300 metres from the wine warehouse and watched the flames roar up and engulf the building. Confident that the building was well alight, he looked around to check if anyone had been watching him, got into this car and drove back to Paris.

Chapter 12

About 200 metres from the warehouse, Julie sat down. She looked back at the burning building which was now silhouetted by the flames from the front of the building. Great clouds of smoke were billowing from the roof, squeezing out of every tile. She heard the distant strain of a fire engine's siren. The sky above was a black cloud being dragged along by the wind, turning the twilight into a storm. In the centre of the building a column of flame was roaring up in the heat dragging the air in and pulling the flames up. She could see roof tiles falling in and the rafters burning. More sirens could be heard and as she watched a rather puny spray of water arched across the flames to no avail. The building was not going to be saved. Julie was in shock; she drew her knees up and hugged herself, feeling pain for the first time from several places around her body.

Surprisingly, she thought of all the wine being ruined, and then stopped herself with a shudder as she remembered that Jean-Paul Chaput was burning up on the floor of the building, and she burst into great shuddering sobs.

After a while she calmed and limped on barefoot further down the dark back lane. Her feet hurt from the burns and scrapes, the lane was rough and she stopped every few metres to pull stones off her feet.

There were several openings along the lane leading out to the main road; she needed to get back to her hotel room without being seen. The first two turns she tried were not far enough but the third came out just beyond the hotel. She took it and peeked out. There was a group of men standing in the road from out of the bar in the hotel – Henri and Lola were with them. They were all watching the fire and none were looking back as Julie crept across the road behind them.

Just as she went through the door Henri turned and saw her but said nothing. He watched the fire for a while longer putting a few things together in his mind; he turned and went back inside.

Henri listened outside her door for a while and heard little. Julie was sitting on the bed hugging herself again. He thought about knocking but decided against it, whatever had happened out there was almost certainly connected to the fire. Was she an arsonist? Unlikely. She was very dirty and her clothes were torn. What the hell is this all about? He needed to know.

His next move was automatic. At some point she would need to clean up, probably sooner rather than later. He opened the door to the linen cupboard and locked it behind him. He slid open the back wall of the cupboard and eased himself into the tiny room.

Julie felt better and safe in the bedroom but she was hurting just about everywhere and need to look at the damage. She inspected her face carefully in the large wall mirror in the bathroom. She was quite shocked at her appearance, any make up was gone, there were black marks all over her face where she had put her hands and her hair had collected debris and twigs and grass from somewhere. She carefully washed her hands and then gently dabbed the dirt from her face. As the dirt came away several red marks appeared, but the skin was not broken and they would soon disappear. She turned away from the mirror and stared to run water into the strange bath.

She sat on the chair beside the bath and slowly and painfully took off the tailored jacket. It was filthy, all the buttons and one pocket had ripped off as she squeezed through the Velux and at some point one sleeve had ripped around the seam such that the shoulder pad was poking out. She dropped it on the floor.

Her white blouse had caught on something and was ripped open around the button holes. It was black and green from the dirt and moss on the roof. Julie again very slowly slipped out of it and dropped in down. Her bra was white, low cut and had a pretty lacey edge. She stood up again in front of the mirror and examined the red welt on her arm that was starting to bleed at the top end at the shoulder. She sponged the blood away and winced at the sting. Henri, no more than three feet away, winced as well.

Her arm was stiffening up and so she was a bit awkward unclasping the bra, but it gave way and her breasts came free. There was another red welt around one of the bra straps which again she sponged with cold water.

She then started to take off her skirt. The top hook had ripped out and the zip was partly down, wrenched and jammed. She wrestled around trying to get the zipper fob down further. The zip wasn't going to move. She bent over and pulled the skirt down tight over her hips and wriggled around so that gradually the material slipped down. She flung the ruined skirt down and stood back again in front of the mirror to see her damaged tights. They were in complete shreds. They came off quickly and she now put her left leg up onto the basin edge and sponged down the black from her knee to reveal an ugly graze still with dirt mingling with blood. There was another long scratch from around the knee up the inside of her leg, which was sore and angry. She inspected it pulling back the edge of her knickers to check the extent. She then took off her knickers and again inspected the inside of her thigh. She bathed the whole length of her leg in cold water, dipping the sponge into the water in the basin.

She now turned around and, looking over her shoulder, tried to check out her back and bottom. There were several marks and scratches and a large red mark on one cheek. She bent half over and backed into the basin and once again bathed the red mark with cold water, resting her bottom on the edge of the china.

The temperature in the tiny cupboard room had risen significantly in the last ten minutes.

Once in the bath Julie slowly cleaned and scrubbed at the black marks and let the warm water soothe the sore bits. She lay there eyes closed and wept quietly.

Henri had been totally transfixed. Never before had he witnessed such an erotic and beautiful vision. He had seen a few others disrobe from behind his double mirror, but he couldn't take his eyes off this woman, so fragile and needy, so sexy without even trying. He wanted to run in and hold her kiss all of the places that hurt and pledge his undying love for her – not necessarily a good plan at this precise moment.

Henri was holding his very large erection still in one hand and he suddenly felt guilty and ashamed. He took a deep breath and his erection faded. He continued to watch Julie for a few more moments and then very quietly left her alone and went downstairs to the bar.

★★★★★★★

Text received in Paris:

All weak links cleared out, no problems, back in three hours

★★★★★★★

Henri sat in the bar. The fire had died down quickly and was under control, there was still quite a large crowd outside but many had now resumed their drinking in the bar. Lola was serving. Everyone was talking about Jean-Paul and whether he was in the building, several were discussing the possibility of an insurance scam. Henri listened to the babble but was consumed by his thoughts. Had Julie started the fire? It was obvious that she had something to do with it. How had she got injured? She was very upset. He couldn't work it out but it felt right helping her, after all he was a policeman, well an ex-policeman. OK a discredited ex-policeman. He still knew what was going on in his town; he still knew the entire police force well, apart from that arsehole inspector that had taken over from him, jumped-up little shit that he was. He would find out what Julie's involvement was in all this, policeman or no.

He was also smitten. He had heard the water running out down the waste pipe sometime before so he reasoned that Julie was now out of the bath and possibly ready to receive visitors. He found a bottle of cognac and two glasses and slipped unnoticed up the stairs to her room. He listened at the door and heard nothing. He hesitated at the thought that she might have gone to bed, but it was still quite early and she probably hadn't eaten. He put the drink and glasses on a table in the hall and went back down to the kitchen and prepared two sandwiches stuffed with every delicious filling he could find. He arranged them with other titbits and took them back up.

He knocked gently on Julie's door and there was no answer. He knocked again a little harder.

Julie was dressed and just lying on her bed trying to work out what had happened and whether she was somehow involved. Seeing someone shot dead was a new experience and she was struggling to allow her mind to remember it. There was a shutter that came down and somehow prevented her from carrying the thought through.

The knock on the door surprised and then frightened her. Was it someone coming to get her? Had the killer followed her? She was relieved to hear the newly familiar voice of the hotel proprietor.

'*Mademoiselle* Webb,' he said, in what he hoped was the right tone, 'I saw that you had come back in and thought you might like something to eat? I have had a sandwich made for you.'

Julie hesitated for a moment as she was still feeling very distraught, but her good 'British' manners made her ease herself off the bed, check her dress was decent and hobble to the door. She did consider saying 'Leave it outside the door' but that was really very rude and so she opened the door to Henri, and saw a comforting face with a large plate of delicious-looking food – and yes, she was hungry.

'May I come in?' he said and walked past her to lay the tray with the food and the drinks on the small desk. Julie stood at the door not really quite sure of the etiquette.

'Now young lady I think you had better sit down and tell me what's going on – don't you agree?' and he poured her a large cognac without her asking and gestured for her to sit on the bed. And she did. He handed her the glass, put one of the sandwiches next to her, sat down on the desk chair opposite her and said, 'From the beginning.'

Julie sat still for several moments trying to work out what was best and what was sensible. She needed desperately to unload, the last couple of days had been too much. She looked again at the man's face and even though he was a stranger she felt that she could trust him and seeing him sitting there she felt safe. Yes, the time was right to unburden herself. She took a deep breath, a swig of the cognac and said,

'OK'.

She spoke without stopping for about fifteen minutes apart from drinking and eating and told him everything. He didn't interrupt, just listened very closely and drank and ate as well.

'Umm,' he said, 'quite a story.' He turned to the desk and

said '…and these keys?' She had forgotten about the keys.

After her bath she had repaired her make up a little, not that she had particularly intended to show her face to the world, but it had made her feel better. Jean-Paul's keys were visible in her handbag which was lying open on the side table. She hadn't remembered putting them in but that wasn't surprising considering the panic.

She told Henri how she had come by the bunch.

'I didn't think they were yours. This one here…' he said holding up a large bronze-coloured intricate key 'is the key to a very expensive floor safe, presumably in the floor of the warehouse under several tons of burning building.'

'I think I know where that is – I saw him through the back door kneeling on the floor.'

Henri switched questions. 'Why are you here in the hotel and not sitting making a statement to the police?'

'I can't go to the police can I? I was supposed to stay in England, one of my bail conditions, and I'm travelling on my sister's passport. If they knew I had run off to France I suspect several things would happen. First, I would be arrested for false use of someone else's passport or whatever, but more important they would probably suspect me of actually being the drug runner as well as Graham. So it would make Graham's situation much worse and we would both be thrown in jail and the key swallowed. So I can't go to the police here because all of my silly, silly actions would be revealed.' And she put her head in her hands and started sobbing. Henri got up from his chair, sat next to her and put his arm around her heaving shoulders.

'Talking to me is almost as good as going to the police; I used to be in charge of the police station here until about a year ago. I had some disagreement with the regional commissioner and so I quit... . If I am honest I didn't have much choice as I had sort of broken the law, which is not really a good trait for a police inspector.'

Julie had stopped sobbing and meekly said from behind her hands, 'From the beginning... .' and smiled.

'Ha ha, well why not. I had run this town pretty much for ten years, crime had come down, and really there was very little of it left. Things got sorted out without too much having to go to court, you know, a close local community, a proverbial clip round the ear for some of the youngsters. But then, last year we had some foreigners in town from the old USSR, gangster types. They rented a large house and they started up a brothel using a couple of young girls they brought with them – who incidentally came not entirely of their own free will. They enticed a number of big players including the mayor into getting into bed, literally. They took photos and threatened exposing their antics to the world. Well you know in France taking a mistress has always been more acceptable than other countries in Europe; but the mayor got a bit frightened that the exposure would be bad with an election coming up and especially for his wife who was the rich side of the arrangement, and he reckoned a divorce would be on the cards and so the plonker paid up. Then it was more demands, more money and so he came to me, off the record.

Well, I took one of my fit young officers and went round to see the guys and a bit of a brawl happened. They ended up getting quite badly hurt as did my young guy. The upshot of it was that they successfully sued for assault and police brutality and got a handsome damages award. I was hauled before the police commissioner because I had gone round without any 'evidence' and endangered the young officer's health and safety. All the charges of running a brothel and blackmail were dropped and to make matters worse, they published the pictures of the mayor, whose wife left him – penniless. I was not the flavour of the month and had to resign.'

'May I ask an indelicate question?' He shrugged.

'Does the young lady behind the bar come from East Europe?'

'Well yes – when the Russians left, they just left and Lola was left behind, with nowhere to live nor means of support and so, as I have this small hotel – which is seldom full I have let her stay here until she can sort herself out. She helps me out around the place... .'

'Yes I have seen her helping – quite competent,' she raised an eyebrow.

'Yes,' said Henri looking a little bashful and not totally sure if she was on to how he collected the rent, and whether some of the locals in the bar came for reasons other than the drink.

Henri was now sitting beside her on the bed but had removed his comforting arm and he changed the subject.

'Based on what you have told me it does seem pretty obvious that the fire and the deaths up at Le Haut are connected... .'

'What deaths?'

'Oh – you won't know – the guys, the police, that is, found both the brothers Montard dead earlier and it seems they may have killed each other.'

'Oh my God, the two that I was with, with the wine, dead'

'Mmm, according to the early report they had had a pretty violent argument in the house, Louis had stabbed Victor in the chest and Victor had shot Louis at close range. Very nasty, lots of blood apparently… .'

'How do you know this?'

'My old sergeant popped in and told me, he keeps me informed of what's going on. I like to know and sometimes I can help him, you know, make some suggestions on how to proceed.'

Julie went very quiet and very white. She had a very good idea that these deaths were connected too and worse, that she was somehow the cause. She felt sick again – not for the first time tonight.

Henri was watching Julie's reaction and went on 'If your deductions are right and these two idiots – and they were idiots – had been the two men that sold the wine to your bloke then it is likely that the wine came from Jean-Paul.'

'Yes,' she said meekly.

'I suppose it is possible that Louis and Victor didn't know what was in the bottles, but were just selling dodgy wine. Except that they had a few bottles – they gave you some and it was good wine and I have to accept that you know your wine, even if you are English'

She glared.

'So even though they were not the brightest on the block they could still work out that there was something odd – selling really good wine at a cheap price. We can assume that

Jean-Paul knew what was in the bottles, in that he set it up. You know, I have known him for years, a shrewd businessman yes, but I didn't have him down as a drug smuggler.

Anyway, it seems the scheme went wrong, that is, you and your Graham got caught with the drugs. It's a good scheme, get someone else to take the stuff through customs, if they get caught, you lose the drugs but not your head. Then some amateur sleuth comes along and blows their scheme out of the water. So they have decided to cut their losses and cut out the team.'

'Are you saying that both of these deaths were about covering up the drug smuggling?'

'Well it makes sense, someone at the top of the organisation, you know 'The Don figure… .'

'Do you mean it's Mafia?' Julie interrupted

'I don't know, organised crime of some sort, if not Mafia then something similar, I suppose. When they realised that these two idiots at the bottom of the pile had started talking about the wine and could therefore compromise the organisation, or they just decided that you were getting a bit too close, they wanted to close the door on it. Jean-Paul and the two idiots were expendable.'

'What you are saying is that because I have seeming stumbled on this drug ring, they have closed it down, I am responsible for the deaths of three people and the case against Graham is still strong?'

Henri gave a Gallic shrug.

They sat silently for a few moments.

'How do you think they were going to get the stuff back

from us? Their plan was good, the chances were that we would get through OK, then off we drive into the night with their stuff on board... .'

'Where were you going?'

'We were going to drive home, back to Reading.'

'I doubt if they could have guessed that but there was a good chance that you would have stopped somewhere fairly close to the ferry, it being a late ferry. A hotel maybe, you would have parked outside, taken an overnight bag into the hotel and left the car with the box of wine in it. Easily broken into by most street corner thieves. If you did live close then again you would have probably just parked in the drive and thought about unloading in the morning.'

'So, they must have had a car waiting our side of the channel – and knew which car to follow.'

'That makes sense.'

'I've just remembered something Graham said – which I didn't mention to the police. He said that the two men had told him that it was good wine but better to let it rack for 3 months. That was an extra insurance – what they were saying was don't try to drink it yet so that would give the pick-up man on the other side time to snatch it back.'

'That was clever; just in case you did decide to crack one open at home, even though it was late.'

They were both getting quite excited working out the possible train of events as this 'could' lead to something important. Henri was loving it – sitting next to a very attractive woman using his police brain again. He felt quite turned on.

Henri went on warming to the analysis, 'I wonder how

sophisticated this gang is – did they just hit any car driving along the autoroute, waiting for anyone to pull in to the lay-by? For instance, supposing a car full of, let's say, rowdy young men came along, the chance of their being stopped would be higher, yes?'

'Probably.'

'So, you come along, a conservative car with – forgive me – conservative-looking people in it. No way do they look like your average drug smuggler. So, choose them and you increase the chance of getting through.'

'If they were really clever they may have even thought about the number plates.'

'Sorry?'

'Well, like on French plates you know where the car has come from. In France the arrondissement number is used, in Great Britain letter codes are used. Each town or region has a group of letter codes which are used on the registration. So they might even have picked a registration that was up north somewhere, and so would know, pretty well, that the car would stop at a hotel – or at their mum's – quite soon after docking.'

'If you are right and they were that sophisticated, then they may have chosen a car or cars with local number plates, knowing that they would get home quickly and so the following car would have less of a problem.'

'Yeh, I suppose, although if they did live close and got home they might have a garage and that would make life a bit more difficult for your sneak thief.'

'This is getting a bit daft. Maybe they are that good but

even if your English registration plates are easy to work out, it's hardly fool-proof you could have hired the car, borrowed it, bought it from a garage somewhere else in the country, or moved house... .'

'OK, but I agree they may have tried to get a car full of middle-aged losers rather than a rowdy bunch.'

'I didn't say losers.'

'Yes I know, but we did get taken, didn't we?'

They sat side by side and thought through those scenarios.

Henri spoke again, 'If I had set this up I would have put a tracking device in with the wine. I bet you a meal out that there's one in the box.'

'Oh, this is important − if they look in the box and find a tracker then that puts Graham in a much better position doesn't it?'

'Maybe.'

Julie slumped 'It doesn't really help much though does it − because I have no way of getting that information into the UK system without revealing where I am and if that is known the shit could hit the fan.'

'No, it's not easy to tip them off but we must assume that the UK police are competent enough to spot a tracking device in the wine box,' said Henri.

'So what do we do now?' she said.

'We do nothing − you go back to England, give your sister back her passport and wait for your Graham to be cleared. I'm sure that sooner or later the events here will be connected and I can maybe put some ideas into the head of the moron that runs the station in town − but I can't promise anything.'

Julie held onto Henri's arm and pleaded, 'we must be able to take this a bit further and maybe find out who supplied the drugs.'

'It's too dangerous for you, and me as well – these guys are serious, they have almost certainly killed Jean-Paul and probably Louis and Victor too, killing you or me if we get too close is not going to faze them.'

'But they don't know about me, you said that – they were just cleaning out their contact trail – I don't exist. That man didn't know I was in the building – it was close but luckily I was the only one drinking wine and I hadn't got much lipstick on and so he assumed the single glass on the table was Jean-Paul's. I think if there had been two glasses he would have found me.'

'Yes – it was close, too close, and so a very good reason why you should go back.'

Julie was in a determined mood but at the same time not really sure why. On the one hand she was thoroughly enjoying Henri's company to the extent that she was probably flirting. He was very – attractive, somehow... very French... very dangerous and in the last half hour and three cognacs she was finding him more and more well, sexy. The episode on the balcony was still very vivid in her mind and oddly, the fact that she now knew that Lola was in fact a prostitute did not worry her or turn her off him. Somehow just the opposite. This whole adventure – and it was an adventure for she had never done anything like this before – was about saving Graham, the man she was with. So how come, if she was 'with' Graham, she feeling attracted, no very attracted, to this

189

Frenchman, a stranger? She was unable to answer any of these questions. She was alarming herself with these thoughts as she sat without speaking next to this man who, it must be said was also flirting with her. She almost got to start thinking it would be rather nice to slide into bed but shut it all down before that thought had a chance to grow. She felt ashamed now and this turned into another spurt of enthusiasm for continuing the investigation despite the dangers, to show the world, herself and Henri, that she really was in love with Graham and would do anything to see him released. Unfortunately she didn't totally believe it.

'I want to take this further if I can, what can I do?'

'Aye ya yah Julie, this is madness.'

She glared at him with one of those looks that only women in a certain mood can do and men who have experienced this know that there is no point in arguing.

'OK, let me look at the keys again.' Henri looked through the bunch of keys and looked again carefully at the safe key. 'This is a very expensive safe – it's burglar proof, fire proof, probably earthquake proof. Only people with a lot to keep in a safe would buy one of these. So it would be nice to look inside it. Tell me where you think it is again.'

'Right at the back of the warehouse, there was a door which led into a kitchen I think and I saw him kneeling behind the door. He had the keys with him and so if you say there is a floor safe – it sounds like that's where it is. In the floor of that back room – under a burnt-out building that by the way is still on fire, surrounded by firemen and police.'

'Let's go and look.'

They went downstairs past the bar door without being seen. There were just two men sitting in there playing chequers. Outside it was very dark, no moon, but there was still a glow over the remains of the warehouse. There was just one fire engine and one police car in the road in front of the site. It was a warm evening and there was a small knot of onlookers across the road, not so interested in the fire but just standing and talking.

Henri and Julie stayed on their side of the street and walked up to the warehouse site. She walked slowly as her injuries were still new and sore. Henri gently held her arm and they looked for all the world like a couple out for an evening stroll.

The front of the warehouse was gone. The big wooden doors had disappeared and the front façade, which was in fact brick-based with wooden boards over, had fallen into the building. The shop area was no more.

They walked up to almost opposite the warehouse site and Henri stood her in the shadows and told her to wait. He crossed the road to the police car.

'Eric, quite a bonfire eh?'

'Too right, Henri.'

'Is Jean-Paul in there do you think?'

'We don't know, my friend, the fire boys won't let anyone near until the heat has dropped off a bit, they just want to play with their hoses a bit more and they will probably go in tomorrow morning. If he's in there, he'll still be in there in the morning.'

'You've got to baby sit them then?'

'Well, you know what the town's like, they're be trying to get in there to see if there's any wine left.'

'Maybe, but the town ain't that stupid, even the drinkers of the gut rot know it's buggered, even if it's still in a bottle.'

'I guess, but I'm here for the night anyway. I have to walk around every half–hour to check but I may nod off in between.'

'I might drop by later with a night cap, see you Eric.'

'Thanks Henri. Oh, another thing that has just come through, you already know about the Montard brothers, don't you?'

'Yeah, I heard, terrible.'

'Well it gets even weirder mate. Apparently the medico had a quick look and said that it wasn't a double self-inflicted killing. They reckon it's murder. They think that the angle of the blade going in and the way the pistol was positioned, whatever, are all wrong, they're saying the bodies were positioned to make it look like they did it to themselves, but in fact they were murdered. What about that eh?'

'Christ, that's awful.'

'You haven't heard half of it yet. The main suspect is a woman.'

'Really.'

'Yeah, some young woman was seen by old Madame Sassin, sitting in a car just up the road watching the farm house, just before they were found dead. What about that?'

'Looks like you've got a real crime on your hands for once, and not just this fire. They'll be asking me to come back soon, eh?'

'Yeah right, somehow I don't think that will happen. Herr

Monsieur Inspector doesn't seem to have much respect for you Henri.'

'Well that's OK, I don't have much respect for him either. Bye Eric.'

'Bye Henri, hey, keep a look out for this strange young woman, she sounds like just your type, ha ha.'

'Yeah, up yours Eric.'

Henri walked on to the firemen and chatted to them for a few minutes. Julie could see the fire chief pointing at the wreckage as his men sprayed water over the hottest part which seemed to be nearer the front of the building than the rear, although completely burnt out, the back wasn't glowing with the same intensity. She could feel the heat from across the road, but still shivered knowing that there was a body inside being well and truly fried and more – it could easily have been her as well.

Henri wandered back, took her arm again and said nothing about the conversation he had had with Eric. They walked slowly up the road.

'What now, we can't get in the building so we will never get to know what's in the safe even if keys do fit?'

'Let's walk around and check it out anyway.'

They slowly walked into the centre of the village, turned left and then left again down a track which lead back to the rear of the warehouse, where only a few hours before she had scrambled out.

It was still very dark but as they got nearer the glow lit up the sky with a warm red. There was a great cloud of smoke hanging over the site but the light wind was blowing it away to the south and away from the track. The smell was almost overpowering, a mixture of soot, dust, chemicals and God knows what else. Julie tried not to think that some of the smell might be roasting person.

They could clearly see the back of the building now, silhouetted by the glow and the spray from the fire engine arcing over and immediately turning into a white steam cloud that mixed in with the black. As Julie had seen from the front, the rear of the building was less charred and in fact the outbuilding where she had seen Jean-Paul kneeling on the floor still had its roof on, a few tiles had fallen in but mostly it was intact.

Henri told her to stay where she was and keep a look out. She looked around and was suddenly petrified at the thought of keeping watch and had no real idea of what she should do if someone came. She tried to say this but he was gone.

He carefully crept up to the side of the outbuilding, noiselessly vaulted over the remains of a low wall, and disappeared. Julie nervously looked around again. A dim different-coloured light seeped from the outbuilding as Henri used his flashlight.

Inside it was filthy with smoke and soot and lots of black water on the floor. The door to the back part was still mostly there although leaning and half open. He pushed it open a little more before it jammed against some bricks, but he was able to squeeze through. His torch showed him the remains of the back kitchen with a counter and an old-fashioned sink. There was a sodden carpet on the floor, now black. He stood the torch on the counter and with two hands heaved it back.

He could immediately see the circular top of the safe. He gave himself a little self-satisfied nod, congratulating himself on correctly identifying the make of the safe. He got down on his knees and felt the cold water go straight through his trousers, but within a few seconds the lid of the safe was open, the heat had not affected it at all. Inside there was a metal cylinder with a wire handle. He slid it up and out of the casing. He hesitated for a moment wondering whether to remove the contents and put the sleeve back or take the whole thing. He decided it was easier to take it all. He would have to carry it back to the hotel unnoticed, but in the dark it looked a bit like a bucket and who out there knew what the inside of a floor safe looked like?

Seconds later he was back outside with Julie. She squealed quietly at the sight of the find and then at the state of his trousers. She held his arm and they walked on as quickly as she could manage back along the same path she had used, to the hotel opening.

They crossed the now empty street; Henri's customers had gone home at last. There was still a small knot of on-lookers across the road from the fire but most of the excitement was gone.

The hotel was closed down with just a few wall lights on in the bar and no sign of Lola. They crept back up the stairs to Julie's room. Henri had somehow thought it a little improper to go to his room plus the fact that it was very untidy and unclean enough to be beyond a line acceptable to polite company.

Julie had forgotten her injuries she was so excited and

couldn't wait to find out what was in there. But Henri was milking the moment.

'Now Miss, this is a serious police matter and the contents of this safe probably contain important and significant evidence in a murder enquiry, so I insist that we are sufficiently respectful of the items herein.'

'Bollocks,' she said and went to pull off the inner lid.

But Henri stopped her. 'Please do not touch anything until I get back,' and rushed out of the room. She was puzzled but did as she was told. He came back quickly with a beam on his face and two pairs of disposable gloves. They put them on and then opened up.

Henri tipped the contents onto the bed and laid out the articles they found. Julie immediately recognized the plastic bag from Carrefour that she had seen earlier upstairs in the warehouse. She went to it first. Inside were about twenty small bags of white powder. Even though she had seen plenty of this recently at customs it still came as a shock.

'Oh' she said 'Cocaine?'

'I guess,' said Henri holding up a large manila envelope 'Look at this,' and he tipped out several bundles of large denomination euro notes.

'Shit, that's a lot of cash; there must be thousands.'

Henri fanned a bundle and did a quick count.

'I would think maybe thirty thousand anyway... .'

'Jean-Paul was seriously into this wasn't he?'

'It seems so and right under my nose, the bastard.'

'You are not the chief anymore, so right under the nose of the new man.'

'OK yes.'

'Look at this,' said Julie picking up and flicking through a small blue book, 'Oh boy, Bingo.'

The book was a diary-come-notebook. It was full with tight and even hand written details, of everything. Dates, phones calls, meetings, all meticulously summarized. The man was a pedant. The two sat side by side and silently read through the pages.

Chapter 13

The following email message was sent to the region headquarters in Pas de Calais and copied on to all to police station in the region, including Querchamps-les-Ardres

Urgent message from UK police – Ashford, Kent

Please be on the look out for Miss Julie Webb.

Description:
White, age 36yrs, long blond hair, 1.6m tall, medium build, speaks very good French, using a passport in the name of Madeline Webb. Driving a dark blue Peugeot 208 license plate CA 229 BG (from Pas de Calais).

Believed to be close to the A14 between Calais and Paris and most likely in the region 60 km from Calais.

If located please detain her and an officer from Kent police will be sent to interview her in France with a view to escorting her back to UK for questioning in connection with a serious drug-related offence.

A photograph scanned from Julie's passport was attached.

★★★★★★★

It was late and Saskia had just made it home. Aariz was already in bed; she undressed and slid in beside him.

'Hi, you're late.'

'Yeah, sorry.'

'What's the latest on my client, or can't you tell me?'

'Well, I think you are trying to use your privileged position, in my bed, to gain an advantage.'

'Since when is it your bed?'

'I think I bought this didn't I?'

'I really can't remember. But seriously what's the latest Saskia, you are going to let him walk out in the morning aren't you?'

'Now that the custom's guy has fessed up we don't really have anything at all on Spelling. He has been officially arrested but no charge sheet has been written, so I think we'll just let him go. Curry was pretty cross about the identical twin thing, it was actually quite funny, the whole idea of trying to pass herself off in front of Spelling. But he could still charge them both with several things if he has a mind to, wasting police time, aiding and abetting. But neither of them are going to be charged with any drugs offences and he'll be set free first thing in the morning.'

'Why didn't Curry release him this evening?'

'It was quite late by the time we got back from Folkestone

with the Custom's guy, and by the time he'd been processed it was very late, and I think he was also quite happy to let him stew in the cell for another night, out of spite really.'

'What just because Spelling and Maddie Webb tried to con him?'

'Well yeah, plus the fact he was a bit pissed off that it was me that first thought that they might be identical twins. Anyway, if you turn up first thing you can get your man out.'

'Right, thanks, I'll see you in the morning then Detective.'

★★★★★★★

They sat in silence. Julie turned the pages as she finished reading. Henri waited patiently. He read faster, which is not surprising as it was in French.

When they had both read about twenty pages, Julie stopped reading and turned to Henri.

'Why did he write this all down?'

'Perhaps as some kind of insurance policy, if they really screwed him then he could produce evidence, at least dates and times which could add up to enough to convict these guys.'

'But it didn't save him did it… ?'

'I guess not.'

'So presumably these people didn't know about the safe otherwise the killer would have come looking for it, and probably found me under the bed with the keys.'

'I don't know, perhaps the killer was a contract and that was all he was told. Go cover the tracks by killing Louis and

Victor and then Jean-Paul.'

'What do we do next?'

'I think we do nothing that is, you do nothing – this is getting too hot. You must go back to England and let the police take care of this. We are fast becoming an accessory to murder here – certainly right now I am withholding evidence.'

'Easy, take the book to the police.'

'Fine. How did I get the book? Where did I get the keys? Oh, says the new inspector, who by the way hates my guts, so you Monsieur Henri were in the building, mmm interesting. So I say, well actually no, there is this very attractive woman who is travelling with a false passport, who was in the building, and by the way she was also out at Ferme de Bray just before the other two were murdered. But she's OK because the shit load of drugs they found in her car were planted... .'

Julie sat quietly for some while.

'So you think I'm very attractive then?'

'Mon Dieu, this is serious Julie.'

'I know, I know, I'm sorry. I'm sorry I dragged you into this.'

'You didn't drag me, I dragged myself.'

'Why did you?'

Henri felt a blush starting up – him a policeman, ex-policeman, blushing because he was thinking about her naked body, and not surprisingly felt it inappropriate to mention seeing her bruised bits at this moment.

'I just saw that you were hurt and in distress and I just wanted to help, OK?'

'OK.'

Henri looked at Julie, thought seriously for a moment about asking if he could stay the night, then thought better of it. She looked exhausted, the adrenalin of the safe-breaking episode was wearing of and she was starting to fall asleep. He checked the time – it was half past one.

He swept the contents of the safe back into the cylinder and said.

'Look, its late, get into bed, and we will pick this up again in the cold light of day.'

She just nodded and as he watched she pulled the covers over herself and immediately fell asleep.

'Well, that answers that question then,' he said to himself and closed the door behind him.

Henri stood outside her door for a moment trying to think clearly about what to do and didn't come to any great conclusion apart from stashing away the loot and getting to sleep.

The most obvious place to put the bucket full of goodies was in his cubby hole through the linen cupboard. It was secret and only he had the key. He put the blue book in his pocket.

In bed he thought about Julie. What Eric had told him did fit in with what she had told him, that she had tracked down Louis and Victor and then Jean-Paul but now they were all dead. Julie was there in both 'events'. She had left England for a pretty flimsy reason, to help release her 'loved one'. But even that seemed a bit out of line as he had the distinct feeling that she was coming onto him. The pheromones were pumping out. Was she really so very much in love with this guy or was the whole thing just a fantastic story and she was in fact an assassin working for the Mafia? With these thoughts he fell asleep.

★★★★★★★

Henri woke with a start out of an amazing dream involving a fire engine. He sat up confused, realised his mobile was ringing on the bedside table and immediately forget the details of the dream. He looked at the screen. It was the hotel's number. Lola was calling him from downstairs.

'Yes.'

'I thought you might want knowing, the police have just been here looking at you.'

Henri looked at the clock. It was 6.30am.

'Do you know why?'

'They ask me if there was an English lady stays here.'

'I say them no. I don't like police so I don't help OK.'

'Thanks.'

He flipped off the phone.

He dressed quickly, looked out of the window to make sure the police had left and ran down the stairs to find Lola sitting behind the bar with a cup of coffee. She just looked at him and gave a shrug, she had learnt that from him.

'I owe you a bonus,' he said and looked out of the door and down the street.

'Did they check the guest register?'

'No, I told them it was in your office and it was locked.'

'I don't have an office.'

'So?'

'I told them you were out drinking all night with your silly pals as usual and you didn't make it home yet. They said they would come back later and talk to you.'

'Where is the guest register?'

'Here,' she said pulling it out from under the counter.

He spun it around, found the entry and filled in the section that showed that Julie checked out the evening before having stayed just the one night. He signed her signature.

'Look you silly girl, she was here but left after one night... .'

'I suppose I didn't understand the policeman, you French all speak so fast...

'Good, well done.'

Upstairs again, Henri knocked on Julie's door, first gently and then louder as he had got no response. He heard a snorting and mumbling which didn't much relate to someone waking up bright and breezy. He used his master key to open the door to find her pretty much where he had left her. He gently shook her awake and she sat up quickly and stared at him for several seconds trying to work out where she was and who he was.

'What?' she managed.

'The police are looking for you. Have you told anyone in England where you are?'

'What?'

'Wake up, wake up Julie. Who knows you are here?'

'No one of course, well yes, but only my sister and even she doesn't know where exactly, anyway she wouldn't tell anyone... I don't think.'

'Get dressed; pack your things, you're leaving. You've got four minutes. Stay in the room until I fetch you.'

'Er, OK.'

'Now! Quickly, this is serious.'

He closed the door again and his phone pinged to tell him a text message had arrived. He flicked open the message file and read it as he ran downstairs.

Henri, thought you might like to know… report came in from England. We are asked to look for and detain an English woman called Julie Webb, on drug smuggling charge? More important WE are looking for a woman driving a blue Peugeot seen at the Ferme de Bray and a woman of the same description going into Jean-Paul's place just before the fire????? Your police friend.

'Oh *merde*' he said out loud. Not for the first time he wondered whether he was being an idiot and influenced by naked bodies. He said to himself 'I've got a load of cocaine stashed in the cupboard and I'm aiding and abetting a woman who is running from the English police because of a drugs bust and the French police because of a murder charge. Not particularly smart Henri.'

****

Once again Julie's heart started pumping, ready to run. She did as she was told and was dressed and packed in just over four minutes when Henri was back at the door.

He knocked and went straight in.

'Where's your car?'

'In your car park.'

'Did you hire it?'

'Yes.'

'Did you use a credit card?'

'Yes, of course, why?'

'The English police are looking for you and so are the French. Have you used your mobile recently?'

Julie was panicking again and had gone white and very quiet.

'Yes, I texted my sister,' she said in a small voice.

'Turn it off and leave it off.'

'It's off.'

'Right, are you ready, let's go.'

'Nearly.'

'Let's go, now.'

'OK, OK, OK.'

He hurried her down the stairs, through the bar and checked the street.

'We are going towards Paris. Follow me. We'll stop once we are clear of the town. Do not break the speed limit or do anything stupid that would get you stopped by the police. Do not use your phone.'

He turned to Lola.

'I have just called you and I got so drunk with my friends last night that I am not planning to get back here until sometime later. I need to sleep it off. I will crash out somewhere, you have no idea where, OK?'

'OK, Henri, but please be careful.'

He followed Julie out of the back door into the car park; he gave her a nod to follow him. They turned left out of the hotel down a lane that looked like it was a dead end. After about 300 metres of rough and rutted lane they came out on to a farm road that took them way from the town. They saw no other cars.

Once the car was out of town Henri relaxed a bit, but even then he kept a watch on Julie in his rear view mirror and made sure she kept up with him. With few cars on the road he was certain that no one had followed them.

Julie drove behind keeping her distance. She calmed down quickly. She was getting used to this.

She kept her gaze fixed on the rear lights of his car. It still wasn't fully light; the sun hadn't really broken through the overnight cloud bank that had built up. The countryside she knew was beautiful but this morning it was dingy and Julie didn't see it. She was stiff from the battering her body had received the night before, both her knees were badly bruised and sore and the driving position was uncomfortable. She constantly wanted to straighten them out, but couldn't easily while driving. Her hands too had grazes and she was holding the wheel in an awkward grip to avoid the damaged bits. She kept fixed on Henri's car and thought about Graham a bit. The odd thing was that although this whole adventure was all about Graham and getting him out of jail, she had thought very little about him since it all started. She had broken the law, travelled on a false passport, had found the drug runners, had been in great danger, had seen a man killed and had escaped from a burning building. It had all been awful, terrifying but very, very exciting and now she was following a man whom she had watched making love to someone and she was now finding him extraordinarily sexy. The horror of the recent hours had dulled into a kind of cartoon, not in the least bit real.

She concentrated on blanking out her thoughts again and was suddenly very weary. She started to fantasise, sexually. The cars reached a deserted stretch of road with woodland on either side. He indicated and turned off to the right into a rough track. She followed. He came to a halt and turned off his lights and engine. She did the same. He came back to her, opened the car door, took her hand and led her out of the car without saying a word. He smiled at her and she went with him. He pulled her down to him onto a rug (that had magically appeared). He kissed her full on the lips. She wrapped her arms around his neck and kissed him back hard. He pulled off her top (she seemingly had no bra on), lifted her skirt (no knickers) she opened her legs wide and her entered her in a single movement.

'Oooh.'

The brake lights in front came on and Julie braked hard to avoid him. She had come back to earth with a jolt. Her heart was beating fast, she was panting and had an odd feeling between her thighs.

Henri had slowed quickly and was now indicating to the right. Julie's heart beat even faster.

'It was happening, it was happening… .'

It took Julie a moment to spot that she was not, in fact, in a dark wooded area and about to be ravaged but was on the edge of another town and parking outside a tatty- looking bar with a string of coloured lights dangling outside.

Henri was at her window. She still wasn't totally sure... she wound down the window.

'We need to talk, let's stop here for breakfast and a recap.'

He opened the car door, took her hand and led her out of the car without saying another word... and into the bar.

They sat at a small table in a corner with a coffee and a fresh croissant. Croissants were so much nicer in France than in England, she mused, why was that?

'Right, Julie, this is getting serious, tell me exactly what you said to your sister.'

'I just text her to keep her in the loop, I have kept her informed of what I have been doing. She is worried about me.'

'What did you say in the recent texts?'

Julie got out her mobile and read out loud the last three texts.

'maddie landed at calais hired car all ok j'

'at hotel in town all ok j.'

'Some progress I think I am on to something j'

'And that's all you said?'

'Yes.'

'What did she say in reply?'

'Very little, she just said "be careful" after the first one and after the second she said "I think U should come home."'

Julie passed the phone across to Henri to 'prove' the text was all she wrote.

He read them and frowned.

'Who else might have seen these texts apart from your sister?'

'No one.'

'Is she married?'

'No divorced years ago, lives alone.'

'OK.'

'Do you really think they have tracked me from using my credit card or do you think it's something to do with my sister?'

'I don't know, but I do know that they are looking for you so they know you were in or around Querchamps. The English police are looking for you by name and the French police are looking for a woman of your description in connection with the murder of Louis and Victor and for arson of Jean-Paul's place. That may also turn into murder if they find Jean-Paul's body in the burnt-out building, which according to your story they will sooner or later. Not good Julie. So how did they know where to find you?'

'Are you doubting me Henri, tell me now?'

'No.'

'OK, the only person who knew where I was going was my sister and she wouldn't be telling anyone where I was, would she?'

'If we are dealing with a very organised set of criminals with good connections, then they may be able to keep checks on things like credit cards. But they still needed to know you were here. So the information is out there and if they knew that you had left your sister's house, they may have been able to track down your credit card when you used it at the dock. They could have guessed that you were coming here to Querchamps – close to the Aire. But there are a lot of ifs in that.'

They sat in silence for a while both trying to think through the situation.

'Tell me about Jean-Paul? How long has he been in town?'

'Maybe five years, he bought the old warehouse site and converted it into a wine depot. I have no idea what his background was. Everyone saw him as a lady's man, charming and dapper. He flirted with some of the older ladies in town, to their delight and to the annoyance of their husbands. But for all of that I never saw him with a woman of his own and when that is realised in a small town like Querchamps, the next thing is that people will talk about him being gay. Certainly I had heard that being said in my bar.'

'Do you think he was gay?'

'No idea, but he was mixed up in this drug business for sure, gay or not.'

Henri took out the blue diary and flicked through some of the pages. Much of the careful writing was in Jean-Paul's shorthand. Dates were understandable but people he had met were just initials. Once again they sat shoulder to shoulder and read the notes together.

'Here is a reference to a meeting with Louis and Victor. He says "5 May. Met L & VM. Discd w deal."'

'Wine deal I suppose… .'

'5 May Phoned P, na, got G. Confirm dates for go as 22 July.'

'22 July, that was last Thursday – the day we got caught.'

'Hate G, threatening old prob if I don't agree. No option.'

'G, whoever he is, had obviously got something on Jean-Paul and in effect was blackmailing him to do their dirty work.'

'So your charming Monsieur JP has a murky past?'

'Seemingly.'

'Perhaps it was something to do with his being gay?'

'We don't know if he was gay and anyway that's not a good enough reason to work a blackmail. He is not your Oscar Wilde you know. It's no big deal these days being gay.'

'Where are we going?'

'We are not going anywhere. You are going to Gard du Nord and getting on the train home and I am going to do a bit of research into these people.'

'No way. I am staying with this and that is final.' Julie had raised her voice. The man behind the bar looked across and raised an eyebrow, he listened for a while, realised it was mad people and carried on with his work.

Henri dropped his voice a little.

'You are hurt. You are being sought by the police. You are involved in a murder. You are also involved in drug smuggling. If you are caught by the police in France you will go to jail. OK. You are going home and with a bit of luck you might get out of this without getting an international criminal record.'

Julie stuck out her jaw.

'The fact that I am now a 'wanted' person is all the more reason to try to get to the bottom of this. If I go through customs now they will probably arrest me and throw me into the Bastille or wherever and this trail will go cold. These bastards will disappear. And…' she paused for affect, 'you are a disgraced ex–policeman. You run a brothel. You are involved in helping a criminal to escape. A criminal who you know was involved somehow in a drug and murder case. If you are caught by the police you will go to jail. OK?'

Henri smiled and gave the smallest of shrugs in recognition of her point and wit.

Henri did not want her to go home at all. He wanted to pull all her clothes off and make love to her across the breakfast table.

Julie did not want to go home at all either. Yes, she was excited by being a detective but she also wanted to pull all his clothes off and make love to him across the breakfast table.

Luckily, neither said anything along those lines.

'What else is in the book that might be of use?' said Julie in order to change the subject, not that the subject as such had been vocalised. She had started to fantasise again about the breakfast table and was starting to flush.

'If we can find out a bit more about this gang then I can probably let the police in Paris know without it linking up with you or the fact that the police in Querchamps are looking for you. I do know a few people still in the Paris Commissariat and they can keep quiet about information sources.'

'OK so where do we go?'

'I am still very unhappy about taking you anywhere, but at least I can probably stop you from doing anything else really stupid.'

'I promise I will be sensible this time, really.'

'Umm,' commented Henri, not at all confidently. He looked again at the book. 'There are two addresses here but no particular reference against them, so they may be relevant. They may be women friends?'

'Or man friends?'

'We can at least drive past and have a look.'

Chapter 14

Aariz Al Arim was at the police station at 8.00am. In his role as appointed solicitor he saw it as his duty to make sure that Detective Inspector Curry released Graham Spelling no later than required by law – twenty-four hours after he had been 'detained for questioning'. He still felt angry with Curry for pulling a fast one by re-arresting Spelling and he did think that there could be a case suing the police for unlawful detention, but he didn't particularly relish the thought of that especially as he was connected to the case through Saskia. Any decision on whether the firm would go for that would not be his call, it would be Sprake's, but he wasn't going to suggest it.

When Aariz gave his name to the duty sergeant at the front desk the paperwork for Spelling's release was already completed and he had no further contact with either of the two detectives. Graham was brought out to the front desk; he signed some forms and was given back his personal belongings, including his phone.

'What happens now Mr Al Arim?'

'Well that's it really; the original case against you is not being pursued at this time – the smuggling of cocaine. That doesn't mean that they can't pick you up again if more evidence is found. They now seemingly believe that you had nothing to do with the drugs found in the wine box, nor with the cannabis under the back seat but it is all technically still 'under investigation' and they would still like to interview Miss Webb, that's Julie Webb, who hasn't been tracked down and there is still the possibility that you might be charged with the minor offence of wasting police time, with regard to your deception over the identity of Miss Madeline Webb, when she was 'impersonating' Julie.'

'I had nothing to do with that. That was all down to her nutty sister.'

'Yes, I am aware of that.'

'Do the police not know where Julie is?'

'I don't think so, they have put out an arrest notice to the French police and they know the car that she is driving, but they haven't found her yet. The police have also returned your car, it's in the car park at the side of the building.'

'Thank you.'

'Here's my card Mr Spelling, obviously if there are further complications we are here to help sort those out.'

The shook hands and Graham was given his car keys and left. Aariz walked in the opposite direction back to his office.

Graham sat in his car and dialled Julie's mobile – it was turned off. He didn't leave a message.

★★★★★★★

They finished their breakfast, paid and left, Henri again leading the way. They had agreed on the first address to look at and Julie wrote it down in case they were separated. Henri drove on to the A26 Autoroute and then east of Arras turned on to the A1 to Paris. The road swings around to the north of the capital and Henri came off the main road into the Paris suburb of Saint-Denis. Henri had his SatNav on and they reached the first address with no problem. It was a suburban street. They pulled up behind each other. Julie moved forward into Henri's car.

'It seems to be that house over there, with the black door.'

'It doesn't look much like a drug operation?'

'They never do.'

'I'm not really sure what I am looking for. If we are right then it's some kind of wine warehouse. But in the back they are putting drugs into the bottle instead of wine. The van that Graham bought from had quite a few cases. Are we saying that they were all filled with drugs?'

'From what you have told me I think not, one bottle would hold several thousand euro's worth stuff. A case full represents a great deal of money, so just one probably.'

'Why only one?'

'Because somehow that case of yours had to be retrieved and that would mean a man in a car for each one. I think it most likely there was only one – yours.'

'Let's go and check if there's a name on the door.'

They got out, checked the road and walked up to the door which was up a short flight of steps, then stood together and read the plaque beside the door.

M. Eric Baud – Avocat

They walked on to the end of the street.

'It looks like he has a swanky lawyer. Why would he write that in this book?'

'I can check this guy out through my CID friend; it may be that he's a bit dodgy.'

'Anyway it seems unlikely that this is where wine and drugs get sorted.'

'No.'

'OK next.'

'The next address is, 17 Ave du Président, St Denis 93210

Ten minutes later they were looking at the building. The street was narrow with mostly three- and four-storey buildings, cars were parked along one side. The address they were interested in was a three-story building, the ground floor was a shop front but the large glass windows were blanked out. The rooms above appeared to be an apartment. Directly next to the shop front there was a large pair of gates leading to a courtyard with some industrial buildings behind. They parked and walked past the front. There was a small sign on the front door – Societé du vin de St Denis.

'This looks promising Henri, can we get your CID pals to raid it?'

'No, they have no reason to and we have no evidence whatsoever. Even if I was able to show them this book, which I can't, it's just an address in a book. Jean-Paul was a wine merchant and he bought wine to resell from places like this.'

'Yes, but you know and I know that he had hidden this little book as some kind of insurance in case these druggies got too rough. You don't go hiding up your wine supplier's address in a floor safe.'

'I accept that, but I still can't get them to raid. We just need something concrete.'

Directly opposite the wine dealer's building there was a 3-star hotel – La Boule d'Or.

The entrance door and foyer looked quite up market and wholesome. It had topiaried box plants in large tubs either side of a new door with heavy-duty brass handles. The door swung open without a sound on to a small foyer with photographs of previous guests all taken with the same short rotund man – presumably the owner. Julie cast a look at the pictures and didn't recognise any of them. Maybe they were all his relations she thought. A second smooth door opened into the rest of the hotel which was pleasant enough but hadn't benefited from the recent upgrade. In fact it looked like it hadn't had anything much done to it since the fifties. Julie pulled a face, Henri didn't seem to notice.

Julie couldn't help but wonder if many potential customers at this point would turn around and leave. The front aspect was impressive enough to get you in, once in you were most probably going to stay, so no waste of money here then.

A short rotund woman, presumably the wife of the man in the picture took some details and swiped Henri's credit card; he didn't think that anyone was looking for him yet, otherwise he might have thought to use cash. Henri asked for and got separate rooms, next to each other, both overlooking the road, directly opposite the wine dealer. The receptionist did not change her expression during the transaction. If she wondered why they wanted front rooms, most wanted a quieter back room, she didn't show it. If she wondered why two people of the opposite sex wanted separate rooms, she didn't show that either.

After dropping off his overnight bag he joined Julie in her room and they stood side by side looking down at the shop front on the other side of the road.

'Well Julie, I suggest we sit and watch them for a bit and maybe something will turn up but I can't think what that could possibly be. If they do have drugs in there then they are likely to be well hidden so even if we got to walk in – and we won't – I don't think we would find packs of white powder sitting on a shelf.'

'I know Henri, it's just doing something to help Graham. Thank you for being here,' she touched his arm and wished she hadn't for she felt the rock hard muscle in his arm and blushed. She removed her hand and carried on quickly.

'I do appreciate it and I have been pretty bloody stupid of late. I should know better, I am a teacher for God's sake. If my head could see me now, all the staff think I'm stuffy and Miss Goody Two Shoes.'

'OK, you stay here, watch who comes and goes, take a picture with your mobile, even if it's a long way off. Write down the times that you see anything. Do not go out, do not do anything daft. OK?'

'*D'accord, mon capitan.* But first I really, really need a shower.'

'OK, I will watch the building opposite from my window, when you've sorted yourself out bang on the wall.

Fifteen minutes later Henri heard a muffled knocking and

returned to her room. He had seen nothing at all across the road.

He saw a new woman, she was wearing a dress, no longer jeans, not a particularly fashionable dress, but it looked good on her or rather she looked good in it, but actually he thought that she was going to look good in almost anything.

He shook himself back to the matter in hand.

'I'm going to see a friend of mine in the Commissariat Central which is close to here and see if I can dig anything up about this business, who it belongs to and whether they have any form.'

'OK, I'll be here. See you later.'

Julie pulled up a chair to the window and put her feet up on the ledge. She could see both the shop door and the gate leading to the courtyard. She thought back over the last day or so and reflected on what she had achieved. In many ways it was a great deal, but Graham was still in jail and nothing she had found out was of any use to him. She thought again about the Montard brothers and Jean-Paul and the dreadful knowledge that all of them would probably still be alive if she had stayed in England.

****

Text message:

Silvie
Running behind schedule. Hope all is well with business. Pick me up from Gare du Nord tomorrow morning. I will

advise exact time when I know.
Pierre.

Silvie walked through the rear of the shop and punched in a code to open the door which ran into the warehouse behind. Gerard was working alongside Ethan sticking labels on a batch of newly bottled vintage Champagne, which was actually an average sparkling wine called 'Mousseux'. This shipment was destined for London and would sell for a ridiculous price, probably to a young city trader with more money than sense, in one of the many 'posh' drinking places. Silvie took Gerard aside. Ethan tried to listen to their conversation but couldn't hear enough, he just satisfied himself by looking at her body from afar and undressing her, not that it took much of the imagination to remove the few clothes she had on, so he just did it over and over again.

'Gerard, Pierre has just texted. He is back in Paris tomorrow. How sure are you that all of the loose ends are now tied up?

'Totally, all three of the team at the Calais end will not be talking again, ever. I don't know what's happened to Ivan, there's been no word. Hopefully for him he will just lie low, but if he gets caught so be it, he can't get back to us. Charlie has gone to ground but he can be brought back in when we need him. The only problem is that we should probably keep clear of Folkestone for a while, but there are all of the other ports. We don't have any insurance at the other ports – that is, we don't have an 'Ivan' anywhere else, unless Pierre has someone we don't know about. But there is no way that Customs can start checking all of the wine boxes going through, it would cause chaos.'

'Pierre will still be upset about losing the roadside drops, so we should at least try to put something into motion before tomorrow. That will help smooth Pierre's anger.'

'Yeah, OK, I have bloke who works for Carrefour he's second in command in the wine department. He owes me. We can deliver the loaded bottles into their warehouse. He can put them aside in such a way that no one should put them out onto the shelves. He will put some sort of label on the box. When an English tourist asks for a box of that wine, he can carry ours out for them. We will label the bottles up correctly and put the transmitter in as usual. It is extra risky in that first it is possible that the box may get out without him knowing, and also he knows me, just as Jean-Paul did. That means that if this one gets rumbled I would have to cut out the middle man again, literally.' And he smiled.

Silvie was well aware of Gerard's talents, but his joke made her shudder. Too much information.

'The other thing Silvie, I am very keen to get rid of the coke we have here. OK, it's hidden away in the underground store which would be difficult to find unless you knew where to look. But even so... Ethan is trustworthy but only because he's shit scared of what I would do to him if he grassed. Look, I think once I've finished this little run on the vintage Champagne, Ethan and I will load up the rest of the coke into the double-skinned Côte de Rhône bottles ready for Carrefour. Then as soon as Pierre gives us the OK on that route I can ship them out.'

'*D'accord*, Gerard. That will at least show Pierre that we are using our heads and moving on to the next stage. Good, talk to your man.'

Silvie went back to the front office and realised that she was also shit scared of Gerard. Thank goodness Pierre wasn't.

★★★★★★★

After about an hour of watching Julie was getting bored. Nothing had happened. Her arse was getting sore sitting in the same position and her legs ached, partly because of her sitting position and partly still from the battering her body had taken at the fire.

She was now having to get up and stretch her legs every five minutes and was getting less and less keen to keep an eagle eye on the building opposite. After about an hour and a quarter, at last, some action – a young man in his early twenties came out of the front door and walked up the road and out of sight. Julie took his photo but wasn't all that impressed with the picture. After about five minutes he came back down the road carrying a plastic bag. She concluded that he was the gofer and had been sent out for some item, like coffee or bananas, who knew.

Another half hour went past and nothing else had happened. Julie decided she needed to do something else. Just as she stood up, the front door opened again and a woman stepped out. She was tall, very tall, made more so by the huge high heels she was wearing. Julie stared at the woman because she was so stunning. Her hair was blonde, long and pulled back into a single plait which reached her waist. She was wearing a very short skirt which made her legs go on for ever, but instead of the perhaps conventional skirt that hugged the thighs, this was loose and flared.

Julie found herself frowning and being very mumsy and saying to herself as if scolding a teenage daughter 'You can't go out in that, if the wind blew everyone would see your knickers.'

The woman's top was no more conservative; it was a tube of sorts, showing her belly button, which seemed to have some kind of jewel or body piercing – at this distance she couldn't tell. The top was quite low cut with thin shoulder straps. She was model thin. Julie immediately hated her and so could now easily imagine this bitch deeply involved in the drugs trade and it was her fault entirely that Graham was locked up in England – with of course no evidence whatsoever.

On impulse, and for no particular reason bar her boredom, she rushed out of the room and quickly down the hotel stairs. At the foyer she slowed, smiled and nodded to the woman at reception. She walked out of the front door with poise and then ran full tilt to the corner, around which she hoped that the leggy thing had gone. At the corner she again slowed and poked just her head around. The woman was striding down the pavement, head held high parting the on-coming pedestrian traffic. Everyone was watching her, men and women. She walked on seemingly oblivious. Julie scuttled behind, keeping her distance, very aware of first, her less–than–tall–stature, second her very flat and unflattering shoes and her womanly curves. In addition Julie was wearing her sister's not–very–fashionable clothes. She hated this woman even more.

By hurrying she caught up and kept pace just a few strides behind and so was able to inspect her back aspect. Julie begrudgingly accepted that this woman looked pretty damn good. She wasn't so thin as to fire off accusations of pandering to the anorexic culture. Her legs were just very long – helped by the very short skirt thing – but they were slim, tanned and well-shaped. As she walked, the movement of her hips made the skirt flick out just a little. Julie realised she was holding her breath and really concentrating on the hem of the skirt trying to see up it, as were the two men walking alongside her. Julie didn't know why she was doing this – she knew why the two men were – but then as she vaguely pondered her sexual orientation the girl wheeled right into a pâtisserie. The man to Julie's right jumped to the left to avoid colliding with the girl and instead banged into Julie who in turn fell into the other stalker who wasn't concentrating on walking at all.

All three of them fell to the pavement in an undignified heap.

Both men were up quickly and together they hauled Julie to her feet with over-generous apologises and great embarrassment. Unfortunately, one of them had been carrying a half-drunk take-out coffee, much of which was now down the front of Julie's dress. There followed that even more embarrassing moment when the coffee man thought he ought to offer to wipe down her dress with his handkerchief, knowing all along that it was an inappropriate gesture. She sent them away, and they both happily obliged. Julie was left sitting on a bench reminded of her sore spots from the fire episode. She kept watch on the pâtisserie door and the small crowd of fall-onlookers had dispersed by the time the girl reappeared from the shop. The girl turned right and continued on down the street swinging a little paper carrier bag. After about fifty meters she turned right again into a small park.

The park was a series of pathways with circular intersections, each with new benches around the edge. The ubiquitous lime trees shaded the paths benches and almost all of the benches were full with people from the nearby offices eating their lunch. The days when Parisians had three-hour lunches was fast disappearing in the unified Europe and many office workers now brought their lunch in a bag or bought it from the shop down the road, as seemingly the girl had done.

Julie again followed as the girl strode through the paths. Everyone, men and women, watched. Men to ogle, women to hate. There were a few unoccupied places on the benches and Julie wondered why she didn't take one, but argued that maybe, considering her outfit, she preferred to sit alone. The girl passed through three intersections and then in the centre of the last she stopped, looked down at her shoe and scraped it around in the dusty surface. Something had stuck to the shoe. She lifted her foot up high and balanced flamingo-like and surveyed the sole, removed a non-existent stone and continued on her way. The whole of the circle sat open-mouthed, sandwich frozen en route to face. The girl had just shown everyone her arse and more besides. Even Julie had seen it all and, as she was standing had a less advantageous sightline. The girl did have knickers on, but perhaps they were best described as 'small' or 'thong-like' or even 'floss-like'.

Julie watched the lunchers, they looked at each other. Most of the men smiled and then laughed when making eye contact with the others and so realised that everyone had seen it. The women huffed and mouthed an indignant 'well'.

The girl walked on without looking back or registering the reactions. Julie smiled, but at the same time was a little sad for this beautiful woman who seemed to have something missing in her life to need this kind of exhibition. She dropped back and followed the legs back to the wine warehouse and the hotel room, where the 'coffeed' dress was exchanged for the original jeans.

Chapter 15

In his many years with the police, Henri had built good relationships with other police officers, mostly in the Paris force. He had trained with some of them and had spent the first ten years in amongst the high-octane world that is the Paris crime scene. Following a whirlwind romance he married a young beauty called Sandrine, whose family came from Querchamps-les-Ardres. She hated living in northern Paris, felt alone and scared, especially as Henri was working long and unsociable hours. Their marriage started to fall apart very quickly and when a promotion opportunity came up in Querchamps, Henri reluctantly took it. However, he got on well there and started to love the small town environment but unfortunately his relationship with Sandrine had already moved beyond the tipping point. Eighteen months of stressful living later Sandrine left to take a teaching job in Spain and within a short while had married a local accountant. Henri had not heard from her since the business-like letter informing him of her remarriage.

Henri called one of his old friends, Frances Bellon, now the Inspector heading up the Brigade des stupéfiants – illegal drugs – part of the DRPJ – the Direction Regionale de Police

Judiciaire de Paris and the northern section of Paris, including Saint-Denis and co-ordinated from the Commissariat Central for the 18th Arrondissement in rue de Clignancourt.

'Hey Frankie, *ça va?*'

'Henri, you old bastard, how is the hotel business?'

'What hotel business, hey I get by. Frankie I need to talk, it's a drug matter, right up your street, literally.'

'OK, when?'

'Now, it's important, but it needs to be off record, nothing strictly illegal, but you will understand when I tell the story.'

'I'm a bit tied up right now, Henri... .'

'No, Frankie, this is a serious drug-related issue and it's on your patch, I need to see you right now.'

'OK, I hear you my friend, sorry, I'll reschedule, how soon can you be here?'

'Ten minutes?'

'Right. Next to our building is a bar called 'Numero Dix'. I'll be in there over on the right in one of the alcoves, it's quiet and very anonymous.'

'Perfect, see you there.'

Henri, parked right outside and found Frankie nursing a double espresso. Another arrived for Henri thirty seconds after he sat down.

'OK my friend, tell me all, it sounds like a "Henri-getting-in-up-to-his-ears" business.'

'Yup.'

Henri needed information from his friend but couldn't tell all, partly because that would compromise both Julie and himself but also because it would put Frankie in a difficult place, aiding and abetting a wanted person.

'I need you to trust me, Frankie, there's a company in Saint-Denis that could be involved in a drug smuggling racket, sending drugs through to the UK. Don't worry, I am not involved, but a friend of mine has become, well let's say, entrapped. They're totally innocent, but it appears that they are – connected.'

'It's not a woman by any chance?'

'Well yes, but that has no bearing on this – I am not involved with the woman... honestly. Why are you giving me that look?'

'Not involved yet, I think Henri.'

'Look Frankie I just need you to dig a little without asking too many questions. If I'm right about this lot, then it would be a huge feather in your cap. An international drug smuggling ring rounded up by the intrepid Inspector Frances "Le Ram" Bellon.'

'I know that I will regret this, but go on ask away.'

'It's called the 'The Societé du Vin de St Denis on Ave du Président 93210. Anything you have on it, company directors, employees, any form on them, anything, and a raid would be good.'

'Oh a raid, I suppose you have a truck load of evidence to use to get permission to go in?'

'Of course... none whatsoever.'

'Then the answer is no, no raid, not based on one of your hunches, but I will find out what I can. OK . But why the great urgency?'

'Oh nothing much. The woman friend of mine is wanted

in UK for drug smuggling and for murder in France, and she is in hiding with me, and probably the local police know that by now, so no great shakes eh.'

'Oh shit Henri. Go away now, I will phone you when I have any info but my friend, don't fuck with me.'

They shook hands. Henri left the bar and headed to the central library where there was an Internet connection that he could use. He tried calling Julie on her mobile but got no connection because, as he had instructed her, it was turned off.

When Bellon got back to his office he called in a junior officer, gave him the name and address of the wine business and asked him to dig around 'an anonymous tip,' he had called it. 'Let me know as soon as you have anything.' When the young officer had gone, Bellon fired up his computer and started scrolling through anything that had come out of the UK recently and also out of the sleepy little town of Querchamps-les-Ardes. Fifteen minutes later he had what he was sure were the answers. A message from a Detective Inspector Curry in Ashford, Kent, UK, regarding an attractive woman – he had the photo – called Julie Webb, wanted for involvement in a possible drug smuggling offence and for travelling on a false passport. Out of Querchamps police department he found that they were looking for an unnamed woman, of similar description, wanted in connection with a double murder of two farm workers and an arson attack on a wine warehouse, and possible murder of the proprietor, one Jean-Paul Caput. He found no mention of Henri.

Bellon leaned back in his chair and sighed, 'Fuck me Henri,

you can pick them.'

The young officer knocked on Bellon's door and entered.

'I have found some things, sir, whether they are important of not, I don't know. The wine company has three directors, Pierre Roche, Silvia Cresson and Gerard Mostier. I have also accessed their tax records and there is one other employee called Ethan Brune. Mostier is the most interesting, he has several mentions in the records and is a nasty piece of work by all accounts. When working for a security firm he was cautioned several times for, let's say, over-enthusiasm in his work. He badly beat up some drunks. He was also given a suspended sentence for possession of a firearm. There is also reference of some trouble when he was in the army. A reference only, as you know, the full records are not easily extracted from the Services. Ethan Brune has been arrested for possession of a banned substance, cannabis and amphetamines, given a suspended sentence and again a year later, same offence, two months in a young offender's jail. Silvia Cresson has no record but her name does crop up a couple of times as suspect in a fraud case and a minor drug incident. We have nothing at all on Roche.'

'Ok, thanks, I'll take it from here.'

'Thank you sir.'

★★★★★★★

Julie had tracked the girl back via another entrance to the park and to the building in Ave du Président. She was now back in the window, watching nothing much.

All she had observed through the day was the young man

getting something from up the road and the woman doing her public exposure act. What else went on in there? This whole operation, staking out the building was a joke; she wondered whether Henri had set this up, sticking her here in the hotel room to keep her out of harm's way? Where was he anyway?

She was getting more and more frustrated being cooped up and not moving anything forward. The people and the business opposite could well be totally kosher, in fact the chances were that it all was. Just a name in a book, just a supplier to Jean-Paul, albeit in a book that was hidden away... .

Getting inside the building was going to prove difficult or impossible – that only left the people to investigate. Julie decided she would again follow the next person to come out of the building and just see what happened. She felt better at this resolve, but would leave a note for Henri. Before she could find a pen and paper, the young man appeared at the door of the building opposite and headed off down the road. Once more Julie scampered down the stairs, slowed past reception, and hurried on to the street some 50 meters behind the man.

She caught up with him as he waited at a bus stop, the 255 which went east as far as Bondy. Julie held back at the corner, just out of sight, and watched for the bus back down the road, when it turned into the street she came out of the side road and walked up to the bus stop, timing it fairly well, joined the end of the queue and squeezed on to the bus someway behind the lad who stood facing away. The bus took about twenty minutes to reach the lad's stop in Bondy by which time many people had already got off.

The district of Bondy was run down and poor   with several

old high rise buildings that really should have been pulled down. Almost all those on the streets were non-European and Julie felt not only out of place but threatened. She followed without being seen.

She had assumed that he was going home and that would probably be it – at least she would be able to get his address and possibly his name if it was on the door. Then she would return to the hotel and meet Henri and then they would argue again about her going back to the UK.

The young man didn't go home, he walked from the bus stop directly to a large, seedy-looking bar. Julie walked past and tried to see in – there were quite a few young people in there and some pool tables. She could go in and pass as a young person – just about – and as her French was pretty good, probably pass as a native.

She stood on the street corner trying to weigh up the pros and cons of following the lad inside. Her mind was made up by the looks three of four passing motorists gave her as she stood alone on the corner.

She pushed open the door to the bar. It was larger than she'd imagined with four pool tables and about twenty small tables, most of which were occupied by a complete cross section of cultures, nearly all under 25.

As she walked to the bar there was one of those difficult moments when everyone stopped talking, turned, and looked at her. She wasn't interesting enough to hold their attention for long and by the time she reached the bar the general hum of conversation had returned. She ordered a beer. This was a top-off-the-bottle kind of bar, which was fine.

The young man from the wine business was already playing pool with another man and a girl. She moved closer to the table and perched on a stool close enough to see the play but not too close to be seen to be interfering. They weren't great pool players. Julie figured she was probably better than all of them, although a bit rusty. When she had lived in France the local bar had a table and as she had spent a lot of time in there, she had learnt quickly and conquered many an alpha male.

The girl at the table made a terrible shot, the ball left the table and hit the wall next to Julie who picked it up and handed it back.

'That was a great shot... .'

'I hate this game, I'm only here because my boyfriend cannot prise himself away.'

'I can see the appeal of this bar – it is full of smoke, smells of beer and testosterone and just the place for a romantic evening with your boyfriend.'

The girl laughed and said

'So that's what turns you on too then.'

'OK' replied Julie, '*touché.*'

'Are we playing or what?' the girl's boyfriend called across.

'Yeh, yeh, yeh,' said the girl who was still holding the pool ball.

'Ask your friend if she wants to make up a foursome' called the young man from the wine business.

Julie pulled a face, shrugged and said 'OK'.

'Boys against girls, OK with you?' he laughed

'Ok with me' said Julie, 'What's the prize for the winners?'

'If you win, we will let you buy us a drink.'

'Ho, ho, ho' said the other girl and turned to Julie 'They're mostly harmless, I'm Yvette, my boyfriend is Jacques and he's Dickhead.'

The lad threw the chalk at Yvette, 'OK it's Ethan.'

'Julie,' said Julie.

'Hello Julie,' said Ethan.

Jacques just gave Julie a chin-up kind of nod in recognition. Ethan got a coin from his pocket, spun it and clapped it on the back of his hand. 'Call,' he said.

'Heads.'

'Heads it is, do you want to start?'

'No, you break,' said Julie.

The first game was very scrappy, the girls lost, mostly because Yvette was extraordinarily inept and so, even with Julie being a lot better, it made little impact on the final score.

'So you girls have to buy the next round.'

'Oh no, no, no,' purred Julie, 'that wasn't the deal. The deal was if we won then we would be fortunate enough to buy you guys a drink, but as you won then it would be reasonable if you bought us one, eh?'

Ethan frowned.

'Err, yes I suppose so… same again,' and went off to the bar.

Julie watched him go and turned to Yvette who just raised her eyebrow. No one spoke but Julie was thinking that Ethan, although good looking wasn't the sharpest knife in the drawer and Yvette nodded as though she had heard what Julie was thinking.

The group played on and with some minimal coaching from Julie the girls did better and ended up a pretty even match. They had all had five beers.

Ethan was starting to get a little drunk; he was getting louder and suggestive towards Julie. Julie was flirting back a bit, but was now back peddling – as he was getting the wrong idea.

They had bought each other drinks in succession and next it was Ethan's turn again. He weaved a little on his way to the bar. Yvette was at the giggly stage and Jacques was groping her a bit. Julie was stone-cold sober, partly because she could handle her drink and partly because she had been pouring about half of each bottle into a plant pot, containing a plastic plant vaguely resembling a real one. Julie had tested the viability of this early on and found that when poured onto the plastic soil surface the beer ran down somewhere into the pot and didn't seep out of the bottom.

Julie watched Ethan at the bar laughing with some of his mates, all who looked about fourteen. Several were of North African descent, probably Algerian, thought Julie.

Julie chatted more to Yvette but was conscious of the continued laughter and looks in her direction from the bar. She guessed that the rather drunk and small-brained Ethan was betting that he could get off with her. Fat chance.

Finally he weaved back to the pool table with four tops-off bottles and handed them round. They all swigged and started playing another game. The girls were well ahead when Julie played an uncharacteristic poor shot which potted one of the boy's balls and gave away a shot. Jacques potted three balls on the trot and only needed one more before getting to the black. Yvette and Ethan made hopeless attempts leaving Julie an easy shot to draw level. She took a long time to cue up finding it difficult to concentrate and hold the cue steady. Finally she played, completely missed the white and fell over, much to the amusement of the other three as well as several boys at the bar who were now watching. Ethan helped her to her feet.

Julie felt suddenly very drunk, the bar swam around a bit.

'I must get some air,' she mumbled, and headed towards the door. But she was unsteady and Ethan took her arm and helped her outside, even though he was just as unsteady. A cheer went up from the boys at the bar. Julie heard the suggestive tone if not the actual words. Outside she felt even more drunk and, like it or not, she needed Ethan to keep her upright.

'I need to get some coffee into you, you've drunk too much' he said close to her ear.

'Yeh, Christ I feel pissed, and I haven't drunk much at all,' she slurred.

'Let's go to my place, it's just over there.'

Julie didn't answer as she was trying to work out why this was not a good idea, but couldn't quite get the facts straight. They stumbled across a rough grassed area and into one of the high-rise blocks she had seen earlier.

Had she been more aware she would have spotted the same signs of neglect that similar-aged blocks in London show. Graffiti, broken and scarred floors, the smell of urine. But it did have a working lift, slow and noisy, but working. Ethan propped her into one corner and hit the button. He then launched himself onto her; he held her face in both hands and kissed her full on the lips.

It was from about this point that Julie had no further

memory. What she did and her reactions would have caused her to be eternally embarrassed. The drug that Ethan had dropped into her bottle had taken effect very quickly and had transported her back into her slightly wild and irresponsible teenage years. When Ethan kissed her she responded, kissed him back with just as much passion, grabbed him around the arse and pulled him to her. Encouraged, he whipped his hands up inside her shirt and grabbed one breast and managed to get his right hand around her back and, with great skill, pinged the clasp at the back and allowed his left hand to creep under her bra onto her bare skin.

This was in fact only the second time that he found himself in this position. The first, with a girl called Angel, had been a huge disappointment to both of them, he had got her into bed and then had come after about ten seconds. She had stormed out with a string of insults aimed at his manhood before he'd had a chance to recover and try again. This incident had scarred him with a total lack of confidence with girls and he had struggled to regain any kind of relationship since. The bra pinging skill he had mastered at age fourteen using one of his mother's bras on a dress-making dummy, and at last the hours spent in his youth had paid off.

He was now very aroused and Julie, on some kind of auto-pilot, was very aware and pleased that she could feel his erection pushing against her stomach. She groaned a little, still mouth to mouth, as the lift finally 'dinged' its arrival on the twelfth floor and was feeling great, young, turned on, free and completely out of control. By the time they reached the flat door she had passed out and he had to carry her to the bed.

Chapter 16

Aariz and Saskia were snuggled up to each other in bed; they had just made love and were still in the afterglow. Aariz was stroking her hair as she liked him to do.

'Do you think your inspector will get Spelling back in and press any charges?'

'I really don't know, most of the loose ends are now tied up. He was pretty pissed off at Spelling and the sister for playing games, but I can't see that there is any great desire to prosecute. It rather depends on what happens with Julie Webb and what she says when we get her back here.'

'So have you tracked down this Julie woman?'

'Not yet, the French police are supposedly looking for her, but with how much effort we can't tell. I did tell you that I've got her sister's phone didn't I?'

'Yes you did. I'm still not sure whether that is legal.'

'Oh shut up Mr Clean Lawyer. We are trying to trace her through the phone in order to protect her, right?'

'Right, OK. So where is she?

'We're fairly sure she went off looking for the bad guys, stupid bitch. So she's somewhere near where the wine scam was carried out, but although she is texting her sister she hasn't told exactly where she is. We do know that she has said that she has tracked down the guys from the lay-by, but we have nothing to pass on to the French police because she hasn't been specific enough. All I'm doing is continuing to pretend that I am her sister and sending messages for her to come home. That's the best I can do for now.'

'Do keep me posted if you can, it's really interesting.'

'But Aariz, you are a spy and by telling you I am breaking zee law; I could be takenz outside and shot. I will only tell you zees secrets for a price.'

'I see Mata, what is your price?'

'You know, my lover... .'

'Again, already, oh vell I suppose I could make some of zee extra efforts, just for you... .'

****

Julie took a long while to wake up completely. Her dreams as she came to were bizarre, as usual. She had been driving along in a white van, the white van, she knew it was that van even though it looked just like her Dad's old Vauxhall Vectra. The man driving was the shorter of the two Frenchmen in the lay-by but for some reason – in her dream– she couldn't focus enough to be able to really identify him, and she knew it was important to do so. The man had started to grope her with his left hand even though he was still driving and she couldn't stop him. Her head teacher was in the back of the car, oblivious to what the driver was doing. Then she was sweating and looking at the ceiling. The dream was still very real. It must have been a British car because the driver was on the right... . How come she was now in bed? Where was the van? It was very important to find the van... . A new horror started to dawn, she didn't know where she was. Julie almost laughed at the cliché. So many times had she seen clips in films where people said 'Where am I?', what a joke, how unreal was that. She paused in her thoughts, still a little in the dream but coming round. She stared again at the ceiling. It was creamish, with swirly patterns of brownish. Obviously at some point water had leaked from the rooms above or the roof. She followed the patterns across the room. Someone ought to repaint that ceiling, she thought.

The smell was unfamiliar, musty, not clean, sweat, cooking, rubber, banana – a mixture of different things, all unknown. A shudder of panic flushed through her. Fuck, really, where was she? The duvet was partly over her. She was completely naked. There was a man asleep next to her in the bed, lying on his back. She jumped up out of her side and stood staring at the man. It was the young man from the bar, from the wine business, the man she had followed, the man she had played pool with – the man she had flirted with. She remembered nothing about the flat. The horror of the situation started to dawn. She had gone to bed with this youth, this fourteen-year-old, this boy. She had made love to him, shagged him, fucked him?

Her head spun. She felt sick and needed to pee at the same time. She needed to suddenly get rid of stuff quickly. Where was the bathroom? Kitchen, cupboard, another cupboard, bathroom at last. She sat on the loo and felt better not standing and took stock. Her pee stank and there was a feeling of acid, sharp, sore. She sat head in hands and thought back to the bar, the beer, the feeling drunk, unexpectingly feeling drunk, the laughter at the bar, the taste of the beer. There was a drug in the beer. The bastard has spiked her drink.

She was also aware of the feeling between her legs. She had had sex, she could feel it. She felt the bile coming up again and took deep breaths and let the anger take over. The bastard had spiked her drink and raped her. Naked, she stood up and out of habit looked at her pee. It was a funny colour, orangey green, definitely not natural. She flushed.

When the cistern had refilled and quietened down she crept back to the main room and found her clothes, which were strewn around the bed, and got into them as quickly and quietly as she could. Her jeans were inside out, he had taken them off her by pulling them straight down, turning them. The man, Ethan, was partly covered sprawled across the bed but in a deep sleep, mouth open.

Julie sat on a chair by the kitchen table looking at the bed and tried to think straight. Her first reaction was to call the police; her second was not to call the police because she was breaking the law, her third was to get even with this little bastard, her fourth was to get information from this little bastard. Her purpose, her whole reason for all this pain and effort and danger and grief was to get Graham off the hook, to prove that there was a conspiracy and they were unwitting mules. So she sat and planned what she had to do to get what she wanted from Ethan.

****

Fifteen minutes later she was ready and took some deep breaths. In front of her were several items she had found around the flat. None were quite what she wanted but she had had to improvise. Once again she was sweating; this was not a normal situation for a French teacher from a rather posh private girl's school.

The items collected were in fact for torture. The anger was still there and she knew that she could do this. There were two long nylon straps which looked like they could have been used to tie a bike or a windsurfer to the roof of a car, a roll of gaffer tape, a leather belt, a large kitchen knife and an old pickle jar half full of orange juice. She also had her phone out and had spent several minutes working out how to use the recorder – she had never used it before along with most of the other features.

'Shit,' she said to herself, 'what am I doing?'. She looked down at the sleeping boy, he looked so young and she started to waiver. 'No, no, Julie, get a hold, this little shit drugged you and raped you, he deserves everything bad you can think of right now... .'

Her anger rise spurned her on and she growled through clamped teeth. First she put her mobile phone on a little shelf above the bed and turned it on to the record mode. It was high above Ethan's head and he wouldn't be able to see it from his position. She took the long nylon strap, folded it roughly into two and wound it round one of Ethan's wrists at the middle point. His arm on that side was close to the bedhead which was wooden with upright spindles on the ends; this left a gap to the main panel, through which she passed the two ends of the strap. At the other side of the bed she pulled the loose ends of the strap through the gap and carefully wound the strap around his other wrist. The loose end from his wrist she fed through the buckle. It was one of those clever non-return buckles which allow you to tighten by just pulling the strap. Ethan's arm was alongside his prone body, so she carefully lifted it and flopped it back against the right-hand end of the bedhead, and by pulling the loose end gently tightened the strap and pulled his hand right up to the spindle. Ethan now lay on his back with both arms above him and securely tied. He stirred and shifted his body and pulled against the ties. Julie moved quickly to his legs and repeated the tie down with the second strap, this time running it under the bed around the legs. As she pulled the strap tight he started to come round.

'What, what's happening, what, hey I'm tied. What the fuck are you doing?'

He was pulling hard on the straps around his wrists and there was a danger that he might be able to slip the cuffs off.

Julie leaned over him and with the most vicious voice she could muster she yelled in his face.

'Stay still you bastard or I'll kill you.'

Ethan stopped struggling and stared wide-eyed at her.

Julie saw that the straps could slip off and so grabbed the gaffer tape and wound it around his wrists several times over the top of the nylon straps. He started to kick and shout and bounce up and down.

This made her even more determined to push ahead. She

brought the kitchen knife up to his face. He got the message and lay still. Panic was starting to rise. As she wound the tape around each ankle, he started to scream.

With gaffer tape across his mouth he stopped and concentrated on breathing through his nose. He was now panting, hyperventilating partly through blind panic and partly because he wasn't getting enough air up his nose.

Julie was now calm again and in total control of her emotions.

The duvet was long gone from his naked body. Julie was somewhat revolted by his nakedness, not that she hadn't seen a naked man before but she was so not attracted to him now that she tried not to focus on any bits at all.

She sat on the side of the bed. He was very scared now and had no idea what she was going to do. He was trying to think clearly and obviously this woman was seriously pissed off with him; it could well be to do with the fact that he had screwed her and maybe she was aware that there was a just a little bit of drug-related help.

He tried to say 'Sorry,' through the gag. She said 'Shut up and listen.'

He nodded.

'I'm going to ask you some questions and I would like you to answer clearly and truthfully. If you do that you may get out of this situation without losing any part of your anatomy. OK?' and in order to emphasise this she again picked up the kitchen knife.

Ethan groaned under the tape and nodded at her a few times.

'I'm going to take off the tape and I don't expect you to call out. Do you understand?'

He nodded again. She pulled the tape off quickly hoping that it would hurt. She felt the resistance of some bum-fluff moustache and he did as well. He gasped and lay back on the bed.

'Now to start with I know that you spiked my drink last night – I guess with Rohypnol or something similar... .'

He interrupted 'No I didn't – and you can't prove that.'

'Yes I can, you see, I have a sample,' and she picked up the pickle jar full of orange juice to which she had added just a little from a bottle of green toilet cleaner which changed the colour to an odd shade, which wasn't really close to the colour of her pee in the toilet but she figured that he wasn't aware of the colour that Rohypnol did turn a girl's pee.

He lay back down.

'So you see when the police analyse this and talk to your friends at the bar, all of which I could pick out, because I took very good notice, plus of course Yvette and Jacques, I think you will go to jail for a very long time.'

She let this sink in for a moment.

'It may be however that I forget all that and let you go or maybe I will just cut some bits off and leave you here. You don't know who I am, and believe me, the police would never find me – and oh, I've done this before.' She added that just for fun and to try to emphasise that she was playing hard ball here.

'What do you want?' he screeched several notes higher than his normal voice.

'Tell me about the Societé du vin de St Denis '

Ethan looked a bit shocked at the idea. He thought back through the events; she had come into the bar and pushed herself into their company so she must have known from the start where he worked and had planned the meeting in order to get information.

'Who are you, who do you work for?'

Julie was ready; she had put down the knife and instead slapped him quite hard across the chest with the belt. The buckle left a red mark on his skin.

'I ask the questions, remember.'

'We export wines all over Europe, mostly to England,' he blurted.

'Go on.'

'That's it.'

'What kind of wines?'

'Expensive, rare ones, collectables.'

'OK, are they all genuine?'

'I don't know what you mean.'

'Are all the bottles that you sell actually the genuine article, or are some fake?'

Ethan relaxed a bit, she was tracking down fake wine sources and maybe she was representing a punter who guessed the wine was fake, or maybe the wine police, nothing more.

'Look I don't know anything about wine, all I do is pack the bottles they give me. I know nothing more really. Do you think the company is selling fake wine then?'

Julie sat thinking about what to say next, she just looked at him and remembered the rape. It was completely possible that his company had nothing to do with the drugs she and Graham had been stuffed with. Maybe Jean-Paul had just listed one of his suppliers, maybe Jean-Paul was involved in the sale of fake bottles and that was why he had hidden away the address in the underground safe. Oh shit, was she on the wrong track altogether?

Ethan was getting restless again

'Look I don't know anything so let me go; and I didn't drug you, honestly… .'

She hit him again with the strap, just because she wanted to. He lay back down again; the red marks on his chest were getting redder and obviously hurt. Well, she now knew he was lying about the drugs in her drink, so there was a fair chance that he was also lying about the other things. She decided to go for it.

'Tell me about how your company smuggles drugs into England.'

She was watching very closely, he hesitated, his eyes stared for a second and the hesitation was a 'tell; she knew now she was on the right track.

'What do you mean, what drugs?'

But it was too late to protest his innocence his body language had told all.

She slapped him again – another red mark appeared.

He yelled out again, 'I don't know anything about drugs, really, nothing at all – we just sell expensive wine.'

'Oh dear – we have to get a bit rougher then. I strongly advise you to start telling me the truth,' and to emphasis this she again picked up the kitchen knife.

Julie's amateur dramatics past was coming in handy but she was hoping to God that he would start talking; the prospect of actually going on to some 'knife work' was causing her to shake a bit so in order to cover the shaking, she said,

'I'm starting to get angry now, and I am not very nice when I'm angry.' Even though this was a serious moment, she nearly burst out laughing at her seriously clichéd comment, straight out of some film or other. However, it had a positive impact on Ethan.

'Look I can't tell you anything, really, I just can't… .'

'You mean you know what's going on but can't tell me because of what might happen?'

'Yeah, something like that.'

'Let me tell you something about the organisation I work for. Have you heard of the Mafia? Of course you have, everyone's heard of the Mafia. Well the modern day Mafia is still quite Italian funded but has branched out into a much more pan–European organisation covering, and indeed controlling, much of the organised crime syndicates. Drug smuggling is by far our biggest earner. We do it very well and in fact, we estimate that we control about 70% of all drug movements throughout Europe– it's quite a business. We don't like other people setting up little scams and so we discourage this. The company you work for, we believe, is pushing its way into what we see as our domain, so we need to stop it… .'

'I can't tell you anything, they would kill me, they would, Gerard would just kill me.'

'And do you think that I wouldn't? You are part of a drug smuggling organisation which I am investigating for my bosses, when they get the information that I have been collecting, you will be closed down, permanently. Oh, and by the way you drugged and raped me. Do you really think that I would hesitate when it comes to killing you myself, um?'

'No.'

'Now, the people I work for like me to follow orders, my orders are not to kill you, and so I am reluctant to upset them. They want me to get as much information from you as possible, and they will do the rest. The other little problem is that you can't let the others know about our meeting. Under no circumstances can you blab if they run off, we will know and find you and that would be very bad for you. Do I make myself clear?'

'If I tell you what I know will you let me go?'

'Yes.'

'How do I know that?'

'You don't.'

'I'm just a packager, I don't buy or sell the drugs, that's Pierre and Gerard, they're the ones that do the deals, not me, honest.'

'And the girl?'

'Silvie, yeah, she gets involved too, she's Pierre's girlfriend, she's a bitch.'

'So what does Gerard do?'

'He runs the warehouse, he's my boss, but he's a thug.'

'Ok, first tell me about the fine wine scam?'

Julie was actually enjoying the role she was creating as the serious bad mother. She hadn't known if there was a wine scam but she thought she would ask just for the hell of it.

Ethan was scared shitless by the Mafia thing and so decided to tell all and hope that Julie was telling the truth about letting him go.

'We get ordinary, but really good bottles of wine and decant it into old bottles that we get made in Poland. They have got moulds that were made from original old wine bottles and they use the exact mixture of glass used in the olden days. We reprint the labels on old paper and distress them. We even get the cork from the same area in Portugal that used to be used, before the plastic and screw tops came in. Then they are sold as the real thing. No one can tell the difference and no one opens the bottles and drinks the wine, it's all about investment.'

'Who buys these bottles?'

'Rich blokes in England, people with more money than sense, pop stars and television people. They all think that buying old wine is going to give them a good return on their money, and maybe it will. Pierre does alright anyway.'

'OK, where do the drugs come into this?'

'It's all about the way the wine is shipped. As these bottles are very valuable – well supposed to be – we send them all packaged up with a security guard. Each bottle is boxed up in loads of foam and stuff and in a big crate to keep it from breaking in transit. We also organise a 24-hour security guard, in case someone tries to nick it. It's all bollocks but the security guard makes it all legit. Anyway Pierre realised that because of all the fuss around it, no Customs Officer was ever going to open the bottle or even get close to examining it. So he decided it was a pretty cool way to ship coke around.

Some of his good customers from the wine investment scam were pop stars and coke users, and so he sent them some drugs instead. The stuff arrives in a security van with a guard – coke delivered to the door. Good idea eh.'

'How long has this been going on?'

'Oh, I dunno, a couple of years I suppose.'

'Ok, now tell me about the stuff going over on the ferry.'

'That's a pretty new scam. Pierre decided that there was only so much old vintage wine that could be 'found' and sold without someone getting suspicious so he switched to packing the coke into ordinary wine bottles and then getting tourists to take them across through Customs.'

'If the tourist has got the drugs how do you get them back?'

'There's a transmitter inside the wine case and there's a bloke on the other side who follows the mark and switches the whole wine box.'

'When?'

'Usually it's pretty soon after they land, most people stop for a drink or something to eat on the other side – especially if they have a long journey. It's easy to break into their car at a café and swap the box with a normal one. Sometimes he might have to follow them all the way home and then break into their car in their drive or even burgle their house the next day. They mostly don't even realise that it's happened because they end up with a case of the wine that they bought.'

'Has anyone ever got stopped at Customs?'

'No, and even if they did Pierre has got some bloke at the dock in England on the payroll. I don't know who it is, it's just an insurance policy.'

Julie had moved away from the bed having got the information from the still trussed up Ethan. She sat on the kitchen chair and ignored Ethan's pleading to be let free.

She was feeling disgusted with herself and scared of what she was capable of, but mingled with this feeling was also one of some elation, she had found out all about the drugs ring. She now had the information that would clear her and Graham of any wrong doing and she could go back to her life. There were however two problems that faced her, first, how on earth could she go about getting the information back to the Customs or police in England without letting on that she had in fact broken the law, or did that now matter? If she could show them all what she had found, would the tiny but necessary offense of travelling on a false passport count at all? She didn't know. The second problem was that she wasn't sure that she wanted to go back to life in England as a 'spinster' French teacher in a private girl's school in September, and with Graham who was 'OK' – did she really want to continue with this slightly dull pedant who spent half of his time on the road in Europe, selling bloody kitchen knives? She didn't know.

She woke from her daydream to realise that Ethan was now making a lot of noise. His problem now was that he was desperate for a pee. She looked again at the scrawny youth, her rapist. Here was another problem. There was a huge danger that if she let him go he would run straight back to this Gerard or Pierre and tell all and they would run off and disappear. Her perfect information would be gone with no evidence. But equally she couldn't keep him here locked in and tied up or take him with her. She had to move, and quickly. She turned to the squirming Ethan.

'Today is Saturday, do you go to work?'

'No, not 'til Monday. Why?'

'Good. I'm sure you will gradually wrestle free, the straps aren't that tight. I am going to report back to my Italian bosses and must remind you that you cannot under any circumstances talk to your people about this discussion. If you do warn them, we will get to know, we have informants throughout the police as well as the underworld. There are two routes that I can instigate, first, I just give this jar of pee to the police and let them track you down, second, I just put the word out and my people will find you and kill you. I think it in your best interest to keep quiet. Personally, I would like to castrate you right now, but my bosses wouldn't like that. Do I make myself perfectly clear?'

'Yes.'

'The straps are not tight – you will be able to work them loose in time. Goodbye.' And she picked up the jar of orange juice and left the flat, closing the door behind her.

'Oh fuck,' said Ethan out loud and pissed himself.

Chapter 17

When Henri got back to the hotel from his meeting with Frances and his session at the library, he had found that Julie's room was empty. He asked at reception to no avail, there was no note left and her phone was still turned off. He switched between worry, anger and guilt. Had she been abducted? Had she just decided it was all too much and headed home – part of him was happy with that idea, part not. He phoned the hotel in Querchamps and spoke to Lola. Yes, the police had been around several times, she had stonewalled them and stuck to story. But it was obvious now that the local inspector was implicating Henri in the crimes, if not the actual murders but with spiriting away the main suspect. They had now put together the two people, the mystery woman seen at Le Haut and outside Jean-Paul's and the woman wanted by UK Police – Miss Julie Webb. Henri's car registration along with the one supplied by Kent police for Julie was being circulated in the whole region.

Henri had spoken again to Frances Bellon who had told him that there was nothing much to go on but that they would be alert to any future developments. This was of no great use to Henri and his Internet research had pulled up very little of use either, and nothing at all peculiar on the lawyer whose office he and Julie had looked at.

He spent a very restless night and even when he got Julie's text early in the morning, it was a relief but didn't calm him down much. He paced up and down the bedroom and looked out of the window every two minutes, hoping to see her walk along.

★★★★★★★

Julie walked down the concrete stairway from Ethan's flat, preferring that to a ride in the lift, which no doubt would have a characteristic smell common with all lifts in tower blocks throughout the world, apart from Singapore.

It was early, still only six o'clock and on a Saturday not that many people on the streets. She stood outside Ethan's flat and turned her phone back on and only then remembered that it had been switched off for almost a day from the time that Henri had suspected the drugs people or the police might be tracking her. A list of missed calls came pinging in. There were six from Henri and three from Maddie. She opened the first from Maddie.

Julie. Where are u? I am very worried. Please come home at the first possible moment. It's very important that you do. Madeline.

Julie grunted at her sister's message then frowned and thought something was a bit odd. She then flicked through to the list of missed calls from Henri. They all read almost the same.

where the hell are you call me henri

Julie had hardly ever used her text messaging and still struggled with the short forms and the predictive text systems, along with many people over thirty. She also struggled finding the capital letters and so didn't bother much, same as Henri she noted. Maddie seemed to have mastered it though.

She texted Henri back

i'm ok lots to tell i will call later julie

She scrolled back quickly through Maddie's texts. The more recent ones were pretty much the same as the first, but one from the previous day was important. It read:

Julie please come home, Graham was released at 9.00am this morning.

Julie had been waiting for that message for days, she should have been elated, but she wasn't. She was confused. These last few days had been all about Graham, and their relationship and now he was free but she wasn't. In fact she was in deeper shit than ever he was, and she couldn't just run home, she would be stopped at the ferry. She had to see it through.

She tried Graham's number and got no answer – his phone was turned off. She thought about texting but didn't. She sent a message to Maddie instead.

maddie had a bad day yesterday but have info now that should clear us all good that graham is ok going back to

watch the wine company in saint-denis from hotel opposite
should be back home very soon julie

She turned her phone back off, she knew that Henri would
try to call her again and she couldn't quite face that yet. She
hadn't really come to terms with what had happened overnight
and what she had done to Ethan and – it was too early in the
morning.

Just down the road from the flat she dropped the orange
juice jar into a skip. She guessed the route back to the bar and
bus stop correctly but the road was completely unfamiliar,
she had no recollection at all of walking along there the night
before. She shivered at the thought and anger started up again,
this time it was more focused at the organisation, not just
Ethan. She now wanted to get back and blow the whole thing
apart. Nail the bastards. Get her life back.

****

On the bus going back to Saint-Denis Julie plugged in her
earphones and listened to some of the recording she had made
of Ethan, telling all. The quality was not great, but all of
his words were audible. She winced when she heard Ethan's
muffled screams. 'Not very nice are you Julie Webb,' she said
out loud, 'deep down there seems to be a rather nasty person,'
she thought to herself. She put that thought away and revelled
in the fact that she 'had them', here was the evidence. She
and Henri had been right, the Societé du Vin was indeed the
front for an international drugs ring, and she, little old French

teacher Julie Webb, had solved the crime – not without some sacrifices and pain, but she had done it. An OBE at least or possibly a gong from Monsieur Le President was in order.

She then realised what was odd about Maddie's texts, as well as learning how to get capitals and to use short forms, she had signed herself, Madeline. A puzzle.

★★★★★★★

In was Saturday, but Saskia and Curry were both in the office. These last few days one of Saskia's first tasks in the morning was to check Maddie's texts, and so it was just before 9.30am when she picked up the message.

She found Curry at the coffee machine.

'We've found her sir, she's in a hotel in Saint-Denis a suburb of Paris', she held up the phone.

'Good, well done, contact that police in France and ask them to go and find her, and tell them that she is no longer a suspect, but we would like to get her back for her own protection.'

From her own desk she sent the message through to France. As she finished the email her phone rang. It was Aariz. She didn't like to take private calls in the office; it was OK in an emergency but was generally frowned upon for anything else. She looked around but there was no one in earshot.

'Hi babe, I can get tickets for that play at the Wolsey Theatre, are you going to be free by say 7.00 o'clock tonight?'

'Yes, I'm pretty sure I'll be home by lunchtime, we're just sorting out a few loose ends and we've tracked down Julie

Webb at last.'

'Oh great, that presumably also puts Spelling totally in the clear. Where is she?'

'In a hotel opposite a wine business in Saint-Denis in Paris, she thinks they are behind the drugs scam. Anyway, we have alerted the French police so they will go around and hopefully pick her up and get her home.'

'Good, I'll get the tickets for the play. See you later.'

Aariz was also in his office, he wasn't usually that conscientious but when Saskia was working he usually went in as well, in that way he could justify taking time out at other times and so spend more time with Saskia.

He knew that Sprake was in too and so he popped his head around the boss's door, to give him the latest nugget about the Spelling case but also to make sure he registered a gold star for working on a Saturday.

'Thought you'd like to know sir that the Webb woman has been located in France she's in a hotel in Saint-Denis watching a wine business across the road. She reckons the company is the base for the drugs ring.'

'Oh OK thank you Aariz, thanks a lot.' And he bent back over his paperwork until Aariz had left.

'Fuck,' he said quietly, got up, closed the door and then phoned a Paris number.

'Hi Silvie,' he said when it was answered, 'it's your old father here.'

'Oh hi papa, long time since we spoke.'

'Yes, I know, sorry. Look something has come up over here and I wanted a word. Are you and that creep Pierre still exporting dodgy wine into England?'

'Well no, not really, only for a few specialist clients. Most of our exports are legit these days. We haven't really done much since that last batch that you bought.'

'Please don't try to imply that I am part of your sordid little business.'

'Do you still have the wine?'

'No of course not… I sold it on as soon as I knew it was fake.'

'So you told the buyer it was fake, did you?'

'Don't be daft girl, I would have lost my shirt. I just sent it all through to Sotheby's and let them check out the documentation. I am delighted that your counterfeiting is good enough to pass muster even with the experts. I even made a small profit. But now listen, this is more serious are you and that Pierre sending through drugs in wine bottles now?'

'No, of course not Papa, we don't have anything to do with drugs, how can you think so and why do you ask?'

'Well there's someone out there in France stuffing wine bottles full of cocaine and getting tourists to unwittingly bring it through customs. A couple got caught last week and the girl is over in Paris trying to track down whoever is responsible. She thinks it's you.'

'What! How can she, and how do you know this?'

'It doesn't matter; even if you are innocent she could still give you some grief. She's in a hotel opposite you right now watching the place. So be warned Silvie.'

'We have nothing to fear, but thanks anyway Papa, see you

soon I hope, bye.'

'Bye.'

'*Putain*,' screamed Silvie into her hands and then ran downstairs to the warehouse, where she knew Gerard was still packing up the last of the cocaine bottles. She rushed in and had to control her emotions quickly because unexpectedly, young Ethan was also there helping Gerard.

'Oh good morning Ethan, you don't usually come in on a Saturday.'

'No, well I knew there was a lot to do and the quicker this stuff is out of the way the better eh?'

'Yes, well good. Gerard I need a word in private please.'

Chapter 18

It was still early when Julie got back to the hotel to find Henri in a froth. It took him some time to calm down and to allow Julie to tell him what had happened the night before. He held his head in his hands when she summarised the difficult bits, but he was still keen to listen to the recording she made.

'Julie, you are a huge liability and you have put yourself in the most terrible danger, for what? But OK we will talk more about this later, right now I must get this recording to Frances, I think it's enough to get him off his arse and have a serious look in there. You must now stay here, first I'm going to a bloke I know to get this recording transferred onto a flash pen and at the same time I will get him to remove some of the incriminating bits. I will be no more than an hour. Promise me you will do nothing Julie.'

'OK, I promise, really Henri, I've had enough.' She gave him a hug. 'Thank you.'

As soon as she was alone she showered and changed in to clean clothes, the last few she had, then once again sat at the window, watching the wine business front door. She had no great desire to do so and was losing heart. She had been through so much and achieved more than she could have hoped for, but the bad guys were still the bad guys and the information that she had given to Henri may not be enough to convince the DRPJ to raid the place and prove it all. She had obtained a confession which of course would not hold up in court, any lawyer with half a brain would get it thrown out – just a tad too much 'under duress'.

She was uncomfortable on the window ledge and as she moved around to ease the numbness she almost missed the figure walking out of the side gate. It was the gate that led through to the warehouse. The stocky figure closed the gate behind him and stood with his back to the gate and swept his eyes along the hotel wall, along the line of first floor windows and stopped at Julie's window and held his gaze there for a moment. Julie stiffened. She knew immediately that this was the man she saw in Querchamps, in the warehouse, the man who shot Jean-Paul. She instinctively stepped back from the window out of sight. She still watched the man although she now couldn't be seen. He was watching the traffic and unhurriedly crossed the road to the hotel side. Julie stepped forward again to try to see him but he was too close to the wall to be seen unless she leant out of the window. The thought suddenly hit her – what if he was coming into the hotel, what if he knew where she was? She panicked, thought about hiding under the bed, went the door to check it was locked and then thought more clearly. There was no way that he could know who she was, or indeed where she was; the French and English police were all looking for her, and even they had only just found out about her and they didn't know where she was… .

She felt a bit braver opened the door and stepped across the hallway to the top of the stairs that led down to the reception area. She could hear voices. She went down three steps and crouched down and was able to see down through the bannister. The stocky assassin was talking to the Madam who was red in the face and had fear in her eyes. To Julie's horror the man turned slightly and the Madam was handing him a key. In his right hand was a gun with a long silencer on it.

Julie turned and quickly and quietly raced back up the top steps and headed back to her room then stopped, realising that he now had a key– the pass key no doubt. She stood undecided, then turned left along the corridor to the first fire door and slipped through. It closed slowly on its gas hinge and she tried to hurry it. The door had a wired glass panel but she daren't stand behind it for fear of being seen. The corridor she had run into was short, very short with just four room doors and no way out. The room maid was in one of them but she knew that if she burst in to that room there would be conversation that would alert the man. There was another door, ajar, with clean linen and towels; it was open because the maid had been getting clean things. Julie squeezed in and pulled it closed behind her, leaving just a crack through which she could just about see her own room door through the glass in the fire door. The man was at her door, he stood listening and then carefully put the key in the lock, turned it and pushed the door open quickly, bringing his gun up level as he did so. He stepped in out of sight. Three seconds later he came back out and looked left and right along the corridor. He knew she was here and close by, he had seen her standing at the window just a few moments before and she hadn't come down the stairs. He turned to the left away from her and she took a breath. She had never been the other way and had no idea where it led. It was only a small hotel and chances were that it was another short corridor, which meant he would return and find her.

Henri was suddenly in the frame of the door window. He stood at the top of the stair well and was looking down the corridor to where the man had disappeared. He was talking. The stocky man came back and stopped at the head of the stairs as well. She could see Henri waving his hands and talking in an animated way to the man. The man then left and went back down the stairs. Julie stayed where she was, in hiding. Suddenly it was all clear to her. Henri must know this man. Henri was the only person that knew where she was. Henri was in on the drug scam. Henri had sent this man to kill her. It had all been a charade. She gasped at her own stupidity, how she had trusted this stranger, told him everything... .

Henri turned and looked up and down the corridor and walked towards the fire door. Julie pulled the linen cupboard door as fully closed as she could, gripping the inside of the panelling with her nails. Henri came through the fire door and opened the linen cupboard easily against her grip.

'Ah, there you are, well done for hiding,' he said in a calm voice. Julie flew at him, nails out.

'You bastard, you bloody, bloody bastard, it was you all along.' Henri had been taken by surprise but had managed to grab her wrists as she screamed and tried to claw him. He held her off with some difficulty as she was in such a powerful rage.

'Wow, wow, stop, what the hell are you talking about?'

'You bastard you told him where I was, no one else knew. He came straight up here after me. He had a gun for fuck's sake. He was going to kill me.'

'I didn't tell anyone, stop, calm down, calm down.' Julie had exhausted herself and she fell backwards into the cupboard and started crying in great gasping sobs. Henri crouched down in front of her.

'You know him, you talked to him,' she said through gasps for air.

'I don't know him; I just happened to have followed him into the hotel and saw him going upstairs. The woman on reception was in a state and just said to me quietly, 'He's got a gun.' And so I guessed what was happening, ran up the stairs and met him at the top outside your room.'

'You talked to him, what did you say then. Nice weather?'

'No, I said, have you seen my dog?'

'What?'

'It was the first thing I thought of. I pretended that I was staying at the hotel and had lost my dog somewhere and I asked him if he had seen it and started to describe what had happened like some complete loony. He decided he'd had enough and left.'

'OK, supposing I believe that, which I don't, how did he know I was here then?'

'I don't know, but I think we should get out of the cupboard and then out of this hotel as quickly as possible, because I think he will come back.' He held out his hand, she took it, stood up, and didn't know what to believe.

Henri looked out through the glass door but wheeled Julie

back away from the stairwell into the open guest room that was being cleaned. The girl cleaner turned around to remonstrate but Henri held up a police badge and said, 'Mam'selle, please stay in this room for a few moments, there is some danger. This lady will stay with you until I can make sure it is safe to come out.' And with that he sat Julie on the bed went back out and down the stairs. The receptionist was not in sight. He looked out of the front door but could not see Gerard and he then called a number on his mobile.

'Frankie, Gerard Mostier has just been in the hotel looking for Julie, he's armed. He may still be outside waiting, or he's gone back across, did you see him?'

'Yes, we saw him come out of the hotel. He crossed over and went through the gate back inside. The gate is still open a little; I think he's watching for her to come out. OK, we're going in. We have ten armed officers to hand. Oh, by the way we are following the girl, she left a while back in a Porsche 911 of all things. And we have the young bloke, he slipped out immediately after Mostier left to go over the road. I am right in thinking you are in the hotel with your woman? The lad was doing a runner. Very silly boy, he was carrying a bottle of wine, which I suspect is not completely full of wine. Mostier is on his own in there, we can take him. We'll keep you posted. Out.'

Henri went back upstairs to the guest room. 'OK you two, all is clear the police, are outside and you are no longer in danger.' The maid said something in Spanish and disappeared quickly down the stairs.

Henri took Julie back to her room and they watched the

action through the window. Four armed police approached the open gate, two on each side. Over on the right another policeman with a pair of binoculars, could be seen in a window that overlooked the yard talking into his mouthpiece. One of the police on the ground threw a small canister through the gap and stood back. There was the loud crack of a stun grenade and two seconds later all four of the police at the gate pushed through into the yard with their machine pistols out and ready to fire. About ten seconds after that two police cars pulled up at the gate, lights flashing, and Gerard was dragged out, bundled into one of the cars and then they both sped off. It was all over so very quickly that passers-by hardly noticed and the street returned to normal within minutes.

The two stood side by side at the window. When the police cars had gone and the other police had moved into the yard and buildings beyond, Julie looked at Henri and said, 'Sorry'. He just nodded.

She then added, 'How come you still have a police badge?'

'Oh, it's a fake, I bought it for 5 euros in a back-street market. It comes in handy sometimes.'

'I do believe that's illegal.'

'Yep. Oh well. What is bothering me is how Mostier knew you were here and I hope you believe me, I didn't tell. Please note, even the police have not come looking for you here yet, even though you are wanted for questioning, for murder.'

'OK, I believe you.'

'Have you told your sister where you are?'

'Not exactly, I kept her informed. I did tell her I was watching a wine business in Paris from a hotel.'

'Phone her now on her landline, I presume she has one.'

'Yes she has, for the Internet. But we always talk via text, it's a lot cheaper, especially from France.'

'Phone her now, on her landline.'

Julie found the number on her mobile and hit the button. Maddie picked up straight away.

'Julie, oh Julie thank God you're alright, I've been so worried. Are you alright really? Where are you? Are you still in France?'

'Maddie, hold up, ssh. I'm fine really. Are you not getting my texts?'

'Well no dear, it's a long story, um, the police have got my phone, sorry, they said it would help to protect you and get you back in one piece.'

'OK, don't worry, Maddie. When did you give it to them?'

'That was, er, Thursday morning. I tried to phone you to tell you about the police having your phone, but stupidly I didn't have your mobile number written down. It's only on my contacts on my mobile. Do you know that Graham has been released?'

'Yes thanks, I knew about Graham. OK Maddie, look, I'll be home soon. I have to go; I'll call you again when I can on your landline. Bye.'

'Do I understand that your sister gave the police her phone and so they have been able to track you?'

'Looks that way, but that still doesn't tell us how Gerard Mostier got to hear, does it?'

'Well it can only be some kind of mole in the police in England. I can't believe that these guys have the technical kit to hack into my mobile calls – well, I don't think so… .'

'But come on Henri, are you suggesting that someone in the police force in Ashford is so in bed with a group of very nasty drug smugglers that they are passing information back in order to shut me up?'

'I know that sounds a bit drastic, but what other explanation?'

Now that Julie had turned her phone back on she saw again the list of missed calls. There were several unread from 'Maddie' plus several from Vodaphone – none from Graham. The messages from 'Maddie' were interesting now that she knew who had sent them. As she read them she was reminded why the first few had seemed odd when she read them before. Maddie was a useless texter, she could never find the full stops and commas or the capital letters – a bit like Henri – and as she had spotted before, she had signed herself as 'Madeline', a name she never used.

The texts read:

Julie. Where are u? I am very worried. Please come home at the first possible moment. It's very important that you do. Madeline.

Hi, Julie, the police know u are in France and it would be much better for all if u came back. Please come back. Tell me where u are now so that I can stop worrying. Madeline. Julie please come home, Graham was released at 9.00am this morning.

****

Henri had talked again to Frankie who in turn had been able to talk to several senior officers in Paris, and they had cleared the way for her to leave France unhindered. Her involvement in the murders in Querchamps had been explained in her long statement and, although she would need to return at a later date, she could leave France for the time being. In addition, the same officer at the DRPJ had phoned Detective Inspector Curry in Ashford and he confirmed that she was no longer a suspect on any drugs charges but still might be questioned on other minor matters – passport swapping for one.

Henri had driven Julie to the station in Paris to get the Eurostar back to London. Her hire car had been returned to a depot in Paris. Henri parked right outside the entrance and pulled a 'Police' sign from out of the glove box. Julie smiled and he gave a shrug. They walked through the main gate onto the mezzanine floor, this overlooked the concourse in front of several of the busiest platforms, and both were lost for words for a while. This was going to be the big goodbye and difficult for both of them.

'I shall miss you Julie,' said Henri at last, still gazing out over the large and busy station.

'*Moi, aussi*,' she replied.

'You could stay a little longer, you are no longer wanted by the police on either side of the Channel. You could do with a couple of day's holiday after what you have been through in the last week.'

'That does sound very nice Henri, but really I ought to get back and see Graham and put all of this behind me.' She was very aware that she was saying things that she didn't quite want to say or believe, plus that nasty word 'ought' had crept in even though years ago she had made a New Year's resolution to never say 'ought' ever again.

She looked up at Henri and wondered whether he would kiss her. His phone rang, he pulled a face, looked at the caller and turned away to speak. Julie gave a resigned sigh and watched the crowds milling through, all knowing where they were going, all heading somewhere, she suddenly felt alone and directionless.

From her vantage point she could see out through the side entrance of the concourse and on to the street beyond. A red open-top Porsche drew up next to the archway. 'You can't park there can you?' thought Julie. A very leggy woman slid out of the car. Julie watched in amazement at the very familiar figure now leaning against the car.

Julie's eye automatically followed Silvie's gaze towards the tall figure with swept- back hair. He was wearing an ankle-length coat and striding from the platform gate with an air of total assurance. Julie watched the man for a few seconds and then put her hand to her mouth and gasped. She turned to call Henri but he had turned away and was talking on his phone. Julie pulled out her phone and hit a number. It rang. The elegantly dressed man stopped in mid-stride and pressed 'answer'.

'Graham!' said Julie, 'I have only just got the news that all charges have been dropped and you are out of jail. Where are you? It sounds busy.'

'Julie, my God are you alright, I was told you were in France. Where are you now?'

'I'm in London at Kings Cross, I've just got off the Eurostar, but where are you?'

Graham paused before answering.

'I'm in the centre of Reading, getting some food in.'

Julie smiled as she in turn paused before speaking again.

'Where exactly are you?'

'Er, outside the Tesco Express in Shinfield Road.'

Julie was enjoying herself.

'Oh Graham, be a love, and pop into Tesco get me some milk and I'll come straight to your flat when I get off the train.'

Right. Semi-skimmed, isn't it?'

They were both playing a game. Julie knew exactly where Graham was and Graham knew that the ring tone would have told Julie that he was not in England.

Graham turned on the spot, surveyed the crowd and wondered… .

'Julie, it's really great to hear your voice, call me as soon as you get to Reading Station and I'll come and pick you up.'

'That would be amazing if you could,' replied Julie.

'Yes… bye then,' and Pierre hung up. He had another quick look around and resumed his path to the Porsche, making a small detour to drop the phone into a waste bin.

The woman, who once again was wearing little to concern the imagination, wrapped her leg around the man and kissed him hard. Passers-by stopped and pretended not to look at her legs that went on for ever, only just finishing under a skirt of sorts.

'*Salut*, Silvie.'

'I've been worried about you Pierre. Is everything OK?'

'Yes, it is now, it's a long story but remind me next time to trust the people in the organisation and not constantly feel the need to check up on them.'

Silvie frowned at him, 'OK, I'll do that. We've had a few interesting days here, I'll tell all when we get back home.

'Good, let's go then.' He threw his suitcase onto the back seat, jumped into the passenger seat and Silvie powered the car out of the forecourt with a screech of tyres.

Henri had finished his call with Frankie. 'That was the inspector, they have followed Silvie in the Porsche to the station here somewhere and they believe that she is picking up Pierre Roche. So hopefully both will fall straight into the trap back at the warehouse. Who did you phone?'

'Oh no one really, someone I used to know.' She turned to Henri, rose up on her toes and kissed him gently on the lips. 'I've changed my mind; I think I will stay for a few days, if the offer is still open.'

'*Bien sûr, ma chérie.*'

And they walked back to his car arm in arm.

'Oh Henri. Whatever happened to all that money?'

'Don't worry it's in a safe place… .'

Printed in Great Britain
by Amazon